Pictures Of Deceit

By

S C Richmond

Copyright © 2016 by S. C. Richmond

S. C. Richmond asserts the moral right to be identified as the author of this work.

This novel is entirely a work of fiction.
The characters and all events in this publication are fictitious. Any similarity to real persons alive or dead is purely coincidental.

All rights reserved. This book or any portion thereof
may not be reproduced or used in any manner whatsoever without the express written permission of the author
except for the use of brief quotations in a book review.

Printed in the United Kingdom

ISBN 978-1-78723-003-3

CompletelyNovel.com

Pictures Of Deceit

By

S C Richmond

Prologue

It was Monday morning, she walked into the office a little worse for wear, she'd drunk more than a couple of glasses of red wine the night before and although at the time it was enjoyable, this morning was proving to be an effort. Drinking two nights in a row just didn't agree with her.

The office was packed with people, she hadn't realised just how many people actually worked on the paper, most of them she knew but a few of them she'd never seen before and it seemed they were all gathered around the desks at the far end of the room. Alex tried to sneak through unnoticed, she just wanted to make it to her desk and drink a much needed strong coffee to stave off the impending hangover. The low level chatter was already getting under her skin and she hadn't been in for more than three minutes. Alex tried to slip in as unobtrusively as possible to her desk which she had eventually come to love but would always fondly think of as her grubby little desk. Fiona spotted Alex and beckoned her over to the group, there was no escape, no way she could ignore it and so she walked towards them forcing a smile. They were gathered around a pile of opened newspapers that had been spread across two desks. "You were at the opening night on Saturday weren't you Alex?" Fiona asked excitedly. The others looked up expectantly. "Yes, it was a great night. Why, what's up?"

"You've not heard the news? Its Masters... he's gone missing. No-one's heard from him since he opened the exhibition."

"Whoa. How? Oh no..." Alex could feel her quiet day slipping away.

"Alex, are you okay?"

"Yes, just a headache Fi." Alex forced a smile, she didn't want to show too much of a reaction in the office but she needed to find out what this was all about. She hung around for long enough to have a look through the headlines in the nationals and see what was going on then made her escape as soon as possible without showing any emotion that would betray her. She reached her desk, sat down heavily and turned on the computer. Now what was she going to do?

Chapter One

Excitement was at an all-time high in Charmsbury and the buzz was being created by Michael Masters, the world famous art dealer, who was holding an exhibition in the town.

Michael had been born in Charmsbury and started to make his name around the town by selling local artists work from a market stall, he sold some of his own work too but where his work was at best mediocre, he recognised that he had a great talent for discovering new artists. By the time he was twenty years old he had got rid of his market stall and opened a shop on the High Street. Michael was the man in the know if you wanted some really good up and coming art. At the age of twenty three he left Charmsbury, the shop remained but the calling took him to London where he opened another shop, following London he opened several more in Milan, Paris, Rome, New York, Bangkok and rumour had it another was shortly to be opened in Shanghai. Michael was a self-made man and possibly one of the most eligible bachelors in Europe.

Now in 2016 he had chosen to bring art back to his home town, back to where it had all started. This latest exhibition was called 'Starlight' and would be opening in the same shop that started his career in the art world, the gossip going around town was that Michael would be coming back to open the exhibition in person. According to an old magazine article, he had kept the shop in Charmsbury so he would never forget where he came from and to remind him to keep his feet on the ground and his head out of the clouds. Over the years it had always stayed as an art shop, it had been rented to a company that specialised in prints by famous artists but recently it had reverted to 'Masters Fine Arts' again. If the rumoured plans were correct then it would be the second time he had publicly returned to his hometown in twenty two years.

Mel had managed to get her hands on two tickets to the opening night and had talked Alex into going with her to keep her company, although, Alex wasn't overwhelmed with desire to view pointless works of art all evening. She had never understood modern art and certainly wasn't inspired by it, on the up side it would make a good piece for the local paper she worked for, the Daily News, even though she wasn't the chosen journalist to cover the opening night, she at least would be on the inside, so would need to try and be as objective as possible about the work on show.

Everywhere she had been that day was making the most of the opening night, she couldn't turn a corner without seeing posters, wherever she looked people were handing out flyers on the street, according to the local shopkeepers that she talked to business was at a record high. There were tourists everywhere and they were all heading towards the shop where the exhibition was being held. They took photos of themselves and their loved ones in front of the big arty posters that covered the windows with the dates and time of the exhibition openings, Facebook and Instagram had been full of these photos for days now. The high end clothes shops were doing a roaring trade, so it seemed that Charmsbury was going to be the place to be seen in a few days' time, as the rest of the world must be suffering from a severe lack of silk and sequins because everyone who was anyone was buying up dresses as if their lives depended upon it. The local hotel 'The Duke' was fully booked and it seemed most of the rooms were taken by television crews and the national press. Alex didn't think she'd ever seen the town so alive, with such an air of excitement.

She didn't know much about Michael Masters as she'd only been a baby when he had left town, what she did know was gleaned from newspaper and magazine articles and things her parents had told her, they had grown up with him being around and witnessed first-hand his rise to success.

The following two days saw Charmsbury slowly overtaken by television crews in their huge vans and journalists from around the world. Everyone was jostling for places, they all wanted to be the first to get the top story, the best dressed celebrity or the new works of art that Michael Masters was about to put on the world's art map.

Mel was effervescent with excitement; she had won the tickets for the opening night on a local radio competition and asked Alex to join her for the evening. They had been friends for the past year since they met whilst Alex had been working on a big story about an underground community and Mel had helped her with some information, now they saw each other regularly and swapped gossip almost daily.

Already it was Saturday; the day had come around quickly. It was the day of the exhibition and Alex and Mel were determined to make the most of it, in the afternoon they were booked in for a pampering session at the local beauticians and then back to Mel's to get changed. It had been a beautiful day and now the evening was rolling in, the weather had stayed clear and warm. They were dressed in the finest clothes that could be found in Charmsbury and were overjoyed with the effect. The taxi turned up exactly on time so they could start the evening in style by going to 'Hearts', the most upmarket bistro in town, which was hosting the pre-show party. The two girls were feeling nicely relaxed by the time they had indulged in cocktails, canapés and fine wines and were feeling ready to attend the opening of the exhibition. The excitement was building, the atmosphere was heady and whilst the rest of the town looked on they would be the ones going inside, if luck was with them they might see themselves on television. There were cameras and journalists everywhere and the cameras were capturing the movements of everyone approaching the entrance.

Chapter Two

As Alex approached the shop front she noticed the effect, it was stunning, it was lit with hundreds of tiny LED lights spelling out the word 'Starlight' in different shades of gold, it was surrounded by more lights giving the impression of twinkling stars ranging from gold's to silvers, even the flat above the shop had been decorated with lights. The clear night sky gave the perfect backdrop and put on its own display of twinkling stars, it couldn't have been more perfect. The shops sign 'Masters Fine Arts' was barely legible, lost in all of the other lights shining from the windows and the golden spotlights shining towards it. There was even a gold carpet laid out on the approach to the shop and Alex and Mel felt like stars themselves, so after watching enough of them on television this was what it felt like going to a movie premier. Alex glanced around to see the other people who were arriving, she had to wonder if all of the insurance companies around the country were nervous as hell, it seemed like all of the best jewellery was on show here, worn by some of the most glamorous women she had ever seen and they were just strolling down Charmsbury High Street. Alex had to smile; the town had never seen anything quite like this before, it was quite a spectacle.

Barriers had been set up along either side to the road so that at all times and from all angles the press could get good unobscured shots of the windows, the celebrities and hopefully Michael Masters himself if he did put in an appearance. From what Alex knew of the man he was a very private person, rarely giving interviews, preferring instead to issue press releases and stay in the background.

Alex and Mel walked towards the shop with the eyes of Charmsbury turned towards them, Mel looked beautiful as she always did with her perfect blonde bob and stunning silver and turquoise sequined cocktail dress and four inch Jimmy Choo's, there were few people that could carry off glamour like Mel. Alex had opted for a long black classic evening dress with gold accessories, her hair up in a chignon now she had let it grow a little longer and four inch heels that brought her up to a towering five foot six, she thought she looked pretty good and she felt a million dollars. The champagne cocktails had given an extra boost and they were out to have fun. Cameras and journalists scanned the faces of everyone heading towards Masters Fine Arts, hoping to find someone interesting that they could get an interview from and feature in tomorrow's news. Alex silently wished them luck; she for once was off duty. She noticed Nick from the office in the press scrum, so that was who they had given the big story to; she smiled and waved at him. He acted up and took a few shots; they twirled and pouted for him to a ripple of applause from the other photographers.

They walked through the doorway of the shop into more golden lighting and immediately a waiter appeared to offer Champagne served from a gold tray, which was gladly accepted, Alex looked around but so far there was no art to see. The shop inside was narrow but long and had been partitioned off presumably so the exhibition would be a surprise until you were in front of the art itself. Alex spotted a huge chocolate fountain surrounded by ripe fat strawberries and instinctively went to move in that direction, Mel pulled her back and nodded towards the side of the room. Out of a sliding door to her left walked Michael Masters he was very handsome, slim, wavy dark hair and soft brown eyes and he was perfectly dressed in a black suit with a gold waistcoat and his trademark gold tipped cowboy boots, he appeared every inch the showman. He walked up to a small stage and Alex grabbed her mobile to record whatever was coming next for Nick, for him being stuck outside would be frustrating, missing the action inside and just maybe it would give his photos the edge having a bit of inside information to attach to them. The speech was short; Michael welcomed everyone to the exhibition and his home town and said how happy he was to be back. He mentioned the artist's names that were exhibiting and wished everyone a good evening. With that he opened the sheer curtains that had created the divide and the exhibition was opened.

Armed with their glasses of Champagne they went off to investigate, Alex took a swerve to the chocolate fountain to help herself to a chocolate dipped strawberry then caught up with Mel to check out the art. There were vast swathes of gold silk surrounding whole areas that held the works of art, there was a breeze coming from somewhere that made the silk shimmer in the most magical way. They walked into the first area which was a brief history of Charmsbury told in paintings by local artists, displaying how the town had changed over the years. Alex thought some of these were really good, she hadn't realised the town held so much talent. She had found her favourite already, a small pen and ink sketch of the now famous Charmsbury well with a huge bramble bush in the background; it brought back some lovely memories of the previous year. In tiny letters in the corner of the work was the artists name 'Jack Adams' and a small triquetra. Alex smiled, she was so proud of Jack, he wasn't around tonight as he had taken Mary away for a couple of days holiday, they were still busy making up for lost time.

She moved on, Mel was chatting to a very elegant elderly lady so Alex went on to the next section alone, there was nothing there that interested her, it was a whole area of modern art and this was something that Alex just didn't understand. She stood in front of a huge canvas that had been painted blue with a black stripe down the middle and a green what can only be described as a splodge in the left corner. She looked at it trying to work out what on earth it was meant to represent. A voice cut through her thoughts and startled her a little "So do you like this one?" Her instant reaction was "God no! I just don't get it." Before she even knew who she was talking to, she turned around to face the voice and found herself looking up towards Michael Masters, he was watching her and smiling, it was a charming smile. "Oh, sorry." She blushed.

"Don't be, it's refreshing to hear someone being honest, can I let you into a secret?" She nodded her reply. "I don't get it either. It's order and chaos, so the artist tells me." They both smiled and any awkwardness was diffused in an instant. "Come with me and let me show you something I think you might like." They walked out into another area towards the back of the exhibition, Alex followed him, he stopped and swept aside a drape of silk and they stepped into a new section. She found herself facing a large canvas, it took her breath away. It was a scene from a market looking out to sea at a stunning sunrise over mountains. It looked oriental from the few people in the foreground at the market, it was beautiful, she realised she had been holding her breath as she immersed herself in the painting, Michael was watching her with a smile on his face "You approve of this one then."

It's beautiful, so much detail and the colours are so rich, almost Pre-Raphaelite in style, this is much more to my taste." Her eyes roamed back to the painting she was enchanted by it. She looked back towards Michael but the space he had filled a moment before was now empty. He had found her this work of art and left her to enjoy it. She glanced at the tag on the wall it said 'Buddha Mountain' 13,000 GBP. She had no doubt it was worth it but she would have to live without it in her life. She turned her attention back to it and again got lost in it, picking out lots of details, totally enthralled. Mel caught up with her and interrupted her relationship with the painting, "Wow that's beautiful, so how was Michael, I saw you talking to him."

"It was more like him talking to me but he seemed really nice, he disappeared once he'd shown me this, he's obviously very good at what he does."

"Really nice eh?" Mel smiled cheekily.

"No. Although he was charming... and quite handsome." She winked at Mel and turned her attention back to 'Buddha Mountain'.

They spent the next hour looking around the exhibition then returned to the welcome area to get a fresh drink. Mel got chatting to a guy who was wearing an ID badge maybe one of the artists, who she seemed quite interested in if her body language was anything to go by, he was a pleasant enough looking man with quite sharp features. Alex sat on a deep plush settee, people watching, there were few celebrities but plenty of local dignitaries and Michael was wowing them all by the look of things, he mixed easily with his guests and left everyone he spoke to smiling. Every so often Mel would flash Alex a big smile, things were obviously going well with her new friend. Michael appeared next to her and joined her on the settee "Are you related to a lady called Janet by any chance?"

"Yes she's my Mum, how did you know?"

"You look exactly like she did the last time I saw her, you have her eyes." This led him onto several minutes of reminiscing about his Charmsbury days, he had gone to the same school as her Mum and to Alex's surprise he seemed genuinely interested in her family gossip, he seemed interested in her career too, she had thought it may make him feel uncomfortable but he just took it in his stride.

Mel was still batting her eyelashes at her companion and they appeared to be getting along well so when Michael asked her to join him for a drink she eagerly agreed and waved at Mel to let her know. He led her through to the rear of the exhibition, through a set of double doors and turned into an office space that looked like it had come straight out of a 1950's movie. It was dimly lit with Tiffany lamps that looked antique, a mahogany leather desk, deep studded red leather chairs and lots of books, Alex was impressed. Michael offered her a drink and they sat down and talked. They discussed his career, friends, enemies, loves and expectations. Alex couldn't believe her luck. It did seem strange that he would tell her, a journalist, all of these details of his life but she listened enthralled as his life unfolded before her. They chatted and laughed, he was great company and it felt like he seemed almost relieved to have shared his story, as if he was shedding a very old, very heavy coat. "I've had a wonderful evening Michael, just one thing, why would you tell me all of this about yourself? I've heard you don't speak to journalists." She didn't want to spoil the mood but felt like she needed to ask.

"You're not just a journalist Alex, you're Janet's daughter and I feel comfortable with you, it is hardly an interview you haven't asked me any uncomfortable questions." Alex smiled and felt better for mentioning it, it didn't seem to slow down him talking to her, he continued on with the outpouring of his life.

Her phone buzzed in her pocket, she glanced at the message whilst Michael fixed her another drink, it was Mel she was heading off to a club with the artist and apparently his name was Lee. She shared this information with Michael and he laughed. "Lee loves the ladies." She sensed a little sarcasm but let it go.

"I hope he'll look after her?"

"I'm sure he will; she'll be safe with him."

Alex sent a message back telling her to have fun, now she could relax and chat for longer; she was enjoying Michael's company.

Chapter Three

Michael leant back in his seat studying Alex; she really did look like her Mother, the same silver grey eyes, the resemblance was uncanny. He felt almost physically lighter having offloaded his story and Alex was a willing listener, he'd enjoyed going through his life and telling her his thoughts and feelings of many of the things he had encountered and he was almost grateful that she was a journalist at least she knew how to listen but he was surprised she had posed so few questions. It was time for Alex to leave, Michael asked his driver to take her home and although she was tempted to refuse, the thought of arriving home in a chauffeur driven luxurious Rolls Royce seemed irresistible and he would not allow her to go home on her own after drinking with him. He showed her to the car and held the door open for her. "Say hello to your Mum for me Alex."

"I will and thank you for an interesting evening Michael." He smiled and pushed the door closed; it gave a satisfying click and he turned his back to her. With that she was whisked away to her home and back to her own life.

The whole evening had been huge a success, the exhibition had gone off without a hitch and he was pleased with the way it had turned out. The locals were proud, the artists happy and there had been better than hoped press coverage, they had come from around the globe to see this. He really couldn't have hoped for a better evening.

Now his work was complete, a story left behind with a willing listener who couldn't believe her luck to have the interview that journalists had been after for years, everyone seemed happy so now he could move on as he had wanted to for some years. He had begun to feel trapped, tired of women throwing themselves at him, artists desperate to befriend him and everyone he knew trying to make money out of him one way or another. He knew a number of them would be waiting at the hotel for him tonight. They would call it celebratory drinks but all they wanted was to worm their way into his world and take a little piece of it for themselves.

  He casually put his feet up on the desk and leant back into his comfortable leather chair sipping his single malt. Of course he would miss all of this, the relaxing in opulent surroundings, the food, the wine, that quiet moment at the end of an evening when something had come to fruition and he could just sit back and enjoy it but now he was sure it was time for a complete change. He was looking forward to the next phase of his life, it would be daunting leaving the money behind, he had no idea how it would all end but he felt he needed to find some peace. He would never be more ready than he was now.

Chapter Four

When Alex pulled up outside the house she asked the chauffer to sound the horn, after a moment the curtain moved and Matt's face appeared at the window, he smiled and came out to join her as the chauffer got out, came to her side of the vehicle and opened the door, lending his hand to help her exit the car elegantly. Matt watched with admiration for the way she was being treated. "What have you been up to that gets you brought home in a car like this?" He grinned whilst he took a good look around the car. Alex cheekily took a photo of the car and chauffeur on her mobile, he obliged and posed for her, she needed something to remember this journey by. They said goodbye and gave their thanks to the driver, watched him drive away and went into the house. Alex loved coming back to a house, sure she missed her flat but her relationship with Matt had moved fast and before she knew it she had moved in with him and couldn't be happier.

Matt arranged himself comfortably on the settee, where he'd been watching a movie and pulled Alex down to snuggle in next to him. "So how did it go?"

"It was great, the exhibition was much better than I had anticipated, Mel met an artist and allowed herself to be swept off her feet and I got an interview with Michael Masters." She paused for effect "Well it was more of a chat, he seems like a really nice guy and he lent me his car and driver to get home."

"Oh… should I be jealous? Isn't he one of the most eligible bachelors in the world?" He grinned his cheeky lopsided grin at her. He already knew the answer, it needed no reply. Her phone pinged, it was a message from Mel, she was having a wonderful evening and apologised for abandoning her. Alex was pleased for her she needed some fun in her life; she returned her attention to Matt, snuggled in closer and settled in to watch the end of the movie and helped him finish his glass of wine.

They overslept the next morning but luckily neither of them had any work to go to, it was going to be a relaxing Sunday, they didn't often get the chance to laze around so they would make the most of it, they went shopping and returned home and Matt cooked a Sunday roast, Alex curled up on the settee to read a book, later in the day they decided to spend the evening in with a bottle of wine or two and a movie. Alex still had to pinch herself from time to time to make sure all of this was real, she couldn't believe how lucky she was and how much she enjoyed the domestic bliss. They did exactly what they'd planned for the evening, curled up on the settee and enjoyed each other's company.

Monday morning rolled around all too quickly and for the second time they both overslept, they raced around trying to grab some breakfast, get dressed and get out of the door in time for work, Matt made it, Alex didn't.

She got into work a little over thirty minutes late and the atmosphere was manic, newspapers scattered everywhere, the level of chatter much too high for Alex this morning. After Fiona had passed on the news of Michael's disappearance she had no idea what to do, she was sitting on a comprehensive story and wasn't sure if she should release the interview or not. It still bothered her that it wasn't technically an interview and that maybe he'd just felt comfortable chatting with her, otherwise why would he have told her all of those personal things about himself. Even though this could make her name as a journalist, put her in the big league but she couldn't bring herself to be hardnosed enough about it to just print and be damned. First thing was to find out as much as she could about what had happened, then she would decide the right thing to do, with luck she could find a way around having to give too much away. He had seemed so kind and sincere and she didn't really want to tell the world all about his life at least not without his go ahead. He had spoken to her as a friend, an equal but there were a few revelations that would make the story shine, what was playing on her mind was the part when he had asked her what life was about. She had no answer for him and he had seemed thoughtful on that topic saying that he no longer saw the point in what he did, that it all seemed so meaningless. She seriously hoped that he wasn't thinking of doing anything stupid.

She thought she should discuss what she knew with Matt and maybe he could help decide what was best to do, he was the sensible one, so far she had told him little of their conversation. First she wanted to speak to her Mum; she picked up the desk phone and punched in the number. "Hi Mum, can I pop round later? I need to speak to you about Michael Masters."

"Hi, of course you can. Did you meet him Saturday night?"

"Yes, I spoke to him and now he's disappeared and I need some advice. I know you knew him, he only recognised me and spoke to me because of you and he asked me to say hello." Alex felt relieved just telling someone about her chat with Michael.

"Wow, okay, I'll see you later but I'm not sure what I can tell you that's of any interest. It was a long time ago." They said their goodbyes and Alex moved on to thinking about Matt, she really should contact him and soon. After a couple of rings he answered but he sounded flustered "Hi sweetheart, can I call you back? We've got the worlds media camped outside the station and everyone is demanding to know what's happened to Mr Masters, we appear to have lost him."

"That's what I'm calling you about Matt, you know I spoke with him Saturday night and now I'm worried, it seems that I may have been the last person to have seen him. Will it be you in charge of the investigation?"

"Not just me Alex, there's lots of involvement at all levels with him being such a big shot but we will be doing the groundwork and we're certainly trying to find him. You've got nothing to worry about, you came home to me and that's a pretty water tight alibi." He laughed "I don't suppose he mentioned that he might be going anywhere did he?"

"No, I kind of wish he had, do you think I should publish what he told me that night?"

"No! Whilst this is under investigation you only need to tell us, it may be nothing but there may be some clues in there that we can work on. Someone will ring you later, okay? I don't want you getting mixed up in anything Alex, when he turns up safe and well that's when you can publish your story."

"Okay, thanks." She was relieved, she had needed someone to tell her how to handle this.

She settled down at her desk and reached for another headache tablet then sent Nick some of the photos she had managed to get for him of the inside of the venue, she chose to hold back any photos that had Michael Masters in them just in case Matt wanted to see them first. She didn't send him the speech that she had recorded either that was going to be her safe story for today, other journalists would have that too and would certainly be publishing it so she may as well hop on the bandwagon with them albeit a little reluctantly but it would keep her toe in the water until she could release more information. This was a big story and she didn't want her editor, Charlie, to miss out on something even though she technically hadn't been working at the time. Her fingers skipped over the keyboard putting together the same story that everyone else would have and she'd never felt so relieved about it. She forwarded the story to Charlie and grabbed her jacket, as she walked through the office Nick raised his hand and mouthed thank you to her. It was time to go and see what her Mum knew about Michael Masters.

Chapter Five

Michael was sitting in a pool of sunlight, starting to relax after the hectic journey he had just undergone, it was hard to believe it was only forty eight hours ago that he had been getting ready to host his swansong exhibition. He glanced up from the table and looked around at the town square, pretty, clean and the heat was incredibly welcome, he picked up his coffee and inwardly told himself to relax, life was now in the lap of the gods. He looked over at the people on the other tables and no-one seemed to be taking any notice of him even though from where he was sitting he could clearly see his own face on the front of at least two of the newspapers stacked in the newsagents rack. He hadn't shaved since leaving Charmsbury, he was wearing tourist issue baggy shorts and a t-shirt, cheap sunglasses and a baseball cap, without the designer clothes and all the trappings of wealth he assumed he must look just like any other tourist. The only thing he was really missing was his cowboy boots, trainers weren't really his style but he was no longer Michael Masters so maybe it was time to find a new style.

Michael had discovered this small town quite by chance and decided to stay for a few days and let the heat die down before taking a chance at moving on. He liked it here it was pretty and quiet as were many towns in this part of France, the town square was tidy with an abundance of flowers, mostly bright red geraniums, the light stone buildings made it seem an even sunnier day than it actually was, he loved the way the light bounced off the stonework, it appealed to the artist in him. He was feeling quite pleased with the way he had managed to get this far so quickly. He had left Charmsbury after the exhibition, being the last to leave so that none of the staff could have seen him, he left by the back door and started to walk towards the hotel, someone he knew had been waiting to talk to him but after their discussion he walked back as far as the car park, which was where there was a car that was already packed and ready to go, nothing flash just a second hand VW Golf, not a car that would attract any attention. He had driven down to the ferry and got a ticket when he arrived there, at the border crossing the officials had barely glanced at his passport, not that it would have mattered, some time ago he had discovered a friend who had a friend who knew someone who could sort out passports in other names. He was travelling under the name of Michael Shaw, he had decided to keep his Christian name otherwise he wouldn't trust himself not to slip up and Michael was a common enough name, maybe along the way that might become a Mike or Mick, for now he was Michael and he was going to relax and enjoy a little freedom. Should anyone ever decide to sell their story about the passport dealings it wouldn't be a problem he had met other associates along the way who were happy to help and he now held three more passports in different names and countries of origin, he could just throw this one away and move on with another. Michael thought he had covered most eventualities and he'd managed to squirrel enough money away to be able to make his travels comfortable but not so much that would have been noticed. He had opened a bank account in every name that he had a passport for and drip fed cash into them for the past couple of years. Financially he should be secure for quite a while but if the money did run out then he'd just have to do what everyone else did and find some work.

   He finished the coffee and wandered contentedly out of the old square to take a look at the rest of the town.

Chapter Six

Mel was on another date with Lee but she was beginning to feel slightly disappointed, it hadn't been so much fun this evening, he seemed distracted and Mel found herself wishing she hadn't made so much of an effort. She was sitting at the table listening to Lee drone on about a piece of work he had done and where his inspiration had come from for it, it wasn't her world and she struggled to get excited about what she didn't understand, she was gazing into her glass of red wine wondering how she could get herself out of the rest of the evening. She was incredibly attracted to Lee but tonight he seemed very different to the man she had met a few days ago, she was struggling with him just talking about himself and his work, she tried to change the subject but he would always find his way back, it was going to be a long evening, she just wished she wasn't so attracted to him physically, when he touched her skin she would feel the electricity course through her, she couldn't resist him. As if someone was listening to her the door of the bar opened and in walked Alex and Matt, she was so relieved to see them, she hoped the evening would liven up if they had company.

Alex spotted them and waved, they got their drinks and joined Mel and Lee at the corner table. The talk turned to the only common ground they had which was Michael and what had or had not happened to him, they all put their theories forward, Alex seemed intrigued in hearing what everyone else thought, that'll be the journalist in her coming to the fore thought Mel, watching her take it all in. Lee seemed to have lightened up a bit too with all the talk of Michael and he too was taking a great interest in the ideas of the others. It turned out that Lee knew Michael well and had known him since he himself was a young artist. Lee was brought up in the next town, Blunsford, and the two of them had gone to school and art clubs together when it was a fledgling interest to them both and along the way they met up with many other big names in the industry. It definitely cheered Mel up to discover that Lee knew many of the famous names in the art world. Alex was finding all of Lee's talk interesting too and appeared to be taking it all in. Mel became aware of Alex watching her, she drained her glass and asked Lee and Matt what they wanted and motioned to Alex to help her carry the drinks. They stood at the bar waiting to be served "I'm glad you two turned up, before you got here the conversation was all about his work and what inspired it, now you two are here he hasn't mentioned it so much, so what do you think of him?"

"He seems okay, he likes himself and if I'm honest I think you can do better, he seems more interested in talking about Michael and himself than anything else but if you like him..." Alex answered.

"Yes he does seem very interested in Michael's disappearance, I suppose they were friends so he must be concerned but I was just a bit fed up with hearing about his work before you two arrived, does that make me bad?" Mel looked down acting as if she was ashamed.

"No but you're right he does seem interested. It is good for me to hear what other people are thinking and I suppose he must be worried about his friend."

"You don't like him much do you Alex?" Mel looked a little downcast.

"I guess I just want you to be with someone who'll make you happy and he isn't at the moment is he? You were looking bored to tears." Alex smiled and added "Come on lets liven things up." They returned to the table with the drinks and Alex took over the conversation and within a few minutes they started to relax and have fun along with a few more drinks and a change of topic. As the evening went on Lee once more turned back into the charming man she had met at the exhibition and they all ended up laughing and drinking far more than was good for them. Mel was relieved that Lee was making an effort with Alex and Matt; it was turning out to be a good night after all.

Chapter Seven

Alex was dreaming about thousands of monkeys banging on keyboards desperate to write something worthwhile, she opened her eyes and the banging continued as her brain caught up with her body. It dawned on her that there was someone at the front door and they weren't giving up, she leapt out of bed and grabbed her dressing gown and moved as fast as her body/mind combination would let her. She'd overslept again and Matt had already left for work, she ran down the stairs and pulled open the front door.

A delivery for her, the driver looked her up and down without smiling and thrust a clipboard in her direction. "Sign there." Not a good morning, sorry to have woken you…. Nothing. She signed the form without even looking at it as he motioned to a large package leant against the wall. "Thank you." She managed to say but he was already walking towards his van. "You're welcome." She sarcastically added knowing he couldn't hear her. She hadn't ordered anything, she couldn't imagine that Matt would order anything certainly not this size without mentioning it to her, maybe he'd got her a surprise. She grappled with the parcel hoping that none of the neighbours were watching her struggling with the parcel whilst trying to maintain her decency. It was a plywood box approximately two meters by one meter and it wasn't easy to manoeuvre, eventually she managed to drag it into the hallway, she went into the kitchen flicked on the percolator for her morning coffee and found a sharp knife. She carefully slid the knife through the packing tape around the edges, she pulled away the plywood and a large wad of bubble wrap and was stunned. For a moment she was amazed, unable to think straight she gazed at the picture not able to grasp why it was in her hallway just glad that it was. It was the painting that Michael had matched her up with, 'Buddha Mountain' she pinched herself to make sure she wasn't still dreaming.

Once she had recovered from the shock she took off the remainder of the packaging, on the back of the picture tucked into the edge of the frame was a small card about the same size as a business card. Alex plucked it out and turned it over in her hand the inscription was 'Thanks for listening – Michael'. So he had sent this to her personally, she needed to find out when this was sent it may just help her find out where he was. There were no more clues on the painting so she went back to the packaging to try to find the couriers details, maybe they'd be able to help.

She phoned Art Cart – specialist couriers but it turned out that they had just had a call from the exhibition to collect it and deliver it, they had only spoken with a member of the exhibition staff called William. She would head down to the exhibition and speak to William herself. She turned her attention back to the card that was attached to the painting, apart from the message there was only an orchid printed on it, he could have got that from anywhere so no clues there. The only thing she could do now was go down to the exhibition and try and find William and see what he had to say, she wasn't holding out much hope but she had to do something.

Her gaze slipped back to the painting and she thought how right Michael had been, this was definitely her kind of art, you could get lost in the blue of the sea and the sparkles of the new days sunlight hitting the water, the mountain in the background was absolutely the star, it was without a doubt a reclining Buddha. She had to pull herself away from the painting, she wanted to drop into work and see if there were any updates on Michael Masters. Charlie would be surprised to see her there on her day off, he had enough trouble getting her there when she was meant to be working. Since the story she uncovered about the tunnel under Charmsbury where a whole community were living, some as long as for fifty years Charlie had gone much easier on her and had stopped questioning her timekeeping so much, although he did like to see her at her desk occasionally. The story at the time had increased the papers readership exponentially and had grabbed the attention of readers near and far, it had also had a great effect on the local tourism.

Once she was dressed and had downed two steaming hot mugs of coffee she was ready to head off into town to try and find William. It was about eleven o'clock in the morning and as she approached the exhibition it seemed very quiet, she wasn't even sure if it was open, there seemed to be someone moving around inside but it certainly didn't look as inviting as it had on opening night, it appeared somehow seedy in the harsh light of day. She pushed open the door and it yielded immediately, she saw a couple of people moving about at the rear of the shop that looked like staff, "Sorry love we're not open yet." A disembodied voice announced from somewhere close to her. She walked towards where she thought the voice had come from. "I'm just looking for William." She said to the emptiness.

"He'll be out the back, go through." She looked around and finally found the source of the voice, a young man hanging a picture behind the silk drape; he'd seen her in the mirror. "Thanks" She nodded and smiled at him and made her way to the back of the shop. Behind a small, modern glass topped desk stood a tall very slim man with greying hair pulled back into a ponytail and sporting a gold and diamond earring. "William?"

"Hi, can I help?" He had a heavy London accent.

"I hope so, I'm Alex Price. You sent me a painting."

"Yeah the lovely Buddha Mountain, is there a problem, don't you like it?"

"No, I love it, it's breath taking but I was hoping you could throw some light on why it was sent to me or even how you knew where to send it?"

"Michael told me to, he left a note with a card, you got the card, right? Told me to find out your address and send it to you."

"My address?"

"Yes his driver told me where you lived."

"Ah, but why would he send it to me, he didn't even know me that well." She mused.

"That's Michael for you, I can't tell you anymore, he just left a note telling me to send it." He looked sad as he said it.

"When did he leave the note?"

"It was on his desk the morning after the exhibition opened."

"So you don't know where he is then?" She knew she was pushing her luck.

"Are you police or something?" He was suddenly wary.

"No, I was just worried, I've heard the news." She crossed her fingers behind her back, knowing she was the something he was referring to.

"No idea, I just hope he's okay, he's a great boss. All I know is he was seen talking to woman the night of the exhibition and then he was never seen again. Anyway enjoy the painting." With that he started to move away from the desk whilst Alex stood there concerned that she may have genuinely been the last person to see him.

"Thanks William, I will." Alex wandered back out onto the street, she was none the wiser and was still playing that horrible thought of 'what's the point' over and over in her mind.

She walked into the newspaper office with the intent of checking if there were any updates on the story but before she made it to the safety of her desk Charlie intercepted her and pulled her into his office. "I hear you got an interview with Michael Masters Alex, why haven't I seen a story on my desk yet?" Charlie was showing deep furrows on his brow, from bitter experience she knew this was going to spell trouble. He'd never completely forgiven her for writing a book about the tunnel community and not giving the paper the full story even though he had got a better story than any of the other papers with lots of exclusive interviews.

"It wasn't an interview Charlie, I don't know who you've been talking to but they've got it wrong. Michael Masters showed me a painting and we talked about it. In no way does that constitute an interview." Alex knew she needed to choose her words carefully, she didn't want to wind him up too much.

"I've been talking to Mary and she told me."

"Oh great so I haven't even spoken to my Nan but you'd believe her. Charlie if I had a story to give you..." She paused she needed to be careful with what she said, she didn't want to lie to him but she couldn't tell him the truth at the moment. She sighed, "Look, I chatted with him about art, remember, I wasn't working that night. Should I report everything I do in my life!" With that she turned on her heels and left Charlie to brood, without looking back. She strode purposefully to her desk and heaved a sigh of relief when she sat down, the whole office had watched her storm out of Charlie's office, the office gossip mill would be going into overdrive, it was only a matter of time before someone popped in to find out what was going on. They were probably picking straws right now.

She clicked the computer on and waited for it to load up, she wanted a coffee but she wasn't going to walk through the office to get one, she wasn't that brave.

The computer gave her little to no information but there were lots of write-ups about the exhibition and a rerun of an old magazine interview with him. There was nothing new and there didn't seem to be any serious sightings. She checked all of the social media sites there was nothing there either other than gossip. She turned the computer off, grabbed her jacket and ran the gauntlet of the office just to get out to the local coffee shop. She made it in one piece.

Chapter Eight

Matt was fully occupied trying to put together a team of volunteers to field the calls that were coming in of sightings of Michael Masters. There was no end of people willing to help and sit in the basement of an office block on their days off but he knew after a week of doing it the flow of volunteers would dry up, they would get bored unless something happened to hold their interest, that would be when his job would become a lot more difficult. Michael had been gone for four days now and apart from a few alleged sightings that came in from a wide variety of places around the country which amounted to nothing there was no news. He did know that Alex could well have been the last person admitting to have seen him, he knew what they had discussed that night and there seemed to be no real clues there, he needed a break. The phone rang and broke through his thoughts he looked at the callers ID and smiled "Hi babe, everything okay?"

"Hi, yes fine, you'll never guess what's happened… I had a delivery this morning."

"Been shopping online again?"

"No, no but if I had you'd have gone mad at me spending thirteen thousand pounds."

"What are you talking about?" He could hear the excitement in her voice.

"The painting I told you about… remember, the one at the exhibition? Well it turned up on our doorstep this morning."

"What… how?"

"It came with a card that just said thanks for listening, signed by Michael. I've checked out the couriers and the staff at the exhibition and they were just given instructions to send it to me in a note Michael left."

"I'll go and talk to them and see if they'll tell me anything they haven't told you, but why would he send it to you?"

"Maybe he appreciated my listening skills." There was a smile in her voice.

"Okay, I'll go and check it out and find out why no-one mentioned a note being left." He hung up a little abruptly, he knew it was stupid but he felt a little jealous.

He grabbed his coat and walked down to the exhibition, when he got there it was open and there were a few people milling around checking out the art but he couldn't see any staff. He wandered around looking at the paintings until he saw a young guy hanging a picture. "Hi, can you tell me where I can find William?" The guy looked up and pointed to the back of the room. "He'll be over there by that desk somewhere or in the office just through that door." Matt wandered off in that direction. There didn't appear to be anyone around, he pushed through the double doors behind the desk and found himself in a small grey hallway with a fire exit at the opposite end, it was a dull drab area in contrast to the shop, to his left was another door. He knocked on the door and walked in, great detective he thought to himself and smiled, he had found the stationery cupboard, he came out and closed the door and went for the only other available option a door on the right. It opened onto a small office area with soft low lighting, an antique mahogany desk and deep leather chairs, tiffany lamps and a wall full of books. It was the room Alex had described to him and she had been right it was like walking back in time to a study in a grand house, it felt warm and welcoming but he still hadn't found William. As if on cue he heard a movement behind him. "Can I help you?" A tall slim man stood there scowling at him.

"I'm looking for William."

"You've found him, what are you doing in here?" He didn't look happy.

"Young guy out front sent me through; can I ask you a couple of questions?" He knew the uniform meant that William wouldn't refuse even if he wanted to.

"Pah!" He still didn't look happy. "Okay."

"We're enquiring into the whereabouts of Michael Masters, is there anything you can tell us?"

"No."

"We've heard that Mr Masters left you a note before he disappeared, can I see it?"

"Sure it's on his desk." William walked to the desk and picked up a couple of pieces of paper and handed them to Matt. The papers were Masters Fine Art letterheads with a list of instructions written on them.

Send Lee the attached envelope and paperwork.
Pay D M Waite 10K from the exhibition Acc No. on file.
Find address for Alex Price – send 'Buddha Mountain'
with attached card.
Send Jasmine flowers and attached card.
Give yourself a bonus 5k on completion of exhibition.
Send attached letters.
- MM

"So who are D M Waite and Jasmine?" Matt took a photo of the note on his phone and looked at William.

"Don Waite is one of our exhibiting artists, quite popular with the traditional art collectors, I don't think I've ever met him but he exhibits from time to time with us. I'm pretty sure he lives abroad. Jasmine is the latest in a long line of Michael's girlfriends."

"Did he leave anything else?"

"Just this list."

"Are you a business partner?"

"No, I just work for him." William was getting bored with the questioning.

"So how is it you're able to deal with the money side of things?"

"He added me as signatory a while ago, we go a long way back, and I guess he trusted me. Can I get back to work now?" William appeared to be being honest and open about things.

"He must have trusted you to put you in that position with the size of his company. Have you done everything on the list?"

"Yes, except paying myself."

"Sorry but this won't take much longer William, I need to ask, if we're going to find him. The reference to attached letters, who were they for, what would they have been and were any of them unusual correspondence?"

"Accountants, artists, that kind of thing, to be honest I didn't take much notice I just dumped them in the post box, there were six or seven. I don't normally deal with paperwork so it would have meant nothing to me."

"If you remember who they were for could you get in touch and let me know and can I have Jasmine's address?" Matt handed him a personal card with his details on, it was all he had on him, William did a double take at the address on the card. "Yes it's the same address that you sent the painting to." Matt smiled. "If you hear anything or have any contact with Michael can you call me please?" William nodded and scribbled Jasmine's details down on a scrap of paper. "Thanks, don't mind if I have a look around the exhibition before I go do you?"

"No, take your time." With that William left the room to presumably continue whatever he had been doing, he certainly wasn't going to waste any more of his time showing Matt around. Matt shrugged and looked around at the expensive looking study one last time. He'd love a room like this at home. There was a row of leather bound books held in place by a pair of bronze hare bookends, he had always believed if you wanted an insight into someone's personality you should take a look at what they read, surprisingly there was only one book on art, that was about the Pre-Raphaelites, the other spines showed medieval history and travel books that spanned the globe but not new editions, so Michael loved his history. These wouldn't tell Matt much, there was nothing specific enough to take any notice of, he took a few random photos of the room on his mobile hoping that Alex might notice something out of place, it was a long shot but he'd take anything he could get at the moment. People don't just disappear off the face of the earth without some clues.

Chapter Nine

Alex pulled up outside the tidy terraced house that she had grown up in, everything was in its place and the house looked as welcoming as it always had to her. Her Mum was opening the door before she had even reached it. "Kettle's on." Was the greeting she got, she followed her Mum into the house. She loved this house, hardly anything had changed since she was young. Visiting always felt like she was wrapping herself in a warm blanket. She threw her bag on the first chair she came to in the lounge and collapsed into the settee. Her Mum came through with the drinks, set them down on the coffee table and settled into the armchair opposite Alex. "You're looking well sweetheart, that man's obviously treating you right."

"Thanks Mum, yes he is." Alex grinned. After the pleasantries were over Alex jumped straight in. "Never mind me, how is it that Michael Masters remembers you so well Mum?"

"I don't know why but we were friends at school, he was always hanging around. Back then he wasn't anything like the man you see now, he was intense and his art was everything to him, every time you saw him he was sketching or reading up about artists."

"But he recognised me because of you, so you must have made an impression on him, or he has a terrific memory that twenty five to thirty years on he can still picture you."

Janet grinned "Well, there was one time."

"Eeeww, Stop I don't need those kinds of details."

"Oh okay, only joking." She winked at Alex. "I think he had a bit of a crush on me, every time he saw me he'd give me those big puppy eyes but he wasn't my type, nothing like your

Dad. We went on one date and held hands there was nothing else; of course if I'd have known that he would grow into such a handsome man maybe I'd have tried harder, he was very different back then. Just after that I met your Dad and Michael was long forgotten."

"That would explain why he remembered you then, his first love or maybe the one that got away, you know he never married?" Alex was beginning to enjoy teasing her Mum. "Was there anything else about him?"

"Not really, I only remember him as a wannabe artist but he wasn't that good. He loved the Pre-Raphaelite artists, Rossetti, Burne-Jones and Waterhouse it was the style he wanted to paint in but he just didn't have the talent, he started to hang around with a few lads who could paint and draw and he got himself a market stall and sold their stuff, I guess he had a good eye for art and a head for selling. The rest as they say is history."

"Yes he definitely knows how to match people up to the art that suits them." Alex mused "He sent me a painting, the one he matched me up with on the opening night. He was right too it was the only one in the whole exhibition that inspired me."

"He just sent it to you?" Janet looked surprised.

"Yes, it turned up this morning."

"I wonder why he would do that?"

"The card that came with it just said thanks for listening."

"Sounds odd, he was never known for his generosity but I suppose I only know him from a long time ago, maybe he's changed."

Alex drained her mug of now cold tea, gave her Mum a hug and headed off for her next source of information, her Nan.

Chapter Ten

She pulled up outside her Nan's house; Jack was in the front garden tidying the flower beds. "Hi Jack, they're looking lovely." She pointed to the flowers. "I loved the drawing you did for the exhibition too."

"Thanks, the drawing was easy compared to what she's got me doing here, weeds never used to bother me but she's taught me the difference between them and plants so now I have no excuse. She's got me well trained!" He smiled at her. Alex had a real soft spot for Jack, he wasn't her Granddad but he was the next best thing and she was glad that after the life he had had with the community that he and her Nan had found each other again after fifty years of separation. Alex walked in through the open door and could smell the welcome, Nan was baking and yet again it smelt like she'd timed her visit to perfection. "Hi Nan" She shouted as she walked through the house.

"Hello Alex, coffee and cake?" Came the reply.

"Obviously!" Alex smiled and walked into the kitchen. "Now what have you been telling people about me getting an interview with Michael Masters."

"Well you did didn't you?"

"No, we had a chat, that's really not the same thing Nan, now I have Charlie on my back for a story."

"Sorry love but I thought you'd got a scoop and I was so proud I had to tell someone."

"Never mind Nan, I can deal with Charlie if I have to, he's just wound up because Michaels disappeared and he thinks I know something but the stuff we talked about I can't use. Who told you anyway?"

"Matt, when I phoned and you were in the bath. He sounded rather proud of you."

"What did you think of Michael, you knew him when he was a boy didn't you?" Alex figured she might get some gossip, after all her Nan knew everyone and always got all of the interesting information.

"Oh he was a sweet boy, good manners and all but he was always hanging around your Mum and trying to get her to notice him, the people he hung around with were an odd bunch." She wrinkled her nose up.

"They were artists Nan, not odd."

"They were odd! There was one skinny little fella who stuck to Michael like glue, but he was a spiteful little thing, always trying to get your Mum out of the way. I guess that's just kids though."

"So what happened with Mum then?"

"Nothing, she didn't like Michael as anything more than a friend and eventually I think he got the message and gradually we saw less and less of him, especially when she met your Dad, from then on she never had eyes for anyone else."

"Oh I'm disappointed I thought I was going to get the family secrets. I spoke with Michael and he seemed really nice, a gentleman, I bet Matt told you about my chauffer driven ride home too?"

"Yes he did, don't be fooled by Michael though." She paused. "Although he's grown up now, maybe I'm being unkind." Alex doubted that, her Nan was never unkind to anyone, even those who deserved it. "Why did he speak to you? I've heard he doesn't talk to the press."

"He kind of recognised me or at least the Mum part of me, he asked if I was her daughter and then we sat together talking about art."

"So you got the interview then?"

"No Nan, I told you we just had a chat, no interview!" She knew her Nan was just trying to trip her up on the off chance she was holding anything back, she always had to be the first to get the gossip.

They spent the next hour discussing Jack's artwork of which her Nan was incredibly proud, their holiday in Devon and ideas for their wedding which was due to happen next summer, both her Nan and Jack were blissfully happy.

Chapter Eleven

Michael was beginning to enjoy his new found freedom, his face no longer seemed to be on the front of every newspaper and as far as he knew no-one thus far had recognised him. He was just beginning to unwind and was no longer constantly looking over his shoulder waiting for someone to notice him. He had found his way to a small town called Seix in the foothills of the Pyrenees it was stunningly beautiful and incredibly peaceful. He pulled the car up in front of a small guest house next to the river, this would be home for the next few days whilst he investigated the area. He was appreciating being able to do whatever he felt like doing, no schedule, no meetings. As he got out of the car and approached the slightly tired looking guest house two walkers strolled past and waved a greeting, he raised his hand in response to them. He'd missed out on this type of easy going life because he chose to chase a career, money and surround himself with false friends, now he was beginning to see what a fool he had been. He stopped for a moment and just concentrated on breathing in the fresh, clean air.

The next few days were taken up with strolling up and down hills, country lanes and along rivers enjoying the simple village life, he also brought himself a sketch pad and started drawing, the work was a bit rusty but it felt good to appreciate the beautiful scenery the only way he knew how, through his art. He was getting himself back together and finally doing the things he loved, knowing it would bring some peace and being alone was making him feel whole again. Now he understood why people went off on retreats but this was far better than any new age therapy and he knew, he had tried them all.

It was the last night in the guest house, he was lying awake in his sparse room thinking that he'd like to stay for another day or two and there was nothing stopping him from doing so. His hosts spoke English well and the smattering of French he spoke was increasing daily so he could organise a longer stay without too much trouble, with that thought he fell into a deep slumber.

He woke up feeling content and well rested, he couldn't remember the last time that had happened, he showered and got dressed and went downstairs to find Pierre. At the small counter where Pierre's guests checked in there was a newspaper in English opened to half way through, it was obviously in the process of being read when Pierre must have been called away to tend to one of his guests. He turned the paper around and looked at the date, it was a day old but that probably wasn't unusual here after all they were a bit off the beaten track. He flicked through a few pages and found himself looking at a grainy photo of himself buying a sandwich at a motorway service station. He felt his heart speed up. He remembered this pit stop well, he had left quickly because he thought he may be spotted when he noticed lots of cameras all over the complex but he had been hungry and needed to get something to eat. Stupid maybe but it was too late to undo it now. The journalist that had written the story revealed that they weren't sure if it was him or not and the picture from the security cameras was not of a good enough quality to prove one way or another. Also to his surprise there was no mention of an interview before he disappeared or anything about him speaking with Alex. 'Trust me.' He thought, to pick the only journalist in the universe that has a conscience, the one time you want them to print they don't. He had thought she would want to claim the glory of getting the last interview with him.

He jumped, startled; Pierre was stood next to him watching him reading the newspaper. How long had he been there? "Bonjour" he said and smiled. "Interesting story?" he looked at the picture then up to Michael. "Looks like you a little, don't you think?" The heavy French accent made every word sound almost romantic.

"Not really, I'd love to have his money though."

"Yes of course you're right, Mr Masters would not stop here he would be in the big hotels in Cannes." For a moment it had winded Michael but it seemed that his host was just making conversation or at least he hoped he was. Feeling a little more at ease now Michael booked another night, had a large breakfast and went out to continue his drawing. Tomorrow he knew he would move on, the encounter with the newspaper had unnerved him and the last thing he wanted was Pierre to get in touch with the newspapers. He must also consider changing his car, if the photos of him in the paper were from inside the service station they were sure to have photos of him leaving and of what he was driving, they would now be able to trace him as long as he had the car. It was a shame, he liked it here but now it felt like it was time to move on and try to get rid of the vehicle. He needed to decide where he would like to go next; he could do that whilst he listened to the water tumbling over the rocks down at the river's edge.

Chapter Twelve

It was already six days into Michael's disappearance and there were still no firm sightings. The national papers had run a story claiming that he had been seen in a service station in Kent but the security camera footage was too distorted to be sure who it was and when he left, the security cameras in the car park hadn't been working so they had no idea what the guy was driving whoever he was. It was just another dead end.

Alex was worried about Matt, his bosses were heaping on the pressure, expecting him to come up with some information. To date there had been a couple of hundred sightings and not one of them amounted to anything. She was still hoping that Michael was out there and nothing terrible had happened to him.

She had managed to do a background story for the paper on Michael's time growing up in Charmsbury, sadly his parents had moved away from the area many years ago and he had no other family close by. His parents had gone to Australia and Charlie wasn't going to stump up for a ticket for her to visit them so she had managed to find their telephone number and tried to contact them by phone but they hadn't been answering their calls. They were probably sick of the press anyway and had more than likely been advised not to speak to them without representation. Matt had been informed that they would be doing a televised plea for Michael's return which would be aired nationally within the next forty eight hours.

Matt walked in from work and looked shattered. "Anything new today?" She asked as she made him a coffee.

"No, sightings have dropped off to virtually nothing and people are starting to forget him already."

"The parents' plea should push the story back into people's consciousness though shouldn't it?" Alex said hopefully.

"Maybe but he's not a rock star or an actor otherwise the story would run and run."

"There'll be some news soon... There has to be." She mused.

"Unless he's dead." Matt added.

Alex had no answer to that and still Michael's statement 'what's the point' went round in her head.

The plea went out after the news on all channels the following day; the parents naturally seemed devastated, apparently they had seen him just three weeks previously when he flew out to spend a few days with them unexpectedly. They said all the things you would expect a parent to say about their offspring. His Mum looked really worried, she was pale and drawn and looked like she hadn't slept since the news broke. His Dad looked downcast but not disturbed by anything that was going on around him, he made his statement and answered a few questions, maybe a bit of 'stiff upper lip' going on here thought Alex.

She was surprised that no-one from the media had been in touch with her considering that she was the last known person to have seen Michael before his disappearance, she had given a statement to the police, well actually to Matt, there had to be some perks of living with a police officer. No grotty interview rooms, just a cup of coffee and a sit down at the kitchen table but still she was puzzled that not one person had tried to contact her, maybe she was just lucky, so far. She sat with her laptop on the arm of the chair and tried to surf through all of the social media sites to see if she could come up with any leads, there was nothing to be found anywhere, even the gossip mills had stopped turning. The painting kept catching her eye and she thought it really shouldn't sit in the hall leant up against the wall any longer, time to hang it, she had waited trying to find the perfect place for it and it seemed pride of place above the mantelpiece was the only place that it should go. She went and found a hammer and a picture hook and started measuring, she always felt better when she kept herself busy. The phone rang and with a huff she put everything down and reached for her phone. She smiled when she saw the name flash onto the screen. "This is a nice surprise Summer."

"Hi Alex, how's things?"

"You don't want to know. Lily okay?"

"Yes she's perfect as always. Alex could you meet me at the tunnel tomorrow? One of the guys wants to see you."

"Sure, what's it about?"

"I'm not sure, I think he may have some information for you but I don't really know."

"Oh okay what time?"

"Twelve." Summer wasn't big on conversation when it came to telephones, she wasn't used to them yet but they managed to talk about Lily for a couple of minutes and she'd see her soon anyway. She seemed happy and after what she'd been through Alex thought she deserved to be.

She was looking forward to going out to the tunnel; she didn't visit the Community as much as she should. She returned to the painting and hung it, then stood back to admire her handiwork. Matt came up behind her and wrapped his arms around her. "Looks great there." He kissed the top of her head. "Who phoned?"

"Oh I didn't know you were in." She pulled him in even closer to her. "It was Summer, she wants to meet up tomorrow and I'm not working, it'll be good to catch up." Alex didn't mention why she was going otherwise Matt would insist on going with her and she wanted to find out what it was about first.

"Want a glass of wine?" Matt asked grinning, whilst simultaneously handing her one.

"You know me too well." She smiled up at him, she still couldn't believe how lucky she had got finding Matt. They settled down together to watch some TV but her eye kept being drawn by the painting. She really did love that picture.

The following day she drove out to the nature reserve parked her car and walked out across the scrubland, which was now a lot tidier than it had been a year ago when she had first come here. As she drew closer she could see Summer standing next to the well waiting for her, when she spotted Alex she walked out to meet her. They hugged and walked towards the entrance of the tunnel chatting constantly about all the things Summer was up to. They went inside to look for Jerry and Mark, the place hadn't changed much and everyone seemed pleased that she had come for a visit. Mark was in the recreation area, he walked over and asked Alex to meet him at the well when she had said her hello's to everyone. The well was the place to go when you needed to talk without anyone else overhearing especially if you had something important to say. No one would disturb anybody who was out by the well, strange how that custom had carried over from Jack.

Mark was waiting patiently for her. "Any news on the new library yet Alex?" Surely he was just making conversation this couldn't be what he'd got her out here for could it?

"Nothing's happening yet, you know I'll tell you the moment I hear anything, Is that what you wanted me out here for?" Mark shuffled his feet and pushed around a lump of dirt.

"No I'd ring you for that info, we've finally got the mobile back off Jack." He smiled "... No it's about that guy that disappeared." Alex was all ears. "Michael? What do you know about that Mark?"

"There was a guy in town who was talking about an incident the night that posh guy went missing in town."

"What guy?"

"Well he's one of the homeless blokes, he's a good guy just down on his luck, I've met up with him occasionally and taken him for a coffee and something to eat, anyway he was down by the bridge that night and saw an argument between two blokes. He thought the one being threatened might have been the bloke from the exhibition, Masters was it?"

"Yes Michael Masters, what did he actually see Mark? There's a lot of maybes in this story. Did he ask you for money?"

"Yes, yes he did but I told him not to bother trying that, I wasn't going to see him fleece a friend." He smiled at her.

"Thanks, so what did he tell you?" Alex was hoping this may be worth hearing.

"He saw two guys arguing, he didn't take too much notice of them and had no idea what they were arguing about, he said he tries to stay away from trouble, living on the streets can get difficult if you don't turn a blind eye sometimes. He took some notice though when he heard the smaller guy threaten the one he thought could have been Masters, he threatened to kill him, which was all he heard. I know it's not much but I thought you'd want to know."

"What time was this Mark?" She might be able to rule Masters out of this story.

"He reckoned sometime after midnight." Alex suddenly felt sick, could it be true? He'd seemed so relaxed and chatty that night not like someone who was trying to hide anything or was worried about anything. She'd have to follow this up.

"How did he know it was Masters?"

"He wasn't sure but he saw his face all over the papers the following morning what with the big exhibition and thought he looked a bit like the guy he'd seen."

"Where can I find your friend, who is he?"

"His name's Georgie but he's moved on, he never stays around long and after what he saw he didn't want to get involved especially when there was no money in it for him. If I see him I'll ask him to meet you, I got the impression it worried him otherwise he wouldn't have bothered mentioning it to me. He's seen enough arguments in his life that normally he wouldn't care."

"Okay, if you see him tell him to contact me, I can give him a little cash if the information's good, anyone else see anything?"

"I've not heard anything else but I'll keep my ear to the ground."

"Thanks Mark, so how's everything going here?"

"It's good, none of us can believe our luck really and we don't understand why people want to part with money just to come and see how we live here although we're very glad they do, it's nice to have a few luxuries in there." He tilted his head towards the tunnel entrance. They laughed about the tourists reactions to the tunnels and Mark had a couple of stories to tell. Alex was glad she'd come out here it was good to see them all again and Mark had given her something to think about. They went back inside to find Summer, she was huddled in the corner of a room with the other ladies, chatting and telling dirty jokes if the laughter was anything to go by. Alex joined them for long enough to have a coffee with them and catch up on their gossip, some of them started to drift away after a short while so Summer thought it was time to go back to town. They walked back to the car and Alex dropped Summer off at her flat before popping into work to see if there was any news that had come in that she may have missed. She was worried about Michael now that there may have been a threat made against him; she hoped Mark would be able to track down Georgie soon.

Chapter Thirteen

Mel phoned Alex for a catch up and to share a bit of gossip, she had spent the night with Lee and thought he was something special, if the way she was raving about him was anything to go by. Alex groaned inwardly, he was not for her but Mel couldn't see it, Alex couldn't work out why it was it seemed that they weren't a fit, it was just a gut instinct. If Mel was happy then there must be more to Lee than she thought and she would just have to accept the relationship and be happy for them. They were going to meet up for a drink later so maybe she could find out more then, Alex just hoped it was a girls only meeting.

She phoned Matt to pass on the news about the possible threat between Michael and an unknown man and to keep his eye open for a street dweller with the name Georgie, she knew he'd pass the information on to the other forces too and with any luck he might get a pat on the back for bringing in some new, if obscure information. Apparently Matt hadn't had any updates on Michael's whereabouts so they were still flailing around in the dark. She decided to stay at home and surf the internet and see if anything new could be gleaned from anywhere. This story just seemed to have gone dead, now you see him now you don't and Matt had been right people were starting not to care anymore. The phone rang again, wow she was popular today, it was Charlie. "Alex do you have anything to tell me yet?"

"What are you talking about?" She kept her fingers crossed.

"You lied to me, you did speak to Michael." Then silence.

"Who's telling you this stuff Charlie, I don't have an angle."

"A contact at the police station told me you'd given a statement, you must have a story for me."

"Look Charlie I'm working every angle I can from here, I don't know any more than you do, yes I gave a statement to the police but only because I spoke to him and then he disappeared, trust me as soon as I know anything the paper will get the story."

"Oh Alex, why is it I get nervous when you say things like that." At least she could hear a smile in his voice now.

The rest of the afternoon passed uneventfully she couldn't find anything online and it had taken up a lot of her time. She started to get ready to go out, she was looking forward to some girl time with Mel and finding out what it was about Lee that was so special. It had been more than a week since the exhibition and it felt like she needed to have some fun, the whole week had been taken up with the hunt for Michael. It wouldn't be all twinkling stars and world class art tonight, more likely a glass of red wine in a cosy bar and that would be fine, hopefully no one would go missing tonight.

Alex went out to meet the taxi that had turned up to take her to 'The Wandering Minstrel' which was an old fashioned pub that had been there for as long as Alex could remember, on the front facing the sea, the shopping centre had been built behind it but not a penny spent on doing the pub up. The taxi driver was an old school friend who she hadn't seen for years so it took longer than usual to get to the pub because they were too busy chatting about their school days and mutual friends, by the time she got to the pub Mel was already waiting for her with a half empty glass of wine, Alex had some catching up to do. After the general work life balance discussion and a decision that work takes up far too much of their precious time Alex moved the conversation on to Lee. "So what's happening between you two then?"

"I've fallen for him." Mel smiled coyly.

"So he bought you a romantic meal here…" She looked around at the cosy but very tired interior, this place was great for a drink but only served basic pub grub and not very well at that. "... That boy knows how to treat his girl eh?" She grinned at Mel but could see that she had caught the sarcasm.

"Well, anyway how's your search for Michael going?" She said abruptly changing the subject.

"Not well, there's no sign of him although there may have been an argument and he may have been threatened."

"There's a lot of supposition in there."

"Yeah it seems nothing is straightforward, I really have no idea what's happened to him, you know about the painting though?"

"No, what painting?"

"Remember the one at the exhibition, 'Buddha Mountain', well it turned up on my doorstep. Michael had sent it to me." Alex couldn't understand why she hadn't mentioned it to Mel.

"Wow, you get all the luck."

"Really! I speak to a guy and then he disappears off the face of the earth... I have that much of an effect on men." The girls laughed and any animosity that had reared its head dissolved in an instant.

"So what do you really think happened to him Alex?"

"No idea honestly, but I'm working on it."

"Oh Lee will be glad to hear that."

"What's it got to do with Lee?"

"He keeps asking me what you know and why the police don't seem to be doing anything about it."

"Sounds like he's really interested in finding out what happened. Does he have any theories?" Alex said not looking up but focusing instead on her glass of wine, not wanting Mel to see the sharp flare of anger in her face.

"No he just asked me to find out what you knew." Alex had to smile, going undercover to get information was not Mel's strong point.

"So what does he think Mel? Has he told you anything?"

"No but he does keep on about it, like all the time and it drives me mad, I know he's worried about his friend... but..."

53

"But what? Does he know something he hasn't told the police?" Alex was all ears now.

"I know I shouldn't have but he had some letters in the flat and he didn't say anything but his attention kept wandering back to them. He wouldn't tell me what they were so when he popped out for some cigarettes I took a peek... It was letters and paperwork from Michael and some of it was recent and some really old." Mel looked a little ashamed of herself for disclosing this but poured herself another drink from the half empty bottle and changed the subject. "So how's your Nan and Jack, are the wedding arrangements coming together?"

Alex followed her lead. "They are like a pair of kids and they're so happy. Never mind that though what was in the letters?"

"Nothing, really I didn't get chance to read any, he came back. Some had official Masters letterheads and were typed and others were just handwritten letters." Alex let it go and the conversation relaxed, Lee and the letters weren't mentioned again but Alex knew they would be especially once she mentioned them to Matt.

Chapter Fourteen

Matt went into work the following morning knowing that the next job was to go and see Lee, he didn't want to, it was Mel's boyfriend, he could do without the hassle of his personal life getting involved with his professional life. There was a perfect excuse though with the paperwork that he knew from William had been sent to Lee, some sort of contract and he needed to find out what it was about along with the other letters Alex had told him about.

Lee's flat was on the outskirts of Blunsford and he was surprised to see it was a tired grubby looking place from the outside, after being let in by someone in an adjoining flat it was tired and grubby on the inside too, chipped paintwork and dirty carpets. He went up the stairs to flat number three and knocked but got no answer and it seemed very quiet, he would wait in the car for a while to see if Lee returned. He sat in the car listening to the radio for thirty five minutes before he saw him ambling down the road with a canvas under his arm. He got out of the car and walked to meet him, Lee seemed surprised to see Matt there and that was soon replaced by embarrassment once he discovered that Matt had been to the flat. "It's just somewhere to crash whilst I'm in this part of the country." He said trying to sound dismissive.

"I need to talk to you about the paperwork that was sent to you from Michael this week."

"What paperwork?"

"I know that Michael sent you a contract and other paperwork and I need to know what it was about, now's not the time to play coy Lee, we need to find Michael as quickly as possible."

"Oh he's probably just gone off on a jolly, he'll turn up."

"Glad you can be so flippant about it, do you know something?" Matt was starting to feel irritated.

"Of course I don't but I just think all of this is over the top, just because he's well known."

"Can we go inside and you can show me the paperwork?"

"No and I told you there's nothing to tell, we were friends and that's all there is to it, why don't you just go, do something useful, find him and bring him home and stop bothering me." Lee strode off leaving Matt standing in the middle of the pavement open mouthed.

Matt made his way back to the station to relay what had happened and he knew this would cause nothing but trouble for Lee and in turn Mel. He was sorry that Mel was mixed up in all of this, he needed to speak to her. She picked up her phone on the second ring "Hi Matt, how's things?"

"Not great Mel, I won't take up much of your time, can you just tell me what you know about any paperwork that Lee received from Michael this week?"

"Ahh..." She paused. "Alex told you?"

"Yes she mentioned it but the truth is I spoke to Lee and now I need to speak to you."

"Okay what do you want to know? As I told Alex, I was snooping, there was a pile of correspondence from Michael some of the letters went back years. The one on top of the pile was handwritten but I didn't get chance to read it, I just looked at who they were from."

"How many letters are we talking about?"

"There were a big pile of them maybe twenty or so, that's just a guess though."

"And you weren't tempted to read any of them?"

"Of course I was." Mel laughed. "But I didn't, Lee came back and we went out."

"What do you think of his place?"

"It's cosy inside, the outside's a tip. You don't think he had anything to do with Michael's disappearance do you?"

"Honestly, I don't know. Thanks Mel sorry to bother you, if you think of anything else please give me a ring." He wasn't getting anywhere fast but Mel had just mentioned that the letter she saw was hand written which seemed a little strange if it was a contract as he had been led to believe, contracts are usually typed and formal but maybe Michael did things differently. It was something for him to think about to take his mind off Lee, the truth was the more he knew of Lee the more suspicious he was. He had told Alex to give the guy a chance when she told him Lee was a loser but he was beginning to see how right she was.

Chapter Fifteen

Alex had woken up to her phone ringing, what is it with people and mornings she thought. She reached over and grabbed her phone, squinting at the screen she could see it was Matt ringing, he'd had an early start this morning, he had a call and rushed out of the house, she had woken for a moment when she sensed him moving around trying not to wake her. "Good morning Gorgeous." she smiled and tried to sound sexy.

"Alex, get down to the river as soon as you can, there's a story for you and I never rang you."

"What?" He had already hung up on her.

She scurried around grabbing clothes and didn't even give herself a chance for a coffee, she rushed out to the car and aimed herself into town, she had no idea what was going on but knew that when she finally woke up properly she would be appreciating the upside of living with a police officer. She finally calmed down and looked at the clock it was 6.15am. As she approached she was trying to keep her eyes open for Matt, he hadn't said which part of the river and she had assumed he was down by the bridge. She needn't have worried, before she got to the bridge she saw the heavy police presence by the side of the river that edged the park, she pulled into the car park, grabbed her jacket and went off to find Matt. He was stood with two more officers, Alex figured they might not be so pleased to see a journalist here so she swerved them and went to where the yellow police tape was stopping anyone from getting too close. The grass was wet with dew and she wished she'd had time to put something on her feet that had more protection than her flip flops, the dew enveloped her toes and made her feet slip against the rubber.

She looked down the slope of the bank there was a body shaped lump with a dark piece of tarpaulin thrown over it. She felt sick and desperately hoped that this wasn't what she thought it was. She felt terrible, it felt somehow wrong but still pulled her phone out to take a few shots of the area and the body, the quick snap photos always helped her when she was putting a story together, it was a habit she had got into. She looked up and saw a policewoman heading her way waving her arms about and shouting for her to move away from the area. Alex moved on before the officer reached her and wandered around aimlessly for a few minutes just to calm herself, hoping, praying that this wasn't what she thought it was. She made her way back to the car and noticed another couple of journalists from rival papers just turning up on the scene so she tagged along with them as they went to speak to a police officer who was now keeping people away. They couldn't get any information from the officer she was stern faced and just doing her job. Alex shuffled off back to the car and sat inside before any of the journalists started trading information. She was deep in thought about Michael and wondered if he would have taken his own life, she couldn't conceive that he really had had enough of life, he possessed everything that anyone could want. Suddenly the car rocked and brought her back to the moment, she looked across and saw Matt already climbing into the passenger seat. "Hi, did you get any pics?"

"Yes so what's the story?"

"You know I can't tell you…" He paused. "That it's a male and that's all we know, drowned, time unknown, approx. 5' 10'. It's looking possible that it could be Michael but there's no positive ID, the body doesn't look like anybody anymore, it's been in the water for a while."

"Oh Matt, this is too horrible. I know he said he had times when he wondered what it was all about but this is no way to end a life. How long before you can identify the body?"

"Hang on don't run away with the idea this is definitely him, it could be any missing male, there are over a hundred thousand of them every year. Until we know any different that's the way it is." Matt looked at her, she read his eyes they said he meant it.

After Matt had got out of the car and returned to work Alex went for another walk around the park, more to quiet her mind that anything but also to just see if there was anyone around watching what was going on. She didn't see anyone but she certainly felt better for a walk. It was approaching eight o'clock and there were quite a few people walking through the park now, some on their way to work others just gawping at the police who were still searching the area where the body had been washed up and a couple of hundred yards either side. Alex didn't think there was anything left to see so she headed to get herself a coffee at the 'Breakfast Bap' where she could listen into what the other journalists were discussing, it would be where everyone was at this time of the morning and true to form the place was packed she had to perch on a stool at the bar in the window, she couldn't watch the comings and goings in the park because the windows were so steamed up from all the breakfasts and coffee being served. She couldn't overhear much gossip either and from the sound of things no one had any ideas apart from the obvious that the body was Michael Masters, she took her coffee and sat outside but there was nothing to watch either, the police were just milling around the area.

After she had eaten she went into work to write up the story about the man's body that had been washed up, making sure to keep with the no positive ID line of thought. There was lots of talk in the office and most people were assuming that the body had to be Michael Masters. Alex had to agree that it seemed like the most likely outcome but for now she could only allow that to be gossip.

Chapter Sixteen

Matt had handed the information about the body up to his superiors. Assuming this was Masters body, it strictly wasn't his case but as the body had washed up in his area he had the feeling it was going to fall to him. He checked in with the already dwindling team that was taking the calls on sightings and he was told that there was still a dribble of calls coming in, it was the only thing that gave him hope that the body may not be Michael. He couldn't take it for granted that it was, not after the amount of missing people that turned up in Charmsbury, he thought that may have ceased by now though. The information from the calls was constantly being passed to the police in the towns the sightings had come from but so far there was no positive identification. Until the forensic team came back with the details on the body there was little he could do. He went to his office to do the paperwork and hoped for Alex's sake if nothing else that the body would prove to be someone other than Masters. He needed to go and speak to Mark at the tunnel and find a way of tracing Georgie, he had to know more about the argument he had witnessed, he also needed to go and see Jasmine and find out about her relationship with Michael. He wasn't aware that anyone had been to see her yet and he didn't know why.

When he arrived at the tunnel Mark wasn't surprised to see him. "Hi Matt, I heard the news on the radio, is it him?"

"So you know why I'm here then?"

"Sure, you want to find Georgie."

"Do you know where he is Mark?"

"No not right now but if I see him I'll tell him to contact you."

"Mark this is serious, I'm not expecting him to pop in for coffee, he could have the information we need to sort this mess out! Where is he?" Matt was getting agitated. This community were so laid back you couldn't make them realise when things needed doing urgently.

"I don't know, the guy's a drifter, he could be back next week, next year or never."

"That's no help, where might he have gone, did he ever talk about places he'd been?"

"No." Mark could see Matt was losing patience but he didn't have the answers.

"Okay, so can you describe him to me." This definitely wasn't a question and Mark knew it from the look on Matts face. He proceeded to tell Matt everything he knew about Georgie, which wasn't very much as it turned out.

Eventually Matt left not feeling like he was any the wiser. He checked his phone it was just after two o'clock, he decided to take a drive out to see if Jasmine was home, it would be a good hour's drive but that was fine he needed the distraction and thought it would be better for him to see Jasmine face to face. He wanted to see her reactions when they were talking about Michael, why would he send her flowers and then disappear. He rang Alex to let her know he'd be late home, this house call could easily take up the rest of the day and fall into his evening too.

It was a lovely day, bright sunshine but as the sun started to lose its power in the late afternoon there was a definite chill in the air, autumn was closing in fast now. Matt arrived on the outskirts of a small village, it looked like a pretty little place with a main road passing through the middle of it, the village had the obligatory pub and church. Turning off the main road he found himself suddenly in the countryside, farmland as far as he could see. The cows in the fields were lying down, so it's going to rain later he thought, they must know something he didn't because as far as he could see the sky was clear, not a cloud in sight, just another old wives tale, he smiled to himself.

His GPS took him along another long, lonely, country lane all he could see was fields, trees, cows and the occasional bank of swans. The road wasn't much more than a track and the car bounced happily along it. Then quite unexpectedly seemingly out of nowhere appeared a farmhouse. Matt knew he'd never have found this place without the GPS he was in the middle of nowhere. He pulled into a lay-by and got out of the car to stretch his legs and had the feeling he would need time to psyche himself up for this conversation and it wouldn't be pleasant, this was the downside of the job, dealing with people's emotions in dark times.

He returned to the car and drove the last few hundred metres up to the house, he pulled up next to a brand new Range Rover and before he'd managed to unclick his seatbelt and step out of the car a woman materialised beside him. A tall strikingly beautiful woman with long dark hair and the biggest brown eyes he'd ever seen. "Hello, can I help you?" she said softly, her voice holding a slight hint of a foreign accent but Matt couldn't pinpoint where it originated from.

"I'm looking for Jasmine."

"You have found her." She smiled, she was even more beautiful when she smiled.

"Hello, I'm Inspector Jones from Charmsbury." He flipped his ID open, she looked at it then slowly looked up at him there was a definite glint in her eye, was she flirting with him? "I've come to talk to you about Mr Masters."

"Have you heard from him, do you know where he is?" Her smile had disappeared now.

"We're still not sure, I was hoping you could help us."

"Please come in, we can speak inside." She strode confidently towards the house. Matt looked around there was no-one anywhere near to overhear them, he shrugged his shoulders and followed her inside. His first impression of the inside of the house was that it was a working farm, muddy boots and wax jackets in the hallway but when she opened the door to the lounge it was more like a show home, not a lumpy comfortable settee in sight. She obviously had very expensive taste, dark leather furniture and teak carved tables, everything matched. There were heavy deep red curtains and matching cushions to add colour and warmth to the room, the curtains framed a picture window that looked out over the Somerset Levels. "Beautiful isn't it." She handed him a mug of coffee, gestured to the table that held the sugar and milk and joined him in looking at the view. "So have you found him, where is he?" She asked in a clipped tone.

"I was hoping you could tell me that, please sit down." He gestured to the nearest seat; she obviously hadn't heard the news yet. "We don't know anything for certain yet but a body has been washed up on the river bank at Charmsbury, I must reiterate we don't know who this is yet and it may have nothing to do with Michael. We do know that before he disappeared he sent you flowers, do you know why he would do that?"

"To you it's Mr Masters" She said abruptly, her whole attitude changing. "If you're implying he may have killed himself then you are wrong, that man was too much of a coward to do anything like that." She stood up and glowered at Matt still he detected a tear welling up in her eyes, she took a deep breath, swallowed deeply and it disappeared.

"I'm sorry but what is that meant to mean." He couldn't believe her reaction, it had shocked him, he had been beginning to feel sorry for her and she had wiped that feeling away in an instant. He placed his mug on the table. "You were in a relationship with Mr Masters?" He was careful to use the correct name, he got the impression that this woman wanted to be looked up to, maybe he was being unkind but she was beginning to fit the gold digger role.

"A relationship... that's not what I would have called it, all he was interested in was escaping the city, he loved to come here and he would walk for hours... alone. If I ever suggested going into London or any city for that matter, he would sulk like a teenager. I felt like I was nothing more than a housekeeper for him then he disappears and all I get is a bunch of flowers!" Matt was struggling to understand her reaction.

"Then why did you stay with him?"

"I really don't know Inspector, maybe I thought things would change."

"Where you the only relationship in his life?" Matt thought with her attitude he would push his luck, she couldn't get much ruder anyway.

"Yes, of course, why would he want anyone else?" High maintenance, arrogant, rude. Matt could think of a few reasons. She stopped and looked at him. "There were occasional letters that he wouldn't let me see, he was very secretive about them."

"Any idea who they were from?"

"No, he would say they were about business and then hide them away, they could have been from another woman I suppose. He probably put them in his safe. That was where he put everything he didn't want to share with me." She said bitterly.

"Where's this safe located Jasmine?"

"In the Charmsbury shop, he still thought of that place as home, his little secret place. He sometimes stayed in the small flat above the shop." Matt was taken aback he hadn't thought to look all around the property, he didn't even realise there was a flat attached to the shop.

"One last thing Jasmine, the card that came with the flowers, what did it say?"

"How is that your business? It was private."

"This is a missing persons investigation, I need to know what that note said. I don't have time to play games." Matt was starting to lose his cool, this woman was infuriating.

"I threw it away, it said we were finished but I didn't believe it." Or didn't want to, thought Matt.

"No clue as to what he may have been thinking."

"I don't care what he was thinking. He said he wouldn't see me again. How much clearer would you like me to be Inspector?"

"One more question, does this house belong to you or Mr Masters?"

"It's mine, nothing to do with him." Matt could see she was getting more irritated by the minute, he'd asked what he came to ask and he wasn't going to get any more information out of her now. Apart from a few more swipes at Michael, Jasmine had little of any interest left to say. Matt was pleased to be able to get away, apart from her obvious beauty he couldn't see why Michael would have got himself mixed up with a woman like Jasmine.

It was getting dark as he left and there were tiny spots of rain on his windscreen. Those cows knew something after all.

Chapter Seventeen

Michael checked out of the cosy little guest house he knew it was time for him to get to a larger town and try to sell his car or at least swap it for something else. Pierre seemed genuinely sorry to see him leave and Michael had appreciated the kindness of his host, they had got on well over the past few days, Michael left him a pencil drawing of the river behind his home as a gift to show his appreciation. He was sorry to be leaving this beautiful area but he drove down into the small town taking in the beauty of it for the last time, he didn't expect to return here, he wasn't going to have much luck in a place with a population of less than a thousand people. He found his way onto a main road, filled up with petrol and headed on to the much larger town of Carcassonne; he hoped he would have better luck there.

It felt like he had been driving for hours when he finally reached Carcassonne, it should have taken a little over two hours but he had stopped for coffee a few times, bought fresh fruit from the market stalls along the road and had lunch so it had taken him five hours, he was hot and tired. He found a space in a car park and it happened to be just in front of a café, he thought he would stop there and have a drink before he tried to find somewhere to stay in town. He didn't anticipate being here long but he really needed to think about where he should go from here. He liked France but he thought he should go somewhere where he was a bit safer, a place he could drop out and no one would take any notice of him, the obvious place was India. He needed to pick up a computer or find an internet café to sort out some flights. A tall man walked past him and looked hard at him, Michael was suddenly aware of how easily he could be spotted in the big town, lots of tourists from all over the world, plenty of galleries here too, he had been here before many years ago. He was also still driving the car, anyone could notice it. He realised how much he had enjoyed the anonymity of small towns but here he no longer felt relaxed and at ease. It also dawned on him that the larger the city the more cameras there would be on the streets, that added to the reason for him wanting a computer. Hopefully if he was spotted he might find out about it online and have a chance of moving on before anyone came looking for him. He was beginning to worry that he was becoming paranoid, maybe not, maybe it was just that he had never had this much time to himself before, too much time to think and worry, he used to employ staff to do that for him and he was constantly surrounded by people. He stretched out his legs, took a deep breath and thought he preferred it the way it was now.

He walked along to the shopping area, a large grid of streets criss-crossing each other, full of shops, one street was predominately tourist shops but everything else could be found on the next street or the one after, sweets, clothes, ice cream, food, bars, shoes it just went on seemingly forever, he finally found a shop with computers in the window and a large departmental store with a computer section, between the two he spent nearly three hours looking at computers, learning a little along the way. The more he learnt the more confusing the choices got, that was why he always had a team of people who would look after his computer system for him but now he was on his own. He eventually settled on a tablet, it would be small enough to keep on him all the time. With his purchase wrapped and bagged he returned to his car to try and find out how it all worked. It was much easier than he had expected, he spent a moment musing over why he had paid anyone so much money to sort these things out when he could have done it himself, although one swallow doesn't make a summer he thought and smiled. With that under his belt he decided to return to the café, it was too warm to sit in the car, he found a table and ordered himself a beer, something he hadn't done for years, in his world it had been wine or Champagne. The moment it hit his taste buds he instantly associated the taste with the word freedom, it tasted wonderful.

He scrolled through his computer and a page flashed up that he needed to log in, there was a code chalked up on the bar door, he entered it into the space provided and he was into the internet, with trepidation he re-entered the world and hoped he wouldn't read anything that may entice him to return to his old life. As he looked around for news he was sad to see his parents plea for his return, he couldn't contact them yet it was far too soon but he would, as soon as the story died down, he was pleased he had been to spend some time with them before he did his disappearing act and he would find a way to let them know that he was okay. He also found a news article that made him smile, yes he had been spotted at the service station in Kent but the footage was terrible and the car hadn't been spotted. Michael couldn't believe his luck; he smiled and ordered up another beer after all there was no rush now.

Chapter Eighteen

The coroner, Dr McAndrews had taken a look at the body that had been washed up on the bank at the park, from the state of it the only thing of which he could be certain was that it was a man. Grey, bloated, most of the skin had peeled off and much of the soft tissue had been stripped away by the water and tides or nibbled on by the fish and local wildlife. Dr McAndrews had never seen a body quite so indistinguishable in all the years he had been doing this job. The only thing of which he was certain was that the body took its last breath in roughly the same place as it was found, the small amount of water in his lungs showed diluted salt water, what worried Tony McAndrews was although there was water in the lungs there looked like a possibility of damaged tissue too, possibly due to bruising or impact with something. He couldn't be sure at this moment, decomposition was too extreme and he couldn't even pinpoint a time of death, could have been a week or a month, the warm weather wasn't helping him. He would have to run a lot of tests to get to the bottom of this one. Yet all the police seemed to be interested in was, is it Michael Masters or not, he was getting requests for updates every thirty minutes or so and all he could tell them was had it been his own brother he wouldn't recognise him in this state, it was going to take time. They were just going to have to wait for all of the procedures to be completed and then he may be able to give them the answers they wanted. He had noticed that Inspector Jones had seemed to be the most eager to get this information, the rumour around the station was that his girlfriend was mixed up in the disappearance and from the way he was acting that just may be true. Tony liked Matt Jones and hoped this wasn't the case and if he could help him out he would but he had no way of speeding up the process, this was going to take many painstaking hours to get to the bottom of. He snapped on his latex gloves and once more turned to the body.

Today he would do his best to find an answer for everyone involved.

Chapter Nineteen

Alex knew there was some serious work to be done, this mess wasn't going to fix itself, if it did turn out to be Michael's body then why and how could something like this happen, why didn't she see it coming? Could she have helped him in some way? Now she was getting desperate for more information. If it wasn't Michael then who was it and why was she beginning to feel like she might be part of a set up? She had an interview that couldn't be used at the moment, Charlie was on her back, the police thought she may be involved and there seemed to be no answers, she had noticed that even Matt was beginning to look worried and now she was feeling stuck and even a little sorry for herself, not knowing which way to turn, even the towns grapevine was quiet, it seemed that no-one knew anything, maybe this Georgie guy would come up with something if the police could only find him. She was full of conflicting emotions and had no idea what to do next. She picked up the phone and called Mel, no answer, then sent her a message to see if they could go for coffee. Minutes passed slowly before she received a reply 'can't do coffee, out with Lee.' Alex replied with a 'Have fun' but felt a little hurt that Mel couldn't just pick up the phone.

To fill time she sat down and wrote out everything that Michael had told her hoping that if it was down on paper the clue would jump out at her. It wasted some time but supplied no answers, she read it and re read it but nothing apart from the worrying 'What's the point?' stared out from it. Could he have taken his own life? She didn't think so, there were easier ways than drowning yourself and although it was a generalisation he just didn't seem the type of person to commit suicide, yes he was definitely disillusioned with life but not suicidal. Alex was stuck. Maybe she should be looking for the smaller guy who threatened him, 'small guy' was a relative term and offered no clues. The only other option was that it wasn't Michael's body, so where was he and why wasn't he making himself known, if he was alive he must have seen the news or something in the media by now. He couldn't have been taken against his will because no one had come forward asking for a ransom. Alex's head was spinning, there were just no clues. She decided to go and see her Nan and Jack, if there was any gossip there was no better source in the area, maybe they could come up with another way to attack this conundrum. She needed some fresh ideas.

On the way she decided to detour to the park and take another look at the river bank, she hoped it may offer some inspiration. As she approached, all that could be seen were the tattered remnants of the police tape fluttering from the tree trunks it had been tied around. Already torn and dirty, that was probably down to local kids messing around, kids never saw the tragedy in life only a way to laugh at misfortune. Now it was quiet, no kids, no police, the sky was grey and unimpressive, offering everything it touched a tinge of misery which seemed to mirror Alex's mood. She walked along the bank but it offered up no inspiration, it was just grim, there was nothing to see, what had she expected? Maybe she thought the answer had been overlooked by the police and it was there just for her to find but that only happened in the movies, she sighed and turned her back to the river and sauntered back to the car. She sent a text to Mel again to see if she fancied a drink later, she could do with some cheering up but it seemed she would have to wait for a reply. She phoned Matt instead but he was too busy to talk. She started the car and made her way to her Nan's, hopefully there would be cake and some sensible advice.

When she got there the door was open as usual, she walked in and could hear voices but there were no baking smells, which was the way her day was going. "Hello" she shouted.

"In the lounge Alex, come through." Jack replied. She walked into the lounge and found Mark sitting opposite Jack. "Hi."

"Hi Jack, Mark good to see you." Alex looked towards the kitchen. "She had to pop out, there's brownies in the tin." Jack smiled it was as if he could read her mind. She headed into the kitchen made a pot of coffee, sorted the brownies onto a plate and went to see what the guys were up to. They were just catching up as it turned out, Mark was bringing Jack up to date on the comings and goings of the community and how well they were doing with all of the tourists that wanted to visit, in fact they were having to limit the groups coming through because it was disrupting life in the tunnel. Life was becoming a lot more comfortable for the inhabitants with the new source of income but they needed to find a life work balance. Alex added her news and her worries about being suspected of being involved with Masters disappearance. "There's been some sightings haven't there?" Mark added.

"Possibly but nothing the police are taking seriously from what I know."

"Oh, I thought I saw something online, I must have been wrong."

"I'm sure Matt would have said something if there was a solid lead." Alex sighed and reached for a brownie, even that didn't have the power to cheer her up today.

"Would you like me to have a look around online Alex?"

"He may be in the morgue but I just don't believe it. Yes if you have time see if you can find anything Mark but I keep coming up empty, if there is anything online you're the only person I know who could find it." She forced a smile in his direction.

Mark had only discovered computers properly a year ago but he was a natural, Alex wouldn't be surprised if Microsoft snapped him up, he could even find his way into the dark net, she had barely mastered social media.

Mary walked in and was pleased to see the small gathering. "Alex, they haven't locked you up yet then." She laughed. Jack gave her a sharp look. "Sorry sweetheart, I was only joking, you don't have anything to worry about do you?"

"I don't know Nan, even Matt is beginning to look worried and I'm certain he knows more than he's telling me." At that moment Alex's phone vibrated, a text from Mel, she couldn't make it tonight. Alex was beginning to feel abandoned by her friend and finding it hard to be happy for her, she needed her friend today however unfair and childish that sounded.

"Come on Alex this isn't like you, is there anything I can do?"

"No Nan just keep baking those brownies and maybe practise baking files inside your cakes." Alex decided to go home she was just bringing everyone down. They all said their goodbyes and Alex went home to do some housework, keep herself busy and try to dream up a way to find out the truth, she was keeping her fingers crossed for the coroners' results later.

She returned home deciding to keep busy with chores, she cleaned and tidied and sorted clothes out for washing, as she emptied Matt's pockets out she found a piece of paper with an address in Somerset, she turned it over and the name Jasmine was printed on it. She put it on the side whilst she loaded the washing machine but it kept pulling at her, she was having trouble ignoring it. She continued with loading the washing machine but eventually gave in to the temptation of a story, folded the piece of paper up and put it in the back pocket of her shorts. She would decide what to do with it later.

Chapter Twenty

Alex woke up early and in a determined frame of mind, she was going to find Michael or to find out if he might be dead, one way or another she wanted answers. She made Matt some breakfast and waved him off to work like a dutiful girlfriend then returned to the percolator and made herself another pot of coffee, she was running low of her favourite brand, so she would need to drop into 'The Red Cup' and get them to fix her another batch. She pulled the piece of paper out of her pocket and leaned back against the cool marble worktop. She looked at the address, harbouring more than a little guilt and hoped it may hold some answers. Matt wouldn't be pleased if he knew what she had planned for today, she couldn't give him back this piece of paper now and he wasn't telling her what was going on at work. Yes, she felt guilty but they had to have some secrets right? Alex felt more positive today now she had something she could do, she did toy with the idea of taking Mel with her, it would be good to have someone riding shotgun in case Jasmine gave her a hard time, Matt had said she was a piece of work and hadn't wanted to give him any information. On the other hand she wasn't sure she wanted to spend the day hearing about the 'wonderful' Lee, she thought a drink this evening would be a better idea. It was odd not to have spoken to Mel for a couple of days but if she was busy there was nothing Alex could do, she just hoped Mel was happy. She tapped out a text '7.30pm - Hearts, see you there' sent it then poured herself a coffee and gazed out of the window, daydreaming for a while before getting changed and ready to drive into deepest Somerset.

She stopped off in town at the 'Red Bean' and put in the order for her blend of coffee; they did it for her there and then whilst discussing Jack and Mary. All of the staff were excited about the upcoming wedding and wanted to hear all of the details of what the loved up septuagenarians were planning and Alex was only too pleased to share the details with them as the engagement had happened on their premises. It was so nice that everyone was pleased for them.

She got back to her car and set out for Jasmine's house. After driving for about an hour she had to stop and check her phone for directions, it seemed she was already a little too far out in the sticks, in a small village, normally she would find the nearest pub and get the locals to point her in the right direction but it seemed that this was one of the villages that had succumbed to high taxes and the smoking ban, it had closed down and the windows were boarded up, there didn't even seem to be a local shop here. She checked the map and headed out in the direction her phone had told her, silently thanking the GPS system, it took her out onto the flat landscape of the Somerset Levels and she drove deeper into it. Eventually she found what she was looking for, the house was in the middle of nowhere and she hoped Jasmine was at home and prayed that she would talk to her. Alex had to admit that she was nervous.

She approached the house glancing at the silver grey Range Rover and knocked confidently on the door, whilst feeling anything but. A tall woman with tanned skin and long deep chestnut hair opened the door to her. "Hello" The woman had a slight accent.

"Hi, Jasmine?"

"Yes, you are?" Alex caught the accent, it was South African.

"My name's Alexandra Price, may I talk to you about Michael Masters?"

"Are you a journalist?" A straightforward question.

"Yes but I'm not here for a story, unless you want to give me one, I just don't know who else to talk to." Alex dropped the tough journalist act, now was the time for honesty. Jasmine looked her up and down, weighing her up.

"You'd better come in." Alex followed her through a hallway to a beautiful lounge area with almost a whole wall of glass surrounded by the richest red curtains she had ever seen, the view was spectacular, she could see for miles across the levels. Jasmine moved in front of her and blocked the view. "What do you want?" She asked abruptly.

"I'm worried about Michael and I thought you may be able to help."

"Were you having an affair with him?"

"No!" Alex was shocked by the suggestion. "I spoke with him, that's all."

"That's a lie." Jasmine stood in front of her defiantly. "He never gave interviews to journalists."

"It wasn't an interview." Alex explained. "He knew my family from way back in Charmsbury, he recognised me because of my family."

"So you used that angle and tricked him into an interview!"

"No, no I didn't, he just wanted to talk." Alex hung her head, feeling defeated and with a deep sigh she said "Will you talk to me or not, I don't want to waste any more time." Jasmine simply walked out of the room and left Alex looking at the view. Alex assumed it was over she had no idea what to do next, maybe she just had to give up. She turned to face the doorway and took a step in its direction; she just wanted to leave now.

"Wait." Jasmine commanded and was standing beside her now, holding out a glass of wine. "I'm sorry but I needed to be cautious, you seem genuine you also seem like you're at your wits end. Please, sit down." Alex gratefully accepted the glass.

They drank their wine and Alex told Jasmine all about the evening of the exhibition and most of what they had discussed, omitting the part about women throwing themselves at him. Jasmine let her talk with no interruptions. "Then I found out he had disappeared and now a body has turned up and I don't know what to think." That was it; Alex had told Jasmine everything of any significance.

"Why didn't you put all of this in print for your paper?" It was the first thing she had said since Alex had started talking.

"Because it wasn't an interview." Alex was at a loss to understand why no one could grasp this simple fact. "He offloaded because he kind of knew me, it was more of a friendly chat."

"But it could have made your name as a journalist."

"I'm not interested in journalism if I have to lie and use people to get a story, Michael seemed nice, kind and genuine, I wasn't going to abuse that. Sure I was tempted but it didn't feel right and my boyfriend, a police officer, agreed that it might not be such a good idea."

"A policeman and a journalist!" Jasmine laughed. "That must be awkward." She should laugh more often Alex thought, it made her beautiful.

"It has its downside occasionally but I think it's Matt that's keeping me from being officially questioned right now so it has its upside too. You met him a few days ago."

"Really, you and Inspector Jones, well done, he's gorgeous." They both laughed and now it seemed that she was ready to talk.

"Have you heard from Michael?"

"No and I don't expect to, his note made it clear that we were over, we had grown apart recently, we were not as close as I would have liked. Michael never got that close to anyone."

"But aren't you worried?"

"Of course I am but what can I do? He dumped me and disappeared." She stared into her glass thoughtfully.

"Was there anything odd about him that you noticed?"

"Not really, as I said closeness wasn't our thing, if I'm honest I think we were both just killing time until someone else came along, I mean we liked each other's company but that spark of intimacy was gone. In the beginning I hoped it would go somewhere, I fell for him quite hard but I don't think he ever felt the same. He could be very secretive and after the initial honeymoon period I realised that he wasn't going to commit to the relationship and we just drifted into our own worlds, I'm not even sure why we stayed together. We had our own lives and lived them just meeting up here when we were free. Don't get me wrong, I love him very much and always harboured a hope that he may one day feel the same about me but I had to accept that that may never happen so I acted the same way as he did and things just seemed to slip away from us. I should have worked harder at the relationship but it's difficult when only one partner is trying, somehow it feels desperate, it's easier to just keep rubbing along together."

"That's sad." Alex really didn't know what else to say but it made her feel very lucky to have her relationship with Matt.

"He loved it here though, he never wanted the bright lights and parties if he could be here instead, it was a bit like a retreat for him, and he loved the silence."

"So there were no big upsets or arguments?"

"No, nothing he just went off to open his exhibition and never came back." Alex understood now why Jasmine didn't seem distraught about him leaving, she knew how not to show her feelings outwardly.

"Why weren't you with him the night of the opening?"

"I had a prior engagement that I couldn't get out of with some artists I was representing. If I'm honest I've been in the art world for years and it isn't as exciting as it used to be, so I wasn't too worried about missing it"

"Oh, what do you do?"

"Just the legal paperwork for the artists to ensure the big boys didn't rip them off, I used to think it was romantic working for struggling artists, now I am tired of hearing their woeful, tortured perspective, they each act as if they are the only worthwhile artist on the planet and why can't anyone see it."

"Like journalists then, prima donnas who can't see over their own egos. Did he ever have visitors here?"

"No and to be honest I found that odd, he would never invite anyone here. One day one of his artists turned up on the doorstep and he wouldn't even let him through the door although to be fair I think that was more about the artist than anything else." She smiled at the memory.

"Who was it?"

"Lee Hohlen, do you know him?"

"Short, skinny, dark hair?"

"Yes that's him, I didn't like him much but him and Michael went a long way back, I think they were at school together."

"Any reason you didn't like him?" Alex was fishing for info to pass on to Mel.

"He was sneaky and he was always where Michael was, I often thought he had a thing for Michael but I guess not, Michael used to refer to him as a bloody nuisance but always seemed to put up with him even if he did try to keep him at arm's length."

"To be honest I can't take to him either, he's going out with a friend of mine and I can only see her getting hurt." Alex admitted.

"He can't be…" She paused. "Doesn't she know…? He's gay."

"Really? Not according to Mel he's not." They both sat looking at each other for a moment, absorbing this new information.

"Well…" Jasmine obviously didn't know what else to say.

"She met him at the exhibition and they've been inseparable ever since."

"But he wasn't exhibiting there, I remember Michael remarking that he had nothing that was up to standard, I supposed that was why he had turned up here possibly attempting to change Michaels mind." Jasmine looked thoughtful. "Does your friend Mel have money?"

"She's comfortable but not rich."

81

"Warn her to watch out, Lee likes to live well on other people's money, he has none of his own. He loves the taste of Champagne when it's free."

"I thought it was odd that he lived in a pokey, rundown flat."

"Hmmm he passes that off as his studio, says he doesn't live there, that he likes the image of it but I've never sent correspondence anywhere else." She glanced at her watch. "Would you like some lunch?"

Alex nodded in reply and Jasmine went into the kitchen to prepare something, leaving Alex to admire the view through the window. Jasmine returned ten minutes later and they continued chatting over a lunch of Caesar Salad and grilled chicken. She told Alex more about her relationship with Michael and showed her photographs of them together in Paris, Venice, Bangkok and numerous beaches around the world. It seemed they had a glamorous lifestyle on the face of it but she held fast that it wasn't like that away from the camera. "I thought he was seeing someone else for a while, as I said he could be secretive, he would receive letters from time to time and go off and shut himself away to read them privately. I'd never see them again and they were never left lying around, I'm fairly sure he kept them in his safe in the Charmsbury flat."

"I didn't know he still lived in Charmsbury."

"No he didn't but he kept the flat above the shop, all of his personal things were kept there, he returned periodically." She paused. "I don't suppose it'll do you any good to know that now, I told your boyfriend about it when he came here. The police will be all over it." Alex could only hope that Matt may share something about it with her when she saw him, he hadn't mentioned it so far.

"So what do you think has happened to Michael?" It was the final question Alex had.

"Honestly, I don't know but if he had been murdered he wouldn't have sent a message to me and I think he's too much of a coward to take his own life so I suppose I think he's disappeared but I have no idea where he'd go. I can't recall him ever having mentioned anywhere he liked enough to run away to." She gazed out of the window thoughtfully. "Are you going to print this?"

"Only if you want me to, I had no intention of making any of this public though." Alex replied honestly.

"Let's keep this between us for a while, will you let me know if you discover anything?"

"Of course." Alex had an idea. "How would you feel if I put an article together, if he's out there somewhere he may see it, he may contact you? You could approve anything I write, if you don't like the idea I wouldn't print it."

"That seems fair but please don't give too much personal stuff away. I don't want to be at the centre of a media circus."

"You will have the last word on anything I write. I promise you that." Alex looked for a reaction. Jasmine trusted her she could see it in her face.

By the time Alex was ready to leave there was a beginning of a friendship forming. Alex liked Jasmine, once she had broken through the hard shell she found just another vulnerable woman who had lost her man, all the money and influence in the world didn't change that emotional rollercoaster.

When she got back to her car she checked her phone, it had been in her bag on silent all afternoon, ignored. Mel had left a message saying she was looking forward to meeting up tonight. Alex smiled this must be her lucky day for friendships.

Chapter Twenty One

She was shattered by the time she returned home, she wasn't used to so much driving, she headed straight for the kitchen with her new pack of coffee, as she filled the machine with water she saw that Matt had left her a note attached to the coffee maker saying he would be late home tonight, they'd had a breakthrough so he didn't know what time. She really wished he had left her a little more information but she would have to wait, she fervently hoped that the breakthrough was that they had found Michael. Alex sat down at the kitchen table to write up what Jasmine had told her whilst it was still fresh in her mind, she didn't know why Matt had not got on with Jasmine, he just couldn't have had enough time to get through that shell she had grown around herself so perfectly. Alex had found her friendly and helpful, maybe it had helped that Alex hadn't been the one wearing a uniform.

She didn't have enough time to outline an angle for an article it was time to get ready to meet Mel, she tried to phone Matt but the call went straight to voicemail so she left a message to say where she'd be if he wanted to catch up with her when he had finished at work. She headed for the shower, in forty five minutes she was ready to go and looking forward to seeing Mel although not to telling her that Lee was a gay gold digger.

When she arrived in the cool, lush bar surrounded by palms, chrome and glass she saw that Mel was already there, she looked up to acknowledge Alex but there was no hint of a smile. Alex walked up to her to give her a hug but she was just shrugged off. "Hey, what's up?"

"Your bloody boyfriend, that's what's up! You never liked Lee did you? You poisoned Matt against him!" Mel ranted,

Alex took a step back not believing the way she was being spoken to and in her peripheral vision she could see heads turning towards them. "Stop right there Mel, I have no idea what you are talking about, would you care to explain what's going on?"

"You expect me to believe you didn't know. Matt must have told you."

"I haven't seen Matt all day so do you want to tell me?" Alex waited and watched as Mel processed the fact that she really didn't know anything, that was when the tears started.

"Matt arrested Lee." She sobbed.

"What for, what does he think he has done?" Alex was secretly relieved that Mel was away from Lee for a while but she couldn't say that to her friend.

"He thinks Lee is mixed up with Michael's disappearance."

"Yes I'd kind of worked that out, but what did he have to do with it?"

"I don't know, no one would tell me anything, they just told me to go home, to my own home, not to his flat."

"Where were you when this happened?"

"An artist's flat above the shop, you know where the exhibition was."

"You mean Michael's flat?"

"Oh..." Mel looked down into her lap this was obviously news to her. "Lee said it belonged to an artist friend of his and he needed to pick up some paperwork from there."

"Mel, Lee says a lot of things. I can promise you that it was Michaels flat, do you know what he was going there for?"

"No, he just said it was for some paperwork. I didn't ask anything else." Then she really started crying. Alex ordered a bottle of wine and poured Mel a glass, a very large glass and waited to see what she would come out with next, she could see Mel was thinking things through. "He said the paperwork was something to do with a painting he had sold at the exhibition, that's all I remember."

"Sorry Mel but Lee didn't have any paintings in the exhibition." Alex wanted to comfort her friend but she also needed her to realise the facts for herself.

"Yes he did, he showed me…" Then the penny dropped. "So you're trying to tell me that that was a lie too?"

"I'm sure it was, I'm sorry Mel."

"How do you know so much about him?" Mel started to look defiant now, there was a spark in her eyes. "Have you been checking up on him because you don't want to see me happy?"

"How can you think that? Everything I found out about Lee was got whilst I was looking for information on Michael, Lee's name just kept cropping up." A thought shot through Alex's mind, her Nan had mentioned a skinny boy who used to hang around Michael a lot, she had said he was a spiteful one, could that have been Lee too? She snapped back to the conversation. "You're wrong Mel, I want you to be happy, but it's not Lee who's going to make you happy, you're too good for him." There she had said it now and Mel was looking confused but she didn't look ready to back down quite yet.

"Stop Alex we're going to be happy and I won't let you spoil it for us, you with your precious Matt and your perfect life. We'll get through this and we'll be happy. Just watch." Mel's cutting remark made Alex feel a flare of anger rise through her body.

"What… With a gold digging, gay boyfriend!" Alex snapped, as soon as the words were out she regretted it, this was not how she had planned on breaking the news to Mel. Mel stood up, looked Alex straight in the eye and slapped her across the face. With that she turned and walked out of Hearts. Alex sat down, shocked. As she eventually raised her head she could see people looking away from her, wondering what was going on but not wanting to get involved just in case any of that bad luck rubbed off on them. She did not feel inclined to go after Mel, she thought she had said too much already so she got up to leave. Just as she did Matt walked up to the table. "Hi, I'm pleased to see you." She leant into his arms and kissed him.

"I just saw Mel leave, she was driving out of the car park like the hounds of hell were on her tail, is she okay?" He frowned.

"You upset her by arresting her boyfriend; I upset her by telling her he was gay."

"Ah that would explain it then." He couldn't help but smile at her. They sat and discussed what had happened over a glass of wine and Matt decided to go and pick up a take away, whilst Alex went home.

Thirty minutes later Matt walked into the house to find Alex sitting cross legged on the rug in the middle of the lounge gazing up at the painting, he didn't get it, sure it was nice but Alex seemed almost spellbound by it. He unpacked the take away and put the containers on a tray and took the food through to her. "Ah just the way I like it." She smiled up at him. She was feeling much calmer now and having the painting to focus on had really helped, they put their feet up, flicked the TV on and ate, the evening wasn't lost after all although she still felt a niggling worry over Mel, she had no idea how this would resolve itself.

Chapter Twenty Two

Alex had to go into work, she hoped she would be able to contact Mel today and see if they were okay that was if she could escape her grubby little desk. For a change Charlie appeared to be happy, she had brought in the story of Lee Hohlen's arrest which she was spending the morning writing up. Truth be known there wasn't much to the story except that he broke into the flat but she could incorporate a few little things that Michael had told her and a few that Jasmine had offered up, she hoped that if Michael was out there somewhere and he did see the story maybe he would consider coming home or at least contacting someone. The coroner still hadn't returned any identification on the body, so there was nothing to report there. With her writing done Alex rang Jasmine "Hi, I'm just letting you know that Lee has been arrested."

"Oh, why? What's he been up to now?" She didn't sound surprised.

"I really don't know yet, all I do know is that the police found him at Michael's flat. When they got there he was inside rummaging through a pile of paperwork."

"What was he after and how did he get in?"

"No idea but I think he broke in, I was hoping you may have some thoughts on it." Alex could have kicked herself for not asking Mel how he had gained entry to the flat.

"Not a clue I'm afraid, he could have been after anything, my guess would be money."

"I am putting a story together now but I hope to know more by tonight, I wanted to put in a couple of things you mentioned yesterday, I won't name you, you'll be my reliable source. I'll mail you a copy before I give it to my editor, okay?"

"Sure, thanks for letting me know Alex." They said they're goodbyes and Alex dialled Mel's number, it just rang out obviously Mel hadn't calmed down enough yet. She turned back to her writing to polish it up a little and sent a copy to Jasmine. Jasmine must have been sat on her inbox, in minutes she had a reply 'Looks fine, good luck'. She pushed it down the line to Charlie.

Now she had some time to catch up with people she had been ignoring since the Masters story had broken. She spent the next hour calling Summer, her Nan and her Mum catching up on a bit of non-newsworthy but still entertaining local gossip. When she had finished she noticed a message on her phone from Matt asking her to ring him, she did. "You'd better get down here Alex, Mel is here demanding to know what's going on with Lee. I managed to get her into my office but I can't nursemaid her all day, I've got work to do."

"Okay, I'm on my way." She hung up and grabbed her bag, thinking this might not be a good idea, she was probably the last person Mel wanted to see right now.

When Alex arrived at the police station the desk sergeant waved her through without a word but he gave her a knowing look and a raise of one bushy eyebrow. She got to the office door, took a deep breath and walked inside. Mel turned around as she entered and raised her eyes skyward, Matt was already facing the door, one look at his face told Alex that he was holding down a seriously black mood, those little furrows between his eyebrows looked deep and angry. "What's *she* doing here?" Mel demanded.

"Hopefully talking some sense into you!" He got up from his desk and walked past Alex without a glance and out of the room.

"What's going on Mel?" Alex tried to sound calm using her best 'talking to a five year old' voice.

"I don't want to talk to you, you don't care what's going on you've just come to spill more poison."

"That's not true Mel, I'll help you any way I can but only with the truth."

"It's not the truth, the things you were saying are lies, and don't you think I'd know if my fiancé was gay."

"Maybe…" Alex's head was reeling … fiancé when did this happen, what was going on.

"I want to know how long he's going to be here, he's done nothing wrong."

"The police must think he knows something or they would have let him go by now." Alex couldn't get the fiancé word out of her head. "Breaking and entering is a crime in itself Mel."

"You don't know anything Alex, so why don't you just go home and let me sort things out here."

"Okay." Alex thought there was nothing more she could do here, Mel wouldn't listen to her, Matt had only called Alex in to try to be kind to Mel but maybe it was time he told her to leave. Alex felt helpless and then suddenly from somewhere deep inside she felt a spark. "Actually no, not okay Mel. Matt called me because he was being kind, I think you've had enough consideration now. I have no idea what's got into you but Lee's bad news and the faster you realise that the better. You've been together for eleven days yet you're acting like you've been together for years. What's he holding over you Mel and engaged! He must want to keep you on a short leash for some reason. He has a reputation and it looks like it's down to me to tell you." Alex went on to tell her all the things that Jasmine had shared with her, all the time she was talking Mel just sat still and watched her, not saying a single word. The words continued to tumble out of Alex's mouth as she told her how she felt about him too even though that was only based on gut instinct but once she'd got started she was finding it difficult to stop. That spark deep down had flared like a firework and just as suddenly it felt like it had been doused. "Be careful Mel." With that Alex turned on her heels and left the room. If it had been a sit com that was when the audience would have stood up clapped and cheered. Matt saw her leave but he was too late to stop her so he returned to his office. Mel was occupied with something in her bag, she didn't look up but as she stood she said "Thank you Matt." He could have sworn he heard the sarcasm in the words but he gave her the benefit of the doubt, mainly because he wanted her out. She turned around and left.

    Matt truly believed he would never understand women.

Chapter Twenty Three

Michael sat gazing at his computer screen not knowing what to do next. Around him hundreds of people came and went, busily checking gate numbers and scurrying off so they didn't miss their flights, others sat around eating and drinking acting as if they had all the time in the world, it was easy to distinguish the holidaymakers from the seasoned travellers but he was absorbed in the news on his computer. He had found it whilst he was taking advantage of the charging station in the departure lounge; he seemed to be forever looking for somewhere to plug his computer into. According to the article he had found, a forty five year old man had been arrested in connection with the disappearance of Michael Masters. It went on to explain that the man had been discovered on the premises of Masters flat in Charmsbury and apparently he was a friend and artist. It didn't narrow it down too much but Michaels gut said it must have been Lee, who else would bother to go to his flat? The article also mentioned that the body that had been washed up in Charmsbury had not as yet been identified beyond it being male. Michael wasn't bothered about Lee, if he was stupid enough to go snooping around his flat he deserved everything he got but the police couldn't pin anything on him because he hadn't done anything wrong, Lee had been a thorn in Michael's side for most of his life and whatever he'd been up to inside the flat would certainly have looked suspicious. Michael had an idea why he had been there but couldn't be sure, if it was to find the letters then Lee would have to look beyond the obvious. At the bottom of the article there was a mention of a woman, 'a reliable source' was the wording used and unexpectedly he felt a twinge of sadness about her, of course it was Jasmine, who else had he sent flowers to before he left. They had never been a match made in heaven but now he had taken a step back he started to realise how good she had been for him, high maintenance maybe but not malicious or money grabbing like some of his earlier girlfriends. It mentioned that he was missed by his family and girlfriend and if he saw this would he please come home. There was a photo of a bouquet of flowers, possibly the ones he sent her. Yes now he had had some time alone he was tempted to change his flight and return to Charmsbury but that thought didn't last long once a few images of his previous life swam before his eyes, money grabbers and liars. A short by-line at the bottom of the piece gave recognition to the author of the article, Alexandra Price, Charmsbury. He had to smile, so eventually she had decided to step into the arena, she'd caught up with Jasmine too, she was following his trail well. He mentally gave her a pat on the back, he was now sure the whole 'chat' would come out eventually and whilst there was a body involved he felt safer, the press would be assuming it was his.

He looked up from his computer screen to the screens suspended from the ceiling above his head, his flight wasn't leaving for another two and a half hours, he unplugged his computer and wandered off to find a book shop and buy a trashy novel to keep him amused whilst he waited.

He had parked his car at the long stay car park at Charles De Gaulle airport but he had no intention of going back to collect it, it was his gift to the French. He had come into the airport with a different passport and booked himself a ticket to Thailand, he quite fancied staying on a beach somewhere with few tourists, if any places like that still existed in Thailand, he hadn't been outside the madness of Bangkok for many years. With this passport he was now travelling as Dominic Michael Waite, he liked the name Dominic but if he reacted when anyone shouted Michael he had it as a middle name so he could explain it away. The added bonus with this passport was that if anyone checked there was a bank account with plenty of money in it, in fact more had gone in recently with the money from the painting that he had sent to Alex and an account that was active was a good account, he had travelled to Thailand before on this passport or at least that's what the stamps inside it said. They had handed him a ticket for the eleven and a half hour flight with no excessive questions or checks. Now all he had to do was to wait for another two and a half hours and he would be on his way to the land of smiles and a peaceful life, or so he hoped.

As he got into the queue to board his flight and was inching forward he was struck by a moment of regret, he should turn back, all of the upset and trouble he was causing wasn't worth it, he wanted a quiet life, an escape, but maybe there was another way. Then in a moment of clarity he thought no there isn't a better way, not now he'd come this far and he handed the passport and boarding card over to be checked. He joined another queue waiting to get on the plane, this was all new to him, he had never travelled economy class before, he made his way through the plane to his seat, he found it and looked at the tiny space that would be his world for the next eleven and a half hours, he silently wished he had upgraded. He squeezed himself into the tiny space and shuffled around trying to get comfortable. In no time at all he was aware of the engines humming and they slowly rolled across the tarmac, gently turning towards the main runway, the engines suddenly roared into life and thrust them forward faster and faster and then the magic happened, they were gently lifted skyward. He looked out of the tiny window as they soared through the clouds and into the sunshine, looking down on the ever changing landscape he promised himself that from now on he would only look forward, what was past was past.

Chapter Twenty Four

Matt was sitting behind his desk, this case was getting messier by the minute now Lee was involved, since they had brought him in he had done little except for offering verbal abuse on any subject he could think of to the police, Michael, the body, women in general. All he did say that was constructive was that he had been in the flat looking for something that belonged to him but he wouldn't elaborate on that, he really wasn't helping himself. All Matt knew was that Lee and Michael had known each other most of their lives and Lee wouldn't open up and tell him anymore. He would go and talk to him again but it was becoming pointless, Matt knew he would have to get some information out of him soon otherwise he would end up having to let him go. As he was musing this over his phone rang, it was Alex "Hi."

"Hi, sorry I walked out on you earlier, did she leave?"

"Yeah whatever you said to her got her moving, are you okay?"

"Sure, I'm fine. I just passed on what Jasmine had told me…" She realised her mistake, she hadn't told Matt about Jasmine yet, she decided to keep going. "And I added a few thoughts of my own." She had tried to cover up her slip but Matt was on it.

"And when did you go and see Jasmine and why didn't you tell me?"

"Ah well, I did some washing and found her address in your pocket and I just couldn't resist." She smiled, Matt could hear it in her voice.

"Okay." Matt shrugged aware that Alex couldn't see him. "I guess that's fair, did she tell you anything?"

"A few bits of gossip but she doesn't know anything about what's happened to Michael, I'm sure of that."

"And the gossip was…?" He waited, it was hard work trying to get information out of a journalist.

"Apparently she says Lee is gay and that she thought he had a thing for Michael although Michael said not, she also thinks Lee's a gold digger and she told me to warn my friend, which I did. It didn't go down well."

"I don't suppose it did." Jasmine would never have disclosed gossip to him. "Oh yeah and as penance for stealing the address I hope you're going to iron those trousers too."

"Really!"

"Yes really and thanks sweetheart, see you later." Matt's mood had changed now Alex had passed on the gossip, she had unknowingly given him a reason to return to Lee with a new line in enquiry. He sat for a moment smiling, he hoped he may have found a motive. Michael spurned Lee's advances so Lee killed him. Extreme but possible and certainly more to it than that but it was a start. He got up and made his way back to the interview room, he was going to enjoy this after the abuse that Lee had been throwing around.

He stood in front of the door with a number three sticker on it, took a deep breath and went inside. It was a small bright room that housed a plain wooden table and four basic plastic chairs, on the far side of the table there was a black tape recording machine, old fashioned but it worked, maybe one day they'd upgrade it. Next to it was a small pile of sealed cassette tapes and sealable plastic evidence bags. On the wall a digital clock and that was everything except for a dishevelled Lee, sat at the table with his hands clasped in his lap and his eyes gazing forward to a blank spot on the wall, as if it may help him in some way. He didn't bother to look up as Matt entered the room. "Lee are you okay, can I get you anything?" Lee just continued looking into space. "Do you want a solicitor yet?"

"I ain't done nothing wrong, I don't want one."

"Okay let's get on with this then." Matt pulled out a chair opposite Lee and sat down, there was still no reaction, Lee had just returned to looking at that spot on the wall. Matt reached over and pressed the buttons on the tape recorder and went through the legal spiel, name, time, place etc.

"Lee are you going to tell me what you were looking for in Michael's flat?"

"No."

"Okay so tell me why you killed Michael."

"I didn't fuckin' kill him or anyone else, I already told you that."

"So what happened to him then and why do I conveniently have a body in the morgue?"

"How should I know?"

"The one thing you do know about is what you were doing in Michael's flat, so let's start there. What were you looking for Lee?" Silence was the only answer he got. "We know that Michael kept a lot of his personal paperwork and things he didn't necessarily want other people to see there, so I'll take a stab at money or papers, which were you after?"

"I've never been after his sodding money, didn't seem to bring him any luck did it?" Matt was surprised, he hadn't expected an answer.

"What does that mean, I thought it brought him plenty of luck and a nice lifestyle and you'd love to have his money wouldn't you?"

"Can't enjoy it if you're dead can you." This silenced Matt for a moment.

"Is he dead Lee?" He said quietly.

"I don't know, do I?"

"So back at the flat, what was it then papers, contract, photographs or letters that you were after?" Lee reverted back to staring at his favourite space on the wall. "Okay so do you want me to start guessing? Just stop me if I get any of this wrong." Matt looked at Lee but got no reaction. "We know you and Michael went to school together and you were both into art, only Michael wasn't much of an artist, you were the talented one weren't you Lee, Michael would hang around you, I suppose hoping that a little bit of that artists flair might rub off on him, did it?"

"A bit." Lee reluctantly admitted. Okay Matt thought, it's not much but it's a start.

"But he was never as good as you was he? Otherwise he'd have been painting not selling, that was what he really wanted wasn't it? Did he rip you off, is that what all of this is about?"

"No." Lee continued looking at the wall.

"Did you have a disagreement? I'm sure you must have been quite close friends after all of those years together. Close friends often argue." Silence was all he got this time. "Did he have you tied into an unreasonable contract and that's what you were looking for at the flat? Had you been offered a better deal with someone else?" Still no reply. "Or did he have possession of something that could cause trouble for you and you thought you could get it back once you'd got rid of him?" There it was, barely noticeable but definitely a reaction, just a slight widening of the eyes but enough to encourage Matt to keep digging. "Come on Lee what could have been so bad that it would drive you to get rid of him just to get it back?"

"I didn't…"

"I'm sorry but I don't believe you, Lee if I had to take a stab in the dark I'd say you had a secret, Michael knew about it and maybe he was blackmailing you or maybe just teasing you enough to tip you over the edge."

"I didn't kill him."

"Okay well we'll just have to keep you here until you give us a reason to believe you and once we have an ID on the body we may just have to keep you a little longer. I don't understand why you don't want to help yourself, I would have thought you'd have wanted to be out in the sunshine with your fiancée."

"She told you?" He looked at Matt questioningly.

"She told Alex, so what's the deal there? All a bit quick or was it love at first sight?"

"She's lovely and yes I do want to be with her." His face wasn't telling the same story as his mouth.

"How much do you want to be with her Lee? I think the love of your life was Michael not Mel, I also think that Michael didn't feel the same way. Was that why you got rid of him, a crime of passion, were you trying to get rid of some evidence at the flat when we turned up, is that it?"

"Where did you get that bullshit from?" He was starting to get agitated.

"I think you'll find I ask the questions Lee, so just think over what you want to tell me next and bang on that door when you're ready to discuss it."

"You can't keep me here!"

"With a body to account for I think you'll find I can keep you here as long as I want to." Matt was starting to feel better about all of this now, feeling like he had the control again, he hoped it would shake Lee up a bit.

He leant over towards the tape recorder and said "Inspector Matthew Jones concluding interview with Mr Lee Hohlen, twelve thirty one pm." He clicked the button, released the tape, peeled off a bag with the aplomb of a practiced magician, pulled the seal across and left the room, all the time purposefully not looking at Lee, he wanted him to sweat a little.

Chapter Twenty Five

Alex didn't have anything planned for the afternoon and there was no news on Michael or Lee, she decided to go and see her Nan, from what she could gather Jack was tearing his hair out with her Nan going on about the wedding, Alex needed a distraction and cake.

Jack wasn't wrong, her Nan was drawing and making notes, looking at materials and designs on the internet for her dress, Jack didn't know anything about designs and colours and was being more of a hindrance than a help. Alex had to smile it was lovely to see a pair of septuagenarians getting ruffled over their wedding plans. "Ah here's someone who will be more use." Mary chastised Jack when Alex walked in, it was all Alex could do not to laugh. Jack looked at Alex, shrugged and said "She's all yours I'm going for a walk." At least he was still smiling as he left.

"Nan, have you picked the cake yet?"

"I'm making it myself as a surprise for Jack, don't tell him."

"Okay I'll keep quiet so long as you feed me cake." Mary went off to get cake and coffee whilst Alex checked out the designs she was looking at and she had to admit her Nan still had serious style. Mary came back with plates overflowing with tiny pieces of cake and two steaming mugs of coffee, "Taste these Alex." Gladly she thought. Chocolate, caramel, coffee, orange the list went on and on, Alex realised she was being used as the official taster for the wedding cake. She was beginning to think her Nan was taking all of this a little too far and then she saw the design for the cake. "You wound Jack up on purpose so he'd go out didn't you? This is amazing." The designs she had been working on were for the cake, the dress designs was a cover story. It was going to be a work of art, Jacks favourite design, the triquetra.

Once they'd eaten more cake than was good for them the conversation turned to work. "Have you heard anything yet about the body?" Mary asked.

"No nothing, except they have Lee in for questioning."

"Yes I saw that in the paper, one of the nationals had a photo of him, he's the one I told you was always with Michael, he was a spiteful one, always jealous of your Mum because Michael liked her."

"You sure it was Lee."

"Yes the skinny little one, wherever Michael was, that guy wouldn't be far away. He was a bit creepy if you ask me."

"Well the police are questioning him now, if there's anything to find out I'm sure they will. You know he was going out with Mel? Turns out they had got engaged too." Alex felt a little sad for Mel.

"Oh, back then I thought he preferred boys, guess I was wrong." Alex raised an eyebrow in reply. "I wasn't wrong was I?"

"Not from what I've been told, no one told Mel though and I think he's after her for other reasons but I don't know what… yet." Alex went on to explain to her Nan about their argument and what Jasmine had told her. Her Nan always loved the latest gossip so she could be the first to share it with her book group. Alex changed the topic of conversation, she didn't want to discuss Mel anymore. "So have you chosen your dress yet?"

"Oh that's already been done but don't tell Jack, his suit is sorted too. I'm getting some fun out of winding him up with stupid ideas."

"Poor Jack, I hope you'll put him out of his misery soon. You seem to be very organised, well except for the cake, oh and I think the coffee and caramel combination will work for that. Could I try a bit more just to be sure?" Alex winked cheekily as her Nan went off to get more cake.

Chapter Twenty Six

Alex sat on the floor in front of the painting breathing steadily looking deeper and deeper into the work, the more she looked the more detail she found and it always managed to calm her, she couldn't believe what a difference art could make in her life. Matt was at work and she had the house to herself today, she had planned to get some work done from home, she would have to go out for a while and check out a protest that was being held to stop plans for fracking in the area and then she could come home, write it up and the rest of the day was her own. She went and had a long relaxing bath and headed out to the site of the protest.

When she got there she found a tent serving tea and coffee and maybe thirty people milling around, there was a pile of banners leant against a fence post and there appeared to be far more picket boards than there were people. She hoped more people would turn up soon otherwise no one would take any notice of the protest, they needed at least a couple of hundred people to make it newsworthy and this should be in the news. Alex decided to hang around for a while, she got herself a polystyrene cup of something resembling coffee and waited, a few more people trickled in and a couple turned up who just wanted to see what was going on. A black Mercedes appeared, driving slowly down the track and stopped, a young man in an expensive suit got out and smiled sarcastically at the protesters. "Is this all you could muster?" They each grabbed their banners and boards and tried to look menacing, circling the car. A van pulled up behind the car and amazingly another twenty people or so appeared from inside it. Alex was watching all of this happening as someone touched her arm, she turned around to see Mark standing behind her. "I have some news, come on." He guided her to a quiet spot by the tea tent. "I have been chatting with a guy online who says he's seen Michael. I didn't believe him initially but he said the guy had left him a drawing and he'd seen him reading something in the newspaper about the disappearance, which was when he noticed the similarity. May be nothing but he seemed convinced."

"Where is this bloke?" Alex had forgotten the protest now.

"France, a village called Seix, he has a guest house there."

"Can I speak to him?" She asked excitedly.

"I guess so." Mark replied.

"Come back to the house with me and use my computer, see if you can get hold of him." Alex turned back to the protestors who weren't making much of an impact but were now chanting "No fracking chance. Not fracking here." The man in the car who turned out to be an executive from Ecoplus, the company who wanted the rights to the land, didn't seem overly worried by them but when an egg flew through the air and smashed on his windscreen just missing his head, he got back in the car to cheers from the small crowd. She would just do a few lines for the paper, it wouldn't be much of a story anyway and nothing else would happen now, the car was moving off down the track. The protesters had done their work and made their point.

Back at the house it took Mark about half an hour to get Pierre on the video messenger service, he was a pleasant looking man of about fifty and he proceeded to tell Alex about the man who had stayed with him for a few days. He held up the drawing that he had been gifted for her to see and told her he was sure it had been Michael Masters even though he was going by the name of Michael Shaw and driving a white VW Golf with British plates, he couldn't remember the registration number except for the beginning HG06 and he wasn't sure but he thought there was an 'S' in there too. Michael had spent his days out by the river drawing and seemed very relaxed until he saw the newspaper article, which had seemed to unnerve him a little. Alex could have listened to Pierre all day with his romantic French accent but he had to go and look after his guests. He promised to email her his contact details in case she had more questions.

"Mark do you think he's genuine?" She asked.

"There's been no reward offered so he has nothing to gain, why would anyone make up a story if it wasn't true."

"I'll pass this information to Matt, he'll have more chance of tracing the car than us, I don't know what else we can do, can you try and find out anything you can about a Michael Shaw and I'll talk to Jasmine again and see if the name means anything to her." Alex looked thoughtful. "Maybe I'll go and see if William is still around he might know something too."

"Okay if I stay here and use your laptop? It's so much faster than mine."

"Sure, I'll catch you later." Alex headed for the door and left Mark to work his magic.

She went into town and managed to park directly outside 'Master's Fine Arts' the exhibition was still running, it had another two weeks to go so she hoped William would still be around. The doors were already open and as she walked into the cool interior she spotted William straight away chatting to a woman who was pointing to a painting, she caught his eye and he raised his hand to show her he'd be five minutes, Alex wandered around looking at the work on show whilst she waited. There was nothing here that could hold a candle to her painting though, the one that had been hung where her painting had been was an abstract brightly coloured fish titled 'Splash'. She kept moving, there was a pretty painting called 'Autumn Leaves' by the same artist as her painting but it still didn't have the same intensity as 'Buddha Mountain', finally William was walking towards her. "Hi, sorry to keep you waiting." She wasn't sure if he recognised her or not.

"Hi, I had 'Buddha Mountain' from you, I wanted to ask you a couple of questions, do you mind?"

"Sure I remember you, Alex isn't it, and what can I help you with?" He paused. "Have you found him, is there any news?"

"No, not yet but I may have a lead, do you remember him ever owning a white VW Golf?"

"Golf! No he only had top of the range cars, his latest was a Ferrari, why would he need a little car like that?"

"That's what I thought, never mind. Have you ever heard of a Michael Shaw?"

"No, who's that?"

"Maybe no one, it doesn't matter. I was just chasing a wild card. Thanks for your help."

"Anytime, just let me know if you turn anything up won't you Alex." He looked concerned.

Alex left the exhibition thinking what a nice guy William was and he was keeping everything going really well if the amount of people milling around was anything to go by. She was going to go and see Jasmine but the thought of that drive had her reaching for her phone, Jasmine answered on the third ring. "Hi Alex, any news?"

"Not much but does the name Michael Shaw mean anything to you?"

"No…" She took her time. "No, I don't think I've heard the name before, why?"

"Maybe nothing, did Michael ever own VW Golf?"

"You didn't know Michael did you!" She laughed "He wouldn't be seen dead in anything less than a Bentley." When she realised what she'd said she stopped laughing abruptly. "Sorry I could have been more tactful."

"It's okay, someone thought they saw him but it looks like a red herring, thanks for your help though."

"Alex…"

"Yes."

"Thank you for looking for him and believing." She sounded sad, as if the news had just hit her. Alex hung up and felt some of that sadness herself.

When she got home Mark was still hard at work hunched over the computer. "Any news?" She asked.

"No, have you any idea how many Michael Shaw's there are on Facebook alone?"

"Hundreds I'm guessing."

"Yes and that'll translate to thousands over the whole internet." Mark was close to giving up.

"Anything on the car?" Alex asked hopefully.

"Nothing, again there are white golf's everywhere, I wouldn't know where to start, I don't know anything about cars. We need a full registration number and we need Matt."

"Email Pierre, he may have remembered something else now he's thinking about it."

Mark tapped away for a while longer, without any luck and finally gave up, he wanted to get back to the tunnel, Alex thought he had a date by the way he was acting. "So who is it you've got plans with?"

"Summer." He blushed.

"Really, Summer, Oh that's perfect. Go now and get ready." Alex was pleased for both of them, they would make a lovely couple, both of them were gentle, thoughtful people. Mark hugged her and smiled as he left for his hot date.

Chapter Twenty Seven

Matt phoned Alex telling her to meet him at Hearts and he'd treat her to dinner. She didn't know what she'd done to deserve it but she was pleased to have an excuse to get dressed up.

When she arrived he was already there waiting for her "You got out of work early today, I was beginning to forget what you looked like." She smiled at him.

"I couldn't do anything else today, Lee's still not talking, the body is no closer to being identified and I thought we could do with treat."

"So, a frustrating day, I'll try and cheer you up." She winked and smiled. The waiter came and took their order and brought them a bottle of red wine. "Any news on the car registration?"

"The only bright spot in my day, thanks for that. The car was registered in mid-2006 in Dorset but beyond that we can't tell much, I've got someone going through second hand sales of cars with that year registration, we really need the rest of the registration. It's a long shot but there's a slim chance, did Pierre reveal anything else?"

"He said the man had stayed a few days and left him a pencil drawing. Michael used to draw and paint but everyone said he was no good but this picture was nice, not complicated, and kind of peaceful."

"Don't suppose he signed it." Matt said offhand.

"I didn't ask, I'll email Pierre and ask him."

"I'm joking, if he's hiding then he wouldn't make that type of mistake, Pierre doesn't seem to mind talking to you so I won't contact him officially until you've spoken with him again."

"It can't hurt to check, we might be able to get something from the handwriting." Alex was starting to feel quite excited at the prospect.

"Sweetheart you really should watch less movies." He smiled and his eyes twinkled. Alex laughed and lost herself in that sparkle, she leant over the table to kiss him at the same time as the waiter arrived with their meal, the moment was lost but Matt was amused at the colour rising on the waiters face.

Alex told Matt all about her Nan's plans for the wedding cake and the fun she was having teasing Jack with clothing and matching outfits, "Jack is thinking this is going to be the wedding of the century and he is terrified. I think he's picturing something on the scale of a royal wedding." From the look on Matt's face it looked like he was commiserating with Jack.

"Have they decided where it's going to be yet?"

"Not sure, Jack wants the registry office, a quiet affair and a knees up at the pub. Nan wants it all to be at the tunnel."

"Well if anyone can organise it, Mary can."

"Yeah, the tunnel would be romantic too." Alex's phone rumbled in her pocket like a small animal trying to escape, she freed it and looked at the screen, it was an email from Pierre. "Sorry I need to check this." She clicked on the heading, it opened up to show all of his contact details and a note at the bottom, 'he signed the picture – click attachment.' She smiled and opened the photo. It was a close up of the signature it read Michael S. Pierre must have been thinking along the same lines as she was.

"What's up?" Matt asked.

"Nothing just too many movies, I guess." She turned the screen to face him, smiling. "I'll check this against the card he sent with the picture when we get home."

"Lucky guess, Pulitzer prize winner." He laughed.

They finished their meal and discussed a holiday in the sun they might go on when this case was over whilst they drained their bottle of wine. Alex was getting quite excited about organising their first foreign holiday together.

When they arrived home Alex went straight to the painting and took it off the wall, turned it around and plucked the card from the back, grabbed her phone and found the picture Pierre had sent her. She held them close together, they were similar but not immediately identifiable as the same hand. Maybe she needed to ask someone who knew him better or someone who was an expert in handwriting, she took a photograph of the card and sent that and the signature from Pierre to Jasmine by email, tomorrow she would go and see William and see what he thought.

Now she just wanted to curl up in bed, it had been a busy, informative day with a lovely ending and she was tired, she trudged up to the bedroom, it seemed Matt had other ideas as he grabbed her and pulled her onto the bed.

Chapter Twenty Eight

She woke up to the phone ringing, she glanced at the clock on the bedside table and it told her it was nine thirty, nine thirty! She leapt out of bed and ran for the phone in the hall before the answerphone could catch it. "Hello" she said a little breathlessly.

"Good morning Alex, sounds like I've woken you." It was Jasmine.

"Morning, yes I overslept."

"The email you sent, it could be Michaels signature, not his normal one but it struck me that I remembered us messing around once, me trying to write left handed because that's what he did all the time and him trying to write right handed the way I did. My attempt was awful but his was okay, anyway that's what this signature reminded me of."

"So he was naturally left handed, I didn't notice. Some intrepid journalist I am." She laughed at her own joke.

"Yes but he practised using his right hand a lot because he was always told as a child he shouldn't be left handed otherwise the devil would work through him or some such rubbish."

"So you think it could be him?"

"It's possible, I hope so…" Alex could hear the sorrow in her voice, she seemed to have lost any anger or bravado, now she was just a woman missing her man.

"Thanks Jasmine, if he's out there somewhere I'll do my best to find him, I promise you that."

"Thank you." Jasmine hung up. Alex was wide awake now and went to make coffee.

She phoned Matt and passed on the information from Jasmine and playfully berated him for not waking her. He got away with that by telling her how beautiful she looked whilst she was sleeping, she was a sucker for a romantic line. She got dressed and drove into work, she still had to write a story on the protest from yesterday and she wouldn't get side tracked if she was at her grubby little desk. As she sat down and opened up her computer, no sooner was she settled than Fiona shouted "Have you seen the papers, there's been sighting in France, there's photos." Alex's heart sank she presumed Pierre had sold his story, damn, she should have offered him some money. She got up and grabbed a handful of the days' papers and there on page five was a photo of a man who did look like Michael Masters staring out at her the only difference was he was wearing designer stubble and a tee shirt. She read the story but it wasn't from Pierre there was no mention of a drawing or the car. It seemed the photos were taken by a tourist in Carcassonne who had recognised him from the photos in the newspaper, there was a quote from his parents too, saying they were hopeful. Alex silently said a little thank you if only because it was looking more and more like he was still alive although that set off a whole barrage of new questions in her mind, the first being why would he leave? All of the information was starting to form a picture but she had no idea what that picture was and still she needed to know about the body. She picked up her phone and called Matt "Any way of telling if the body was left handed?"

"Hang on I've got the reports here, an update came in this morning." She heard him rustling paper and could picture him scanning the report.

"Yes it looks like a possibility that he was, it says that 'the left arm was slightly better developed than the right, which would lead us to assume that the man was left handed' is that what you wanted to hear?"

"No, not what I wanted to hear at all, anything else in there that might help?"

"Not really but I know they're trying to contact his dentist in America for dental records."

"Of course he wouldn't have had a dentist here like everyone else would he." She was starting to feel like they were back to square one again.

"It's okay we'll get the answers soon."

"I hope so." Alex ended the call feeling her hope had been dashed.

She needed to get the protest story together before Charlie started shouting about her lack of output. This wasn't turning out to be the day she had hoped but she tapped away at her computer without interruption for an hour and got the story done and sent it off to Charlie. She went on to spend the next hour pointlessly trawling through the internet trying to match up the name Shaw with VW Golf's, a fruitless search but it kept her mind off the body. The rest of the day turned up nothing, Alex tried to contact Mel but she was still not accepting Alex's calls, so she moved on to calling Summer and after a brief catch up she asked the question "Have you seen Mel?" There was a brief pause as if Summer was deciding how to answer.

"Yes, she's not happy with you."

"I did give it to her with both barrels but she was closing her eyes to everything Summer, someone had to tell her."

"What did you say to her that made her so mad?"

"Did she tell you about Lee being arrested and that she turned up at the police station demanding information about her fiancé?"

"What… No she didn't! Fiancé? When did that happen? What's she got herself into Alex?"

"She'll have to tell you that Summer but I just wanted to know she's okay."

"Apart from being mad at you and looking sad a lot of the time I think she's okay."

"Try and get her to accept my calls if you speak to her, please."

"I'll take Lily round to see her and see what I can do."

"I owe you Summer, give Lily a hug from me, hope I'll get to see her soon too."

"I can get over to yours next week with her, she'd love to see you too, you're her claim to fame. She's always talking about her famous Aunty Alex."

"Hardly famous." Alex laughed

"To her you're a journalist, an author and the person who brought her Mum back."

They said their goodbyes and Alex chalked today down to being a bad one, although Summer had cheered her up with her talk of Lily.

Alex was hoping tomorrow would bring some answers.

Chapter Twenty Nine

Michael had been in Thailand for two days and he was enjoying the heat and being amidst the madness of Bangkok and he finally felt completely anonymous. He loved it here, everyone was too busy to notice yet another tourist and he knew none of the language so he was left alone on the whole. The famous tuk tuk drivers could spot a tourist a mile away and they were the only people who tried to capture his attention, relentlessly, wanting to take him to a temple or out to a shop their brother owns, where you were sure to buy many things you never knew you needed. He knew he wouldn't stay here too long he could get a train from Hua Lamphong Station to anywhere in the country and once he'd decided in which direction he wanted to travel he would be on his way, eventually he knew he would go south but he may travel around first. For now Bangkok was amusing him with the smells of food, car fumes and the unique aromas from the markets that seemed to be everywhere and he could wear his Rolex again without worry, everyone had one in this city and they were so good that you couldn't tell the real thing from a fake. He had spent the day walking around the beautiful Temple of Dawn, browsing the craft stalls and eating from the street vendors. He'd only ever eaten in hotels in Bangkok before and the food on the street was much better than the overpriced western food that was served up in the five star hotels. He was like a child in a sweet shop trying everything as he walked amongst the tourists that wanted to photograph the food in preference to eating it. He found himself smiling a lot and he noticed how the locals would all smile back at him, this was how he wanted his life to be. He slowly drifted away still taking time to admire the architecture and the Buddha carvings, he gradually made his way back to his room on a small street that backed onto a Chinese temple. It was basic but it was clean and it had air conditioning, he had no idea how anyone managed without it in this city but when he looked around for a room it seemed that it was only supplied for the tourists, the Thais got by with a fan although he didn't know how, he was constantly moping sweat from his face. His only other concession to western life had come when he tried to sleep in the bed, it was hard, as hard as sleeping on a plank of wood, he had immediately gone out to a local market and found himself a roll of foam and a sleeping bag to place on what they described as a mattress, with that in place his life felt very near perfect and he was happy. The only thing now that dimmed his happiness was the constant pull of checking his computer regularly for updates on what was happening in Charmsbury. From what news he could glean Lee was still in custody but the big news today was the photographs of him in Carcassonne, he knew he shouldn't have hung around there for as long as he had, he had been aware of cameras everywhere but it ended up being a tourist that had spotted and snapped him, he was glad to have got away from Europe, no one here seemed to care who he was or where he had come from. He unrolled his sleeping bag and foam and lay down on the now comfortable bed; he was exhausted from walking around all day in the tropical heat. The smell of garlic wafted through the room as the stalls outside cooked their food and he drifted off to sleep to the constant noise of Bangkok traffic and the incessant hum of the air conditioning.

   The following morning he was woken early by the continuing sound of traffic and people setting up for work, he glanced at his watch, it was five o'clock in the morning, he went to the window and lifted the hanging material that was tacked over the glass to keep out the light, they laughingly called it a curtain. Directly outside his window was a noodle stall preparing food for a monk clad in saffron coloured robes who was standing to the side of the stall, serenely holding his alms bowl, the noodles were bagged up and the offering dropped into the bowl, the monk said a few words which Michael couldn't hear and if he could he wouldn't have understood and the monk walked away as another stallholder stopped him to offer food from her stall. The monk went down the road collecting food from all of the stalls that offered it for as far as Michael could see. He returned to his bed once the monk was out of sight but could no longer sleep, the noise coupled with the heat made sure he was awake, it was even hot at this time of the morning. He pulled on a t shirt and some shorts, this was the time to get out and sort himself out for the day, he had a feeling it was best to do what the locals did, they knew how to handle the heat, get started early, now all he needed was to find some coffee. It was still dark outside but the amount of activity that was going on meant everything was lit up almost brighter than daylight, Michael found a Chinese coffee vendor, he could smell the coffee before he saw it and he followed his nose. The coffee was thick and dark and incredibly sweet but it did the trick and woke him up fully. Today he was going to get on his computer and decide in which direction he wanted to travel, he also wanted to get himself a real Thai massage it was one thing he had promised himself when he arrived here. He bought himself a Thai pork omelette on steamed rice and headed back to his room, already he was looking forward to the cool air from his air conditioning kissing his skin. The Wi-Fi connection was better than he expected this morning and he managed to get a good idea of the country and decided he wanted to go south without travelling around first, so after his massage he would go and check out the trains. With his day planned and his stomach full he lay back and fell asleep for another hour.

Hua Lamphong station was a huge imposing building obviously not inspired by Thai architecture, instead designed by two Italians, it had a large open lobby area, there was some seating available and stalls selling food and books around the sides, there was another level above him that housed the travel agencies and cafes. The seats were not all taken but many people it seemed preferred to sit on the floor in the tiled area without seating, as he was watching he heard some English speaking tourists talking to each other and as he looked towards them they waved and nodded to him. He smiled and waved back then walked away to the stairs and up to a café to get a cool drink and avoid the tourists. The last thing he needed was to make friends and end up with travelling buddies he couldn't get rid of. The lemon soda assaulted his taste buds as the cool liquid hit his mouth and slid down his throat, he happily lost himself in the heat and the noise of the railway station. He sat for a while enjoying his surroundings until a couple of American tourists turned up and sat at the table next to him and started talking about their travel plans and asking him where he was headed, he told them he hadn't decided and made his excuses to leave, he walked off towards the ticket office, he looked at his options and decided four and a half hours on a train was enough for one day so booked himself a ticket to Hua Hin in two days' time, as he paid he thought he must have misheard, ninety four baht, just a little under two pounds, this country just kept getting more and more hospitable.

Chapter Thirty

Alex woke up to the rain and the temperature had dropped substantially, she thought it was definitely a day to go to work. She needed to write up an article on a new range of make-up and a few tricks to make you look ten years younger. Not her idea of fun but Trina who normally covered the beauty section was on maternity leave, so Alex was figuratively speaking left holding the baby. She felt like she needed the dull hum drum of the office to get through this type of writing.

She arrived in work and as usual everyone was chatting, a few of them looked over at her and waved, for a change she stopped to chat before she headed for her desk, whilst her computer loaded up she hoped Matt would get a lead on the car or that Pierre might email her miraculously remembering the car registration. Her computer opened and she started writing the article up, getting lost in chocolate and pineapple lip gloss that promised to give you a pout that would make your partner of ten years look at you like a new woman. She knew Trina loved this job because of all the freebies that came along with it and Alex was beginning to see why, she wouldn't need to buy anymore make-up for at least a year. "Nice to see you at your desk Alex." Charlie appeared next to her, snapping her out of her musings.

"Hi." She smiled up at him.

"Anything new on Masters?"

"Maybe soon Charlie, I don't know anything for sure yet."

"So is he dead or are you holding on to the belief that he's been kidnapped or run away?"

"Stop teasing! I'll let you know when I know anything, I haven't written him off yet."

"Remember I've heard that before. Anyway that's not why I'm here, what are you doing for the next few days?"

"Nothing much."

"Okay we've been given the job of covering a story that will go out to all the local newspapers across the country and I need a reporter in Paris, do you fancy a few days away... paid?"

"Of course, what's it about?"

"A follow up on how France is healing itself after the bombings of last year. A few interviews, a few photographs and the rest of the time will be your own."

"Sounds like my kind of job, I'd love to do it." She almost jumped out of her chair to hug him but he moved fast enough that she got away without looking too undignified. "Charlie, when?" She shouted after him.

"Tomorrow, stop by my office before you leave." With that he walked away. Alex was over the moon and then she wondered how far Seix was from Paris, was there any chance she could go and see Pierre just to see if there was anything else she could find out? She calmed herself down and turned back to what was now looking like an irrelevant article, she just couldn't get back to feeling inspired by eyebrow pencils, she threw together the rest of the article feeling guilty for not giving it her full attention, she was sure Trina would understand. She phoned Matt to share her good fortune with him, he wasn't quite so excited because he knew the police wouldn't give him the time off to accompany her but he seemed pleased for her. Finally she emailed Pierre asking for details on the best way to find him, adding that she would mail him as soon as she knew her schedule. With that done she happily grabbed her bag, swung it over her shoulder and virtually skipped off to Charlie's office. He looked up and smiled. "And what are you looking so happy about?"

"I've got a great boss who's sending me off on holiday."

"Work, Alex. Work." He emphasised.

"Okay, work... so tell me more. Do I get a pay rise too for being your international correspondent?"

"Oh Alex, don't make me wish I'd picked someone else."

"Okay boss." They both laughed and Charlie proceeded to tell her the travel plans and the list of people she would be meeting. Handed her the print out of the tickets for the plane, her itinerary and a taxi had been booked for her for eight o'clock the next morning. She would pick a hire car up at Charles de Gaulle airport when she arrived. She got up to leave when Charlie added. "Don't kill yourself."

"Hey, my driving's not that bad." She retorted.

"Have you driven in Paris before?" Alex shook her head "Just be careful." He added.

She got home, Pierre had emailed and sent her all the information she needed to find him, she was surprised it was such a distance but confident she could fit it in, if she stayed an extra day or two in France. She thought she would phone Mel and see if she would like to go too, it might be a way to help heal the friendship but after trying Mel's number three times and getting voicemail three times, she left a message but with little hope. Then she went and packed a small bag, she heard Matt come in; at least they could spend the evening together.

That was the plan but it turned out he'd had a bad day, he was trying to convince the magistrates to allow him to hold Lee for a longer period of time. He wasn't getting anywhere with him, the longer it all went on the more abusive about Michael he was being, it turned out he may have to release him tomorrow but before he did he was going to have another go at trying to get some fresh information out of him. Also there was nothing on the car and the coroner was no further forward with the body. Matt felt like he was treading water.

Chapter Thirty One

Alex landed in Paris and whilst she waited for her bag to come off the plane she turned her phone on and put it back in her pocket, it normally took a few minutes to log into a new network but almost immediately the phone started vibrating, she checked her phone there were messages coming through constantly, voicemails and emails. Wow, I'm popular she thought. She checked her messages first whilst keeping an eye on the presently empty baggage carousel. The first was from Mel, short and to the point 'Leave me alone'. She added to her initial thought, maybe not that popular! The next three were from Matt all saying a variation on 'don't leave the airport until you've spoken to me. Her voice messages were from Matt too, the emails were all people trying to sell her things except one from Pierre with more detailed directions and a welcome to France message from her phone provider finally pinged its way through.

It took another ten minutes before her small bag came sailing along the baggage carousel waiting to be claimed. She grabbed it awkwardly and moved to a quiet area to phone Matt. "What's up? I've arrived."

"You okay?"

"Sure, what's going on?"

"The police there will be looking out for you."

"What!" She went hot and cold at the same time and her skin prickled with fear.

"Don't panic, they want your help, you'll be working on my behalf. They have found a car in the long stay car park, I need you to take a look at it and get some photos, it could take forever for them to get around to filing a report and sending it on, can you do this for me?"

"Of course, don't scare me like that though, what's the car about?" She started to calm down.

"We think it might be Michael's although we can't be sure but it's an abandoned white Golf and it's the right year."

"Why the panic if it only might be?" She was curious now, this could still be anyone's car.

"It was booked in with the name Michael Shaw. Lee's been talking this morning finally and he's saying the body may have something to do with Michael."

"Okay, I'm struggling with this, you think Michaels here so what's the body got to do with him?" Alex was confused.

"I'm not sure but Lee is implying they're linked, I've got to go back and speak to him again."

"I'll sort the car this end and speak to you afterwards." Alex ended the conversation not knowing what to think. She walked through the customs gate and was instantly met by two police officers, she was relieved to discover that they both spoke English.

They drove her to a huge car park that was surrounded by wire fencing, she looked around, there were a lot of cars here and still it was maybe only half full, the police car pulled up in front of a dirty white VW Golf with a big official looking sticker on the windscreen. Alex rummaged through her carry-on bag and retrieved her camera, an old and trusted Nikon that she used for serious work, as she got out of the car she was already snapping pictures, she covered the car from top to bottom and recorded the police opening the car up for her to continue her photography of the interior, she left nothing to chance. One of the officers got her attention and called her round to the passenger side, he had opened the glove compartment and with his latex covered hand he carefully removed a piece of paper and unfolded it, holding it up for her to photograph. She took pictures of it without really looking at it, she just wanted to cover every movement of the police for

Matt, when she stopped and looked, her breath caught in her throat. What was written there proved the body did not belong to Michael.

> *'Tell Lee not to bother looking, he'll never find them. He'll understand and going out with that woman won't help him either. I won't tell anyone. Ssshhhh! I could write all day but I have a plane to catch.*
> *Michael'*

Alex was speechless, questions and realisations crowding her mind. Michael was alive and it looked like he was settling scores, so where was he now?

She asked the police some questions about when the car was found and when it had been dropped off and finished her photography, there were fingerprints all over the car and they promised her that they would get all of the information off to Inspector Jones as soon as they could. They dropped her back at the airport, she collected the car that Charlie had rented for her and sat in the car park and phoned Matt to relay the news. She also called Mark to see if he could look for possible flights that would have left after the car was deposited at the car park then called Pierre to apologise for the inconvenience but she wouldn't be visiting him, something had come up and finally Jasmine. "I have news."

"Tell me it's good Alex."

"I think so but confusing, Michael is still alive, you were right."

"That's a relief." Jasmine's voice changed, she genuinely sounded relieved.

"There's a note implicating Lee in some way, if you can think of anything he's ever told you about Lee or if you have any idea of where he may be will you call me?"

"Of course I will…" She paused. "Alex."

"Yeah."

"Thank you." It sounded like she might be crying.

Chapter Thirty Two

Matt was sitting opposite Lee again in the interview room, this could be his last chance of getting any information and after getting the news from Alex about the letter he thought he may have a chance of finally getting somewhere. Lee was sitting looking at the same spot on the wall as he had every time they had been together in this room. "Come on Lee, there must be something you want to get off your chest."

"No."

"Okay well I'm going to show you a photograph of a letter that's been found and then you might change your mind." Matt opened a folder that he had on the table in front of him and pulled out a printed copy of the photograph of the letter that Alex had sent him. He handed it to Lee and watched his face carefully. Lee picked it up, read it and laughed. "So." Matt asked.

"So what? He's just trying to stitch me up."

"What for?" It was a double edged question, an answer either way would be an improvement on what they had now. He paused, waiting for Lee to say anything, there was nothing but silence. "Tell us what he has over you Lee, we might be able to sort this mess out." No reply. "The letter implies that you went out with Mel as an alibi for something. Is that it?" Still nothing. "Why was he blackmailing you Lee?" Lee didn't say a thing and Matt had, had enough. "For God's sake, why won't you talk and get yourself out of this mess, anyone would think you'd killed someone ..." Of course, as soon as the words were out of his mouth Matt couldn't believe he hadn't thought of it earlier, was it Lee who was responsible for the body that was lying in the morgue? "Did you kill him Lee?"

"What are you talking about now?" Lee snapped.

"The body, who is it?"

"You're asking all the wrong questions to the wrong man."

"So who should I be asking?"

"Michael of course!"

"But he's not here and you are." Matt couldn't believe he'd got Lee talking, not shouting or swearing, just talking and he was beginning to sound tired.

"Well find him, I'm sure he'll give you all the answers."

"Do you know where we can find him?"

"Not a clue but it'll be somewhere warm... Bastard!"

"Help me understand Lee, I don't know what's going on."

"Why don't you stop talking to me like a child and go and do your fucking job and find out!"

"Exactly what I'm trying to do Lee but you need to help me." Lee turned his attention back to the wall and didn't reply. Matt was learning from experience that he wouldn't get anything else out of Lee now. He concluded the interview and went back to his office, the magistrates would give him more time with Lee now this letter had surfaced. He picked up the coroner's report from his desk and read it again, the body had been dead before it hit the water, there wasn't too much water in the lungs and there were damaged skin particles that could be associated with bruising but it was uncertain due to the state of the corpse. Matt was becoming more and more certain that the body was Lee's responsibility, now the magistrates would surely have to give him an extension on holding him. Matt wouldn't let him get away with this he just needed to work out how Michael fitted in to it.

Chapter Thirty Three

Alex was busy, this had been a lot of hard work, two days solidly filled with interviewing the families of people who had died in the Paris bombings of 2015, it was incredibly sad work, although it was also inspiring how these people damaged beyond most people's comprehension by life were picking themselves up and rebuilding what was left. She had hundreds of photos and many heartfelt stories yet still she couldn't get Michael out of her mind. She phoned Mark "Hi, any news?"

"You still in Paris?"

"Yes. Heading home in a couple of days after I've written my interviews up, thought I may do some sightseeing."

"Do you want me to email the news or should I tell you?" Mark teased.

"Tell me." She laughed.

"Your Michael Shaw seemed to disappear after he dropped the car off, I can't find any reference to him anywhere."

"So what are you saying?"

"I'm saying he either didn't catch a plane anywhere or he's changed his name."

"So how do I find him now?" She asked.

"I'm working on something Alex, I'll email you later, don't tell Matt though, I shouldn't be doing this. Okay?"

"Sure Mark, I can keep a secret." She had no idea what he was up to. "Mark… how's Summer?"

"She's perfect Alex." She could hear the smile in his voice.

"I'm happy for you." They said goodbyes and Alex's mood was elevated she really was happy for them. She was also excited that Mark may be onto something, she hoped he wouldn't be too long emailing her, she needed to know what was going on.

She spent the rest of the day writing up her interviews and downloading photographs, it was grim work and she emailed the first couple of stories off to Charlie, he would be pleased to know she was actually doing some work. As she was ready to close her computer she received an email from Mark.

>To. Alex Price
>From. M.A.R.K.
>
>I have assumed if he changed his name he has stayed with a British sounding name and that if he was running away he would go on a long haul flight. I may be wrong on all counts but this was how I would think if it were me and I had money. I have compiled a list of people's names that may fit on flights that went out that day. If there's nothing in this attachment that catches your eye I can work on the short haul flights. See what you think & let me know.
>Good Luck
>Mark
>P.S. Summer says hello and to tell you that Mel is okay.

Alex couldn't believe the trouble Mark had gone to for her, she opened the attachment. It showed a list of flights with passenger names, he hadn't cut it down too much there were hundreds here, Charles De Gaulle is the second busiest airport in Europe but it was a place to start and she didn't have any better ideas. First she decided to phone Mel maybe she would be calming down, Alex could only hope. This time Mel answered. "Didn't you get my message?" Her tone was sharp.

"I did but I wanted you to tell me yourself, not in a text."

"Stop ringing me!"

"Okay I will but first ... have you heard from Lee? Has he bothered to contact you?" There was silence on the line for a moment.

"No but how could he anyway?"

"Mel, he could get a message to you if he wanted to, you know that don't you?"

"It's none of your business Alex."

"It is Mel, I don't want to see you hurting like this."

"Is that all you have to say, I'm going now."

"Mel, ring me if you need to talk, please." Alex felt a small amount of relief at least Mel was talking to her again, however strained it was. This was progress, she hoped that it could only improve now, she missed her friend. She was also missing Matt, she knew he was busy at the moment with Lee, the magistrates had extended the time that he could hold Lee and he was working hard to get enough evidence to find out what Lee was hiding. She sent him a text just letting him know she was thinking of him then turned her attention to the flight list.

She whispered to herself almost in prayer 'come on Michael where are you?' Took a deep breath and started at flight one, they were arranged in time order, she quickly became disheartened there were just too many places he could have gone she had dismissed the early USA flights because he'd have needed time to buy a ticket, check in and have time to clear security and it would have all taken a while but apart from that he could have gone anywhere. The world was a big place when you're looking for one man. She skipped up to the late morning flights and started studying the names rather than worrying about the countries, she hoped there would be a clue. Eventually she went down to the hotel reception and used their printer, it would be much easier to sort through the lists on paper. She returned to her room and started methodically going through the names. Finally it was too much Alex fell asleep.

Chapter Thirty Four

Lee was desperate, he didn't know what to do, it looked like Michael had stitched him up properly and disappeared, all he wanted were his letters back, he'd done nothing wrong and now it looked like all of the evidence was stacking up against him for killing a man. He wasn't capable of killing anyone but the police weren't believing that and he couldn't tell them what he had been looking for because they would never believe him, after all he had a fiancée now, how on earth did he get himself into this position? He couldn't believe Michael would leave him in this situation, this must have been his plan all along or else why would he have invited him to the exhibition, Lee hadn't wanted to go because even after begging, Michael wouldn't accept his work into the show but still he had asked him to attend the opening night. He knew he had been acting rashly but picking up Mel had been an idea he had when he saw her friend Alex with Michael, he wanted to make sure he had someone with him in case Michael was planning anything and now Mel had fallen for him and he didn't know what to do about her, he was still reeling from the idea of marrying a woman. Even if it had been her idea he should have just come clean, it was too late now and look at the mess he had got himself into, just because he had spent his life in love with the great Michael Masters. He should have walked away when he knew Michael was straight but he didn't chose to love him that was just the way it was, he could no sooner change that than grow wings. He should have tried harder and saved himself almost a lifetime of misery. Now he was in either a police cell or an interview room with the police trying to link him to the body that had washed up in the town. He had a fiancée who wasn't even rich and Michael was gone, what a mess. How he wished he had never come back, never followed Michael but it was what he had always done.

The police, it seemed to him, didn't have a clue what to do with him but he couldn't talk to them, there was no way in his mind that he could put this right now he didn't know how, Michael had always been the brains behind every scheme. This time it was him who'd been stitched up and he had no way of finding out where Michael had gone to try and sort things out, he wished he'd never written those letters to Michael, no, even more he wished he'd never even set eyes on him.

Chapter Thirty Five

Alex woke up on top of the bed, she had fallen into a dead sleep, the clock was showing 7.33am but today she had nothing to get up in a hurry for, the interviews were done and she still had a few days to catch up on some sightseeing and the last few photographs she wanted for the paper. The list of names and flights were still strewn across the bed, she reached over and randomly picked up a list, how on earth was she supposed to find this needle, in this haystack. The room she was in had a kettle and sachets of instant coffee but she needed some real coffee this morning, there was a small café opposite her hotel so she showered and got ready putting the list of names in her bag and went to find good coffee.

She sat at a table just outside the door of the café and watched the world go by whilst she waited for her order. She got the list out of her bag together with a pen and started systematically going through the names. Her café noir arrived in a small cup accompanied by a glass of water and was eye wateringly strong but tasted delicious, she had ruled out a lot of names for no other reason than she didn't like them, hovering intently over names that included Michael but surely he wouldn't keep his own name, or would that be the way he expected people to think. She didn't even know if he had gone on a long haul flight, he could be anywhere, even here and the longer this went on the less likely people were to recognise him. His appearance could be changing rapidly he may have facial hair, or have shaved his head. She put her head in her hands she had to admit to herself that she had no idea what she was doing, she felt a hand on her shoulder, looked up and the waiter was standing over her looking concerned. She reassured him that she was fine and ordered another coffee, he walked away looking unsure, turning around to check on her several times. She returned to the names, she had got to the Asian flights now and she started thinking how good it would be if Matt and she could visit Vietnam or Myanmar for their holidays and get some well-earned sunshine. She continued to scan the list whilst imagining the heat and the sand between her toes, she stopped, Waite, Dominic M, flying to Bangkok. That name was familiar, very familiar.

She found her phone and called Matt. "Hi Darling are you at home?" she asked him.

"Yes just ready to leave, are you having a good time?" He sounded like he'd just got up and that made her miss him.

"I've been interviewing traumatised people who don't know how to cope with their days and photographing bomb sights, what do you think?" She retorted.

"Oh okay, I hope you're getting bit of relax time as well."

"I've got most of it done now so today I'll just do some photography, no interviews booked for today. Can you do me a favour?" She hoped he didn't ask too many questions but she did feel bad for snapping at him for no reason.

"Of course."

"Can you check the name of the artist on the painting?"

"Sure." He paused for a minute she thought strange how people don't talk whilst they're walking. "D.M. Waite. Why?"

"Oh nothing, I'd just seen some art out here and I couldn't remember his name, thank you. Any luck with Lee yet or the body?"

"Not really but Lee does seem to be loosening up, just a matter of time I hope. The body is a work in process."

"I'll ring you later, good luck with Lee today."

"Miss you Alex."

"I'll be home in a couple of days, I'll make it up to you."

They hung up and Alex looked back at the list, could it be true, had she found Michael? It was an amazing coincidence if not. She sent an email to Mark and asked him if he could find out anything else about Dominic Waite. She didn't know what to expect but if anyone could find anything Mark could.

Feeling a bit more hopeful now she decided to go for a walk and take in a few of the sights of Paris, she wished Matt was with her after all it is the city of romance and he would love it here. The art markets enthralled her and the churches bewitched her, she would definitely be coming back with Matt. She got back to her hotel room exhausted, there was a hand written note pushed under her door, 'Please contact reception' was written on it, she picked up the phone and the receptionist apologised for missing her when she had returned, there was a message for her. "Who from?"

"Mark"

"Okay and what does it say?"

"Ring me." Was all she said.

"Okay is that all it says, no explanation?"

"No that is the entire message Miss Price."

"Thank you." Alex hung up and smiled, that had been an awful lot of work for a 'ring me' message. She rummaged around in her bag to find her mobile and rang Mark.

"So what have you found?"

"Your Dominic Waite, I have found him and lost him again."

"How, I mean what's the story Mark?"

"He is an artist who had a degree of success in the 70's and 80's but he had a hard time by all accounts of dealing with it, he left the UK and went to live in Thailand. Not many people heard from him again for quite a while."

"Thailand… Is that what you said?" Alex knew immediately that her painting had come from there, the whole thing looked oriental and she had been right.

"Yes, a place called Prachuap if that's any help."

"No but carry on, where is he now?"

"He returned to the UK, Oxford to be precise and has been there ever since although he doesn't get seen much, he likes his own company."

"So a bit of a hermit then?" Alex asked.

"Yes from what I can gather, he spends his time painting and rarely leaves his home."

"Any link with Michael?" She kept her fingers crossed.

"Yes, he has a contract with Michael, I'll send you the link to the page on the internet, it was quite big news when Michael managed to sign him up, the art world thought he'd given up on painting."

"Thanks Mark this is brilliant. Do you know where in Oxford?"

"Yes the address is in your inbox, good luck Alex. Like I said I've lost him again, apparently no one has heard from him for a while but that's not completely unusual, I'll keep looking."

"Thanks Mark, let me know if you find anything else won't you." Mark promised to keep searching and they said their goodbyes. Alex sat back with a deep sigh of relief, maybe there was a way to trace Michael after all, her Dominic Waite had flown to Bangkok. All sorts of ideas ran through her head but she would have to go to see Dominic herself and find out what he knew about Michael's whereabouts, or was it genuinely him that had gone to Bangkok? It seemed a long shot that he would have travelled from Paris at the same time as Michael was known to be there but maybe that's why he hadn't been seen in Oxford, unless he was helping Michael, she returned to the flight list but there were no more familiar names on that flight, she would keep looking through the flight lists but if nothing else jumped out at her it would come down to a flip of the coin Bangkok or Oxford she'd already decided she had to go to one of them.

Chapter Thirty Six

Matt couldn't get hold of Alex this morning, he had no idea what time to pick her up from the airport and he wanted to share some news with her. Lee had started to talk, Matt didn't know if it was from sheer exhaustion or he'd finally realised it was the only thing he could do but he looked a mess now and had bitten his nails down to ragged stubs, even Matt was starting to feel sorry for him. None of it made much sense but Alex had been right, Lee had been in love with Michael and followed him around throughout his career even though he knew Michael was straight. He had hoped one day that Michael might just give them a chance and never gave up, which had left him open to being involved in all sorts of scams according to him, he told of crooked contracts loaded in Michael's favour and unpaid artists all over the world and much worse but he wouldn't say what that was, yet. Matt was still sceptical but it sounded a lot closer to the truth, he said he had no idea where Michael was, which Matt was now starting to believe, he had also admitted to him that he had only got involved with Mel because he thought Michael might be up to something so he wanted someone else around and the thing with Mel had just got out of hand, she was needy and he agreed to be there for her, he hadn't at the time realised what she had meant but when she started telling people they were engaged he didn't know how to tell her it couldn't happen.

There was also some news on the body this morning, the body turned out to be a little older than they had first thought, more like sixty years old rather than fifty, this ruled out Michael Masters, although it didn't bring them much closer to discovering its identity. Matt knew he'd have to start trawling through the missing persons lists which was something he had done a lot of in previous years, so he knew how to handle that line of work. If the elusive Georgie had been right about the argument he had another crime to solve on his doorstep, he still needed to find him and the other local forces hadn't managed to come up with anything so far. His phone pinged interrupting his line of thought, he had an email, it was from Alex she was staying for another day, Charlie had found her some more photography to do, she would call him later. Great, he thought sarcastically, he'd planned a romantic meal for this evening, he'd really missed her being around. He emailed her back telling her to ring him when she could, he had news. Lee was finally talking and not taking the note into consideration the body couldn't be Michaels and he hit the send button. Knowing that he shouldn't have written that down in case anyone else saw it, Alex would know not to keep an email like that. He hoped. He always found his work difficult when it came to Alex, he couldn't lie to her but he shouldn't hand out information, sometimes he couldn't help himself he knew how much this story meant to her.

 He opened up his computer and started trawling through the missing person's lists, just like the old days he thought.

Chapter Thirty Seven

Alex had told Matt a lie and she didn't feel good about it, she knew she would have to tell him everything if she spoke to him otherwise he just wouldn't understand and she couldn't tell him without getting Mark into hot water, this was turning out to be a huge mess and she didn't know what to do next. She would stay in Paris an extra day until she had decided, she phoned Charlie and came up with some half-baked story about needing more photographs but he didn't seem bothered either way, she'd written up her interviews and there was nothing pressing for her to do back in Charmsbury for a few days, In fact 'enjoy yourself' were his parting words, she thought that maybe Charlie knew her too well. She had received an email from Matt so it looked like he'd have his hands full with Lee for the next few days, the news he shared of the body not being Michael's was now old news to her, she knew he was out there she just had to find him and get to the bottom of why he had gone in the first place. She was beginning to feel like the more she knew, the farther away from the truth she was getting.

She had contacted Mark again and it turned out he'd been busy trying to find Dominic Waite but the news wasn't helpful. She decided to phone him, emails were great but she needed to hear his voice whilst he told her what he'd found out. He answered on the first ring. "Any news Mark?"

"Yes as a matter of fact but I'm not sure how much help it'll be though."

"Go on, at least it may help me decide what my next move is."

"I contacted a friend of mine in Oxford and asked him to check up on Dominic, there doesn't seem to be anyone at home, a neighbour said he thought he had been away for a month or more, it was difficult to tell because he so rarely came out, he doesn't know where as the guy never spoke to anyone locally and always kept himself to his own business. The neighbours just think he's odd and keep out of his way."

"So it could have been him on that flight then, maybe just a coincidence that we're looking for Michael at the same time." She felt despondent.

"You don't really believe that do you? Although if it is him on that flight I'm sure Michael was with him. I wish I could get seat plans and find out who he sat with but that's a step too far for me."

"Well I guess there's only one way to find out." She added, her mind now made up. "Thanks Mark and don't tell Matt we've spoken or he'll want all of the details, I'll message you when I find out anything else. Are you and Summer still doing okay?"

"Oh Alex she's amazing, how did I not see it sooner, I'll send your love."

After their goodbye's Alex turned on her laptop and started to make plans, although what she was going to say to Matt would take some strategic planning, he wasn't going to be pleased.

Chapter Thirty Eight

Michael arrived in Hua Hin after an eventful train journey, the train out of Bangkok had been very pleasant although not entirely comfortable and he had gazed out of the window as he watched the city diminish in the distance, leaving the lights and noise of Bangkok behind, the seating arrangements had started off cramped but as they moved outside Bangkok the train started to empty to the point where everyone finally had a seat, rather than having to sit anywhere there was resembling a seat, steps and parcel shelves were fully utilised. He had begun to wish he'd paid more and got a more comfortable seat or at least something more than an unpadded bench.

After Bangkok was long behind them the train trundled along at a sedate pace and people who were going further than him started to spread themselves out to claim their sleeping spaces where they could, due to this being Thailand they were all eating before settling down for the night. Michael had never seen so much food and when they stopped at a place called Ratchaburi hoards of people boarded the train, selling all manner of foods and drinks, most of the items on sale Michael couldn't even begin to guess at, there was lots of bags with dark liquid and things floating around in it, even bags of what looked like bugs. Everyone else must have known exactly what the food was because it was selling out fast. He watched mesmerised, a Thai lady of about fifty years old touched his arm and pointed to a bag of what looked like noodles, she said something to him in Thai but he had no idea what she was saying. He smiled up at the young man selling the noodles "How much?" The man didn't speak any English but before Michael could get any money out the lady who had encouraged him to try them handed over a note and took the noodles handing them to Michael all the time smiling. "Try, try." She urged him. "Gift for farang."

"Thank you." Michael was touched by her kindness, he got the gist of what she said, he believed the word farang was a term for foreigner. He opened the plastic bag to try the noodles, they were warm and he realised how hungry he was. As suddenly as all of the food vendors had appeared they disappeared back onto the platform, the doors slammed shut and the train moved off, the lady was right the noodles were delicious, the smells of chilli and garlic permeated the carriage and in that moment Michael began to fall in love with Thailand, he looked up at the lady and smiled. They fell into conversation about Thailand but with his none existent Thai and her limited English it wasn't easy, he showed her his map and she pointed out some things he should see whilst he was travelling, when he told her he was going to Hua Hin she told him the shopping was good there. He felt better knowing that he was now anonymous, just another tourist finding their way around this vast country. Most of the carriage was getting ready to sleep after they had eaten but he knew his stop couldn't be too far away now, he'd heard the rumours about the trains and timekeeping but that was of no issue to him, he'd get there when he got there and that would be fine.

The train rolled in just over an hour late, he said goodbye to his travelling companion and disembarked into the madness of Hua Hin, from the moment he stepped off the train the noise, heat and the traffic swallowed him up, it was like a mini Bangkok from what he could see. There were markets and street food in every direction and lots of white faces, this already felt like a tourist area and he'd only been here for ten minutes, he walked along a couple of streets and found a bar, put his bags down and ordered a beer, he still needed to find a room for the night but he had already decided he wouldn't stop here for too long. A man sat down next to him and started talking to him in broken English, his name was Oli he had travelled from Sweden and before long there were another three men that joined them, he started to make his excuses and told them he needed to go and find somewhere to stay for the night. As a group they were having fun and he didn't want to leave them just yet, it had been a while since he had had company but he couldn't sleep in the bar. "Don't worry." One of the men said "We have rented an apartment, just five minutes' walk away, stay with us." The others nodded in agreement, Michael was pleased it was the first time he'd felt sociable since he arrived in Thailand and these guys were fun, no questions were asked of him, they were just out to enjoy themselves. The night continued through into the early hours of the morning, chatting and drinking, one of the guys had drifted off with his Thai girlfriend leaving the four of them to pay the bar bill, Michael noted that him and Oli were left to pick up the majority of the bill but if they were giving him somewhere to sleep why should he worry.

Eventually they all left the bar, the air was a little cooler on the street than when he had arrived and the noise was less now it was so late, except when they walked past a couple of late night bars that were still full of people partying their holidays away. They turned up into a quiet road, "Only a couple of minutes and we'll be there." Someone shouted from up ahead he was feeling tired now and would be happy to get some sleep, the alcohol had helped that feeling.

They piled into a house where they were reunited with the Thai lady and her boyfriend, the party continued for another hour until they were all exhausted, the bearded guy called Jon threw him a sheet and nodded towards the settee; that was the only direction he needed as soon as he lay down and pulled a fluffy cushion under his head he fell into a deep, dreamless sleep.

When he opened his eyes it must have been very early or very late because the house seemed quiet to the point of silent there were just the muted sounds of some building work going on somewhere close by, a ray of sunshine was lying across his chest and it was hot, he needed to find the air con or a fan to cool himself down. His hair felt damp against the cushion under his head and the sheet had been long ago cast to the floor due to the heat. He swung his feet down onto the floor and stood up, he felt okay and thankfully there was no hangover or belting headache, he wondered if the other guys were still asleep. He walked around to the kitchen area, as he walked past a table he saw something that stopped his heart, he stifled a scream but he could not stop the sickness he felt rising from his stomach as he bolted for the door scattering chickens in all directions and threw up whatever remained from what he had eaten yesterday. Standing in a patch of sun leaning against a palm tree it was hard for him to comprehend what he had just seen, he had to force himself to return to the kitchen. He stepped gingerly through the door, not wanting to look but having to. Some of the chickens had returned to their pecking of the body, he wretched, he looked down and there was Oli lying in a pool of blood and there were dried blood patches on the side of his head where it looked like his head had been caved in with something heavy. He knew from looking at him that he was dead but he reached down to feel for a pulse in his neck, hoping, but nothing. What was he meant to do now? He shooed the man eating chickens out into the garden and grabbed the sheet he had discarded in the night and threw it over Oli's body. He couldn't see a phone and he didn't have a mobile, he would have to find the rest of the guys, he ran through the house banging on doors and after all the doors had been knocked with no reply he went back and flung all of the doors open, yelling for them to wake up. Nothing, not a sound, he realised that this was his problem now, they'd gone, they'd killed Oli, he slumped into a squat and put his head in his hands. Why?

He went back to Oli's body and checked to see if there was any form of ID on him but there wasn't, in fact there wasn't anything on him at all, the bastards. He needed to get his computer and contact the police, it was the only thing he could do, he hesitated, thinking, but then they would find him too. He went to get his rucksack but there was an empty space where that had been, his clothes, computer, wallet, in fact everything he owned, he looked around in case it had been moved but no, it was gone, stolen. He'd been stitched up, they'd left him to take the fall for this, he knew he couldn't, he needed to get away from this house, this area and quickly. The only ray of sunshine now was that they may have taken his wallet but he was still wearing his money belt and that was where his cards and majority of his money was but his passports had gone. He almost laughed at that, they were going to be very confused to find out there was more than one passport in more than one name. He apologised to Oli's poor broken body as he sidled past and went outside, he pushed the door shut to stop the birds from getting back in, the chickens scattered as he moved through them and out onto the street, he hung his head and walked fast into the town, he was sweating, the heat was too much and his hair stuck to his head in clumps, but still he did his best to get lost in the crowds of shoppers. He found a stall that he could sit behind to stop and have coffee, possibly the worst coffee he had ever tasted but surprisingly his stomach started to calm down and he began to feel more human. In fact on reflection it wasn't the worst thing that had ever happened to him, he just had to make sure he didn't get picked up. He didn't think hanging around and trying to find the rest of the group was a wise idea and he couldn't remember the other guy's names except for Jon and there had to be a lot of Jon's on holiday in Thailand at any given time, he looked around the stall and as if in answer to his quandary he was almost facing the railway line. Yes he thought, time to move on, I'm sorry Oli but what can I do.

   A train pulled into the station and Michael got on it in approximately one hour he would arrive where he should have gone in the first place.

Chapter Thirty Nine

Alex was still avoiding talking to Matt, she had no idea what she would say to him. She had her flight booked for this evening, it was always pretty easy to get a single seat wherever you wanted to go, Thailand was no exception, she even managed to get a window seat so she could wake up and look down on the clouds. She had to stop for a few hours in Delhi but that was no hardship she'd still got articles to finish writing from Paris and a good book to read. She looked longingly at her phone, she was missing Matt but however much she wanted to she knew she mustn't, instead she phoned her Nan. "Where are you?" Alex guessed Matt had been in touch with her, she sounded worried.

"Paris, why?"

"Matt called said he couldn't get hold of you, we were worried."

"Sorry Nan, could you not mention that you've spoken to me?" There was silence on the other end of the line.

"What are you up to Alex?"

"Nothing I just don't want to speak to Matt right now, he'll want me to come home and I can't just yet." She hoped that would stop any more questions but was fairly sure it wouldn't, when it came to being nosey her Nan ranked high.

"Have you argued? Oh Alex you get yourself a good man and…"

"Stop Nan, there's been no arguments, nothing's happened, I just need to do something and Matt would try to stop me. Can you keep this conversation to yourself? Oh and can you get my computer from the house, I think Mark might come and see you and want to do some work for me?" She heard the intake of breath.

"How on earth do you expect me to do that without telling Matt anything?"

"Oh I don't know maybe there's a wedding file on it you need access to or something."

"Okay, okay, I'll get the computer, I assume Mark knows what's going on and at a guess I'd say it involves Michael Masters, be careful Alex, can't you just come home and let Matt handle everything?"

"No Nan, if Michael's involved me I want to know why and look him in the eye when he tells me. If Matt finds him I'll only get to hear what the lawyers want me to hear.

"Okay I don't want to know anything else, just keep in touch and let us know you're okay. Be careful Alex."

"Thanks Nan."

With that done she packed her small bag and checked out of the hotel, her flight wasn't until late so she was going to treat herself to a little retail therapy beforehand.

She walked around the shops for a while but couldn't find anything she wanted so found a coffee shop and emailed Mark to let him know that it was safe to go to her Nans and her computer would be there waiting for him to use. She needed all the help she could get now. She also pre booked a hotel in Bangkok for a couple of nights and spent some time familiarising herself with Thailand. Mark emailed back a thumb's up and told her to take care, that was it, now it was time to head to the airport. She was nervous but only because she so desperately wanted to talk to Matt and now she was travelling further away from him but she knew he would try to stop her, she left Paris with a heavy heart.

Chapter Forty

The body belonged to a man named Dominic Michael Waite and he had been murdered, the news came through onto Matt's desk first thing in the morning, under normal circumstances he would have been over the moon with this discovery but today he didn't care as much as he should, all of the details swam before his eyes but none of it made much sense. He had been trying to get hold of Alex to find out when she was coming home but there was no reply, he had been trying for over twenty four hours and now he was worried about her. He knew she could take care of herself but had no idea why she wasn't speaking to him, what had he done to deserve to be treated this way, she had seemed fine when she had left. Even Mary and Jack had no idea where she was, although he had thought it odd that Mary wanted Alex's computer just as Alex dropped off the radar but weddings always made people do odd things, he'd handed it over without an argument.

He turned his attention back to the paperwork on his desk, trying to concentrate, so Mr Dominic Michael Waite he thought how the hell do you fit into all of this mess? He wondered how many people knew that this man was mixed up with Michael Masters, he just couldn't fathom how they had got this mess on their doorstep. He kept glancing at his phone, still nothing. He knew Waite was an artist, He remembered Alex asking him to look at D M Waite's name on the painting, had she known something before he did and why hadn't she mentioned anything to him, what exactly did she know? He started to feel a rush of panic, had someone hurt her, was she in trouble? He calmed himself and put a call through to the hotel where she had been staying. It turned out she had checked out yesterday morning and was going to the airport to catch a flight, they had printed out the tickets for her. The receptionist was reluctant to talk at first but when Matt pointed out that he was a police officer he got the information he needed. The receptionist said she had not been there at the time but remembered her friend saying how much she would love to go to Thailand, she envied Alex her trip. His worry turned to anger, he felt helpless. He got up and walked out of his office, slamming the door behind him, no one dared try to stop him when they saw the look on his face.

He pulled up at Mary's house and banged on the door, Mary answered his knock. "Why didn't you tell me Mary?" The anger was subsiding and sadness was overtaking him.

"Tell you what?" She said.

"Oh please Mary, couldn't you have told me she'd gone to Thailand, do you know why?" Mary looked genuinely shocked.

"I didn't know Matt, what's she doing in Thailand?"

"I don't know, can I come in?" He looked past Mary but there was nothing to see.

"I was just heading out for a coffee, would you care to join me? The Red Bean and I'm buying." She hoped that would convince him as Mark was in the lounge on Alex's computer and she didn't need the hassle of trying to explain that to Matt.

"Sure."

They walked towards town, saying little to each other, both lost in their own thoughts. They had a coffee but were both relieved to get away afterwards, the conversation was stilted; each of them thought the other was holding back some vital information but were loathed to start accusing each other. He watched Mary carefully but it seemed like she too was genuinely surprised at whatever Alex was up to. There were no answers here, they walked back to the house then parted company, promising each other that as soon as they heard anything they would be in touch. Matt went back to work and Mary returned home.

Mark was hard at work when Mary returned, he was still trying to locate Dominic for Alex but he wasn't having any luck. Mary stood behind him watching his fingers skip across the keyboard "Mark, you can stop." He turned around to face Mary. "Dominic's dead, the body washed up at the river... it was him."

"Shit..." Mark breathed the word and hung his head, the default position of the beaten. "So we were wrong." His head snapped up. "Mary we need to get Alex home, this feels wrong, we have no idea what Alex is getting herself into." He turned back to the screen and rapidly typed an email to Alex telling her to come home and passing on the news about Dominic.

Mary was worried before Mark brought her up to date on what was going on, knowing what was happening wasn't making her feel any better. Jack walked into the lounge and saw Mark with his head down scanning screens on the computer, he turned to the opposite side of the room to see Mary slumped in the armchair gazing into space. "You alright Sweetheart?" He was concerned he'd never seen her looking like this before, he walked up to her and gathered her up in his arms, she freely wept in his embrace. "I'm scared for Alex, Jack, she's on her own out there and I'm frightened what she'll find, there's no one there to protect her."

"Out where? What's going on?" Mary told Jack everything she knew. "She's strong, I'm sure she'll be okay, she'll ring soon." He kissed the top of her head, she needed him to be strong for her now but he was worried too.

Chapter Forty One

Alex walked out into the arrivals area of Suvarnabhumi Airport with nothing more than her small case and her jacket slung over her arm. There were hundreds of people milling around pulling suitcases or hauling huge backpacks and there were rows of taxi drivers holding up cards with names on them lining either side of the walkway, unfortunately there was no one there to meet her, she would have to find her own way around. In every direction she looked the hall was teeming with people it felt a little intimidating but she put her head up and walked through the terminal as though she owned the airport, stepped outside into the tropical heat of Bangkok and joined the queue for a taxi. An hour later she was deposited at the door of her hotel, it was beautiful, the foyer was full of expensive shops with jewels glittering in their displays, the staff wore traditional Thai outfits and as beautiful as everything was she was nervous, possibly something to do with having to ring home imminently.

After a warm welcome she settled herself into her room which was spacious and luxurious, she fired up her computer and sent Charlie an email to let him know where she was although not why yet, she knew he would be furious with her but he was the least of her problems. Then she phoned her Mum who thankfully was out and the answer phone kicked in, she left a short message just saying she was well and would ring back later. So far so good and she was well aware she was putting off the most difficult phone call until last, Matt, what would he be thinking, how angry would he be? She knew he wouldn't be happy. She opted for a more pleasant call first and before it even rang out she heard her Nan's voice and instantly she felt calmer. "Hi Nan."

"Oh Alex, I'm so pleased to hear from you, are you okay? I have so much to tell you. Have you spoken to Matt?" It all came out without her Nan even taking a breath.

"I'm fine, I'm in Bangkok, No I haven't called Matt yet, is everything okay there?"

"Yes except Matt's not happy and Mark's here he wants to talk to you."

"Okay put him on."

"Alex, have you found anything out yet?" From the sound of his voice she guessed he had.

"No Mark I've only just arrived." She laughed.

"Well I have, the body belonged to Dominic, so it looks like you're following Michael, I don't like it Alex it feels wrong, come home or at least be very careful." He sounded really worried.

"Wow okay, so now we know why no one knew where Dominic had gone, any idea how he ended up there?"

"No but I'm guessing that was the argument that Georgie saw happening the night of the exhibition but I'm still trying to find out anything I can from here, I can't track Michael and there's been no sightings as far as I can tell but Matt might know more."

"I'll be careful, don't worry Mark, I won't be here long. Can you try and find out about this Prachuap place where he had a house and see if he still owns it or if he sold it before he went back to the UK? Oh and can you go down to the exhibition and find a guy called William, just tell him Michaels alive but don't tell him anything else."

"Of course I can and I'll do my best to find out about the house, I'll mail you." Mark said his goodbyes and put her Nan back on the phone.

"Will you call Matt sweetheart? I'm worried about him and I know he's worried to death about you?"

"Of course I will, I'm going to call him right after I put the phone down from you, I just wanted you to know I'm not coming back until you make some more brownies." They both laughed and all of the tension drained out of the call. After she put the phone down she opened the mini bar and poured a miniature bottle of vodka into a glass and added a splash of coke, medicinal she thought and picked her phone up. It rang out for a minute before she heard "Alex, where the hell are you?"

"Promise not to shout Matt."

"Why, what have you done and where are you?" He sounded sad, not angry and that somehow made her feel even worse than she already did.

"I'm in Bangkok."

"Why?" He didn't sound as surprised as she expected, had he known already?

"I think Michael's here somewhere." She proceeded to tell him what she had found out and how it had led her to Thailand, although he got angry and shouted a little, he soon calmed down and shared what little he knew with her about the body being Dominic, she didn't have the heart to tell him she already knew and he told her they were fairly sure that Lee had killed him but Lee was still holding back on what reason he had to do it, he just wouldn't part with any information to help them and he didn't seem interested in helping himself either. They had arrested him on suspicion of murder and he would be going before the courts within the next couple of days to see if he would be granted bail but they expected that he would go on remand, no chance of bail in his view, not for murder. "I miss you, why couldn't you tell me where you were going?"

"Matt you'd have tried to stop me and I needed to follow my hunch, I think Michael's here and I needed to try and find him for myself, I couldn't sit back and wait for the police to find him. Michael involved me in this and I want to know why."

"Be careful darling, I want you back as soon as possible and in one piece, we don't know anything about Michael, it seems that he moves in some dodgy circles, sounds like he's a regular conman. I'll come out and come with you at least I'd know you were safe."

"Matt I love you but no, I'll be fine I just need to do this, I'm sorry I didn't tell you before but you can see why I didn't, can't you?"

"I guess so but I don't like it, ring me all the time and if you need me tell me Alex don't try to so independent. Oh and ring your Nan, she's worried too."

"I will." She answered with her fingers crossed. She hated lying to him but she couldn't say she'd already rung her.

Alex needed to go before she got too emotional, she really wished he was there with her but she hadn't come this far to run home now. They talked for a while longer and by the time the call was finished she felt much more relaxed if a little tearful, her adrenaline was starting to run low but she thought that now it was all going to be okay.

Chapter Forty Two

Michael had found the town he had been looking for and checked into a backpacker's bed and breakfast by the railway station, even though his backpack was long gone. The man at the desk looked him over, carefully assessing whether or not he was going to be trouble, they obviously weren't accustomed to seeing people with no luggage at all, Michael tried to explain that he had left his luggage on the train, eventually he must have decided he could cope with any trouble from this tourist because he handed him a key in return for the cost of a night's stay, with a shrug of his not inconsiderable shoulders. Michael was still shaken by what had happened in Hua Hin but he was beginning to feel better now he had put some distance between it and him, he was still wondering if there was any way he could inform the police without giving himself away. He did feel awful for leaving Oli on that kitchen floor and running away like a coward but what choice did he have? He went into his room, no air con here, just a fan, and the room was just a bed, chair and a table but it felt like a huge relief just to lay down on the bed even though it was another hard mattress, regardless of the heat he slept all afternoon and most of the night, he woke up in the darkness of the following morning feeling better and brighter.

The first thing that needed attending to was to go and find something to eat and then he needed to go shopping for some new clothes, he had nothing but what he stood up in and he wanted to have a look around the town that he'd heard so much about over the years. As soon as he went out onto the street the heat hit him and sweat prickled across his body, yet it was still early and only just getting light, he sat at one of the tables at the front of the bed and breakfast and ordered his breakfast as he watched the world go by, people starting out their day nothing unusual for them to face, delivery men, shopkeepers, waitresses he envied them the normality of their lives.

His breakfast arrived it consisted of ham, egg and a slice of toast but at least the coffee was good and the juice was fresh. After his light breakfast he moved away from his lodgings and walked up towards the crossroads, on his right was a stall with newspapers piled high but he had no chance of knowing what was going on, there was not one newspaper in English on the stand. He would have to keep a low profile until he got more information. He turned onto a main road and found plenty of shops and roadside stalls ready to sell him a clean set of clothes, he took his time choosing, the air conditioning inside the shops was a blessing.

He walked around the town for a while, getting to know his surroundings, he could see why Dominic had loved it here, it had everything, a vibrant town, a beautiful coast and everybody smiled. He hoped he could spend some time here, as long as he didn't get involved with any unsavoury characters again, that had taught him a lesson and he would return to looking out for himself, he was much better at that.

He needed to try and find the house too, it was somewhere in this town but he had never managed to get an address for it, Dominic was very precious when it came to his home here, he wanted to ensure he never had anyone turn up for their holidays. He had said that here was the only place he could be truly left alone. Michael had no idea how big this town was and very few clues as to where to start looking for the house. He made his way back towards his room, as he walked along the streets he spotted an internet café, he wanted to catch up on the news if there was any and it looked pretty comfortable inside with big plush armchairs and he could see the air conditioning units outside the shop, he opened the door and the cool air hit him, he was more than happy to stay here for a while.

The internet threw up some useful information for him, Oli's body had been discovered in Hua Hin and the Swedish embassy had informed the family, the police had arrested a man, the picture was blurred as was his memory of those people, so he couldn't tell if it was one of the men he had been drinking with or not. There was no mention of them looking for anyone else but he still needed to be careful, the passports that had been in his bag would come to light at some stage unless they were already on the black market. There was also news from England, the police had finally identified the body that had been discovered in Charmsbury, he was suddenly relieved that the passports were gone, now he no longer had anything on him to connect him to Dominic the other side of the problem was he had nothing on him to prove who he was either, without a passport he couldn't own a mobile phone in fact he shouldn't even be on the street. If he was asked to produce it he could be in a lot of trouble in this country.

He returned to his room only to be asked for his passport information again, he blundered his way through trying to explain that it had been left on the train in his bags. That seemed to placate the man but it wouldn't work for long, he said that the police would be contacting him about it soon, so he should try to get it returned as soon as possible and told him to go to the station and report the loss. Michael knew he would have to find somewhere else to stay over the next couple of days, he couldn't afford for the Thai police to get involved.

Chapter Forty Three

Mark was still trawling through any information he could find to link Michael and Dominic, so far he was struggling beyond the obvious of the art world, he wondered if Matt had learnt anything from Lee but he was reluctant to get involved with him after the Georgie incident, Matt could be hard to work with when it came down to it, he thought any information belonged to the police and had never been flexible in that respect. Then it struck him, why hadn't he thought of it earlier. He closed the computer down and grabbed his coat, shouting to Jack that he'd be back later. If nothing else he needed some exercise after all of Mary's cakes he'd been eating, he could see why Alex visited so often.

He arrived at the flat and knocked on the door, Mel opened the door just enough to put her head around it, she didn't look like she'd slept in a week and it didn't look like her hair had been brushed in as long. "Mel, are you okay?" He was shocked to see her like this, she always looked so glamorous to him.

"What do you want Mark?"

"Nice welcome, I'm trying to help everyone out of this situation, will you talk to me?" He wasn't holding out much hope.

"You mean you're trying to help Alex, I'm not interested." She went to push the door but Mark was quicker and got his foot in front of it.

"Why, don't you want to help Lee either?"

"He's making a fool of me too." Then she started crying. Mark wasn't used to women crying and had no idea what to do, he felt like a fish on dry land. He pulled his phone out of his pocket and rang Summer. "Can you come to Mel's, I'm out of my depth here?"

"Of course, is she okay? I'll be there in a few minutes." Mark heaved a sigh of relief. Summer would know how to handle this. He hoped. He opened his arms out to Mel who was still standing in the doorway crying, she pushed open the door and moved towards him. "We should go inside." He bundled her into her flat, she clung onto him as if her life depended on it. He held her, murmuring words that he thought would comfort her until Summer was able to take his place.

Within ten minutes Summer arrived and tried to calm Mel down, Mark admired the way she was handling the situation, it was far better than his efforts. When the crying subsided, Summer started the conversation. "What's going on Mel?"

"My life's a mess, I've been stupid and now everyone hates me, all I did was fall in love."

"No one hates you, so tell me why you're so upset."

"Lee dumped me." She let out another sob. Summer and Mark looked at each other exchanging relieved glances.

"Do you want to tell us what happened?"

"I thought he loved me and now I've just made a fool of myself, Alex tried to warn me but I couldn't see beyond Lee, or at least I didn't want to, I thought she was just trying to … oh I don't know what I thought. I really loved him." This time her tears rolled silently down her cheeks.

"What can we do to put things right?" Summer asked.

"Nothing I just want to be left alone."

"Sorry that's the one thing we can't do."

"I haven't forgiven Alex and I won't, she was cruel."

"Okay we're not asking you to forgive her, we're here to try and help but we need your help to sort things out. I know you hadn't known Lee long but did he share anything with you about his life?" Summer tried to take the conversation away from Alex, the last thing she wanted was to antagonise Mel.

"Like what?" Mel seemed to be getting herself together now, which was making it easier to talk to her.

"How he knew Michael, or Dominic, were they friends? Just that kind of stuff." Mark had butted in but he felt like some questions needed asking.

"I never heard him mention Dominic and I don't know much about him and Michael except they were friends since school."

"What was he trying to find in Michael's flat?"

"I really don't know Mark, I wish I did, sorry." With that she started crying again, it took them another half an hour to comfort her enough that they felt happy to leave her on her own and with a promise that Summer would bring Lily to visit at the weekend.

They went off to the Red Bean for coffee to relax and talk things over, Mark was happier than he'd ever been now he was with Summer but still the thought of Alex out in Thailand on her own worried him. They took their coffee and went to the corner table. "She knew nothing about him, how can that be when they were supposed to be getting married?" Mark asked.

"I suppose she just fell for him and thought everything else would come along in time."

"Really…." Sarcasm dripped from his lips. "How could she act so desperately, I always thought she was stronger than that?"

"I don't know, I just feel sorry for her, she doesn't have a clue what's going on does she?"

"So I still have nothing to help Alex with."

"How about a trip to Oxford and see what we can find out there?" She asked.

"No there's no point, I've had a friend do that for me, we won't find out anything that he couldn't."

"So that leaves…" She hesitated.

"Matt." Mark finished the sentence for her. "Oh I really don't want to do this. I suppose you couldn't think of anything else could you?" They laughed but Mark didn't want to see Matt. Summer just shrugged.

They left the café and went their separate ways. Mark headed for the police station. Matt's car was in the car park so he had no excuse to back out now. Matt met Mark by the front desk and showed him up to his office. "So what can I do for you Mark, this is not somewhere I expect to see you so I'm guessing it's important."

"Yes I think it is, you've spoken to Lee, what's the connection between him and Dominic." Mark was nervous around Matt and just spilled the question out, he hadn't meant to, he'd hoped to be more diplomatic.

"You know I can't tell you that don't you?"

"Sure but I thought you might be able to shed some light on it so I can help Alex out."

"What has Alex got to do with this?" Matt's face changed suddenly he looked wild.

"You know she's looking for Michael? You know where she is? I'm just trying to help." He felt like this had been a mistake. "You want her home safe don't you?"

"Are you trying to blackmail the information out of me Mark, that won't go down well in court you know."

"Calm down Matt, I really am here to help Alex, please is there a connection?"

"Get out Mark before I have to throw you out, do you think I'd tell *YOU* about Dominic, Lee and Michael's business dealings. I'm quite capable of looking out for Alex." Matt swivelled his chair round towards the window and turned his back to Mark. Mark took the opportunity, walked out and didn't look back.

He was getting nowhere but at least he knew that all Matt knew of was business details. So he could guess that Lee wasn't talking much. He headed back to Mary's to email Alex and tell her of his lack of information.

Chapter Forty Four

Alex spent her second day in Bangkok looking over maps. Mark had sent her a lot of information about Prachuap and where it was and what to expect when she got there, now she needed to decide how to get there, that was something she'd have to do for herself. She had had another email from Mark telling her that he'd got no further information and that he may have upset Matt. She would ring Matt later and find out about that, for now she needed to find her way to Prachuap, she thought about hiring a car, it would be the quickest way of getting around, from what she'd heard the trains were slow and there didn't seem to be an airport close to the town. Finally she left the hotel and went out onto the street to take a look at her surroundings, no sooner was she out of the door the tuk tuk drivers were waving and shouting over to her, she put her head down and kept walking feeling intimidated already, the traffic was at a standstill and horns were blasting from every direction and people were everywhere, everyone looked hot and bothered and in a rush to get somewhere. There was a shopping centre close by, she ducked into the cool complex and relaxed, she spent an hour browsing antiques and handmade Thai costumes they were certainly proud of their history here. She fell in love with lots of carvings but sense prevailed, she knew she'd never get them home in one piece. Maybe she could pick one up on her way home. She made her way back to the hotel this time just ignoring the waves and calls from the drivers and returned to the calm of the lobby. On her way to her room she picked up all of the English speaking papers and a few snacks from the small shop next to reception, it was time she caught up on the news.

Once in her room and relaxed again as she sifted through the papers, she had the Telegraph, the New York Times and two papers from Thailand written in English offering news to the ex-pats that lived here, Bangkok Post and The Nation. There was nothing of any interest in the Thai papers it was all tourism and business news, the New York Times had little to offer either but the Telegraph had a story about a Swedish man who had been murdered in Thailand the man had lived in Wales whilst attending University there, he'd gone to Thailand on an extended holiday, Oli Petersen, twenty years old. People never expect anything bad to happen on holidays, the thought made Alex shudder, these should have been his happy days. The paper was a day out of date so she would have to go online to find out the rest of the story. She also needed to get online and book some transport to get her south, the idea of driving herself was already long forgotten, as soon as she had seen the road outside the hotel she knew she couldn't drive in this country, just the thought terrified her. Paris had been bad enough. It was too hot and there were too many cars on the road. After trawling around the internet looking for quick transport she decided a taxi was the best way to go and it didn't seem too expensive so she booked one for the following day, she wanted to see if her hunch was right and that Prachuap was where she would find some answers or maybe even find Michael, she also looked around for more details on the young man that had lost his life whilst on holiday. An ex-pat community chat room was discussing it, it seemed he was in a place called Hua Hin, travelling alone but had been last seen in a bar with a few other men drinking until the early hours, it transpired that no one was coming forward saying he had been with them, so there the trail got cold but they were looking for several European men.

She looked at her watch, it was two thirty in the afternoon, she felt bad she'd wasted so much time in her room but outside it was so hot and she promised herself that she would go out in the evening when it was cooler. At least now was a reasonable time to phone Matt he would just be getting ready for work. He answered on the first ring. "Alex, are you okay?"

"Sure, why wouldn't I be?"

"Mark was around yesterday, he gave the impression you were in some kind of trouble, and he wanted information to help you."

"Take no notice Matt he just worries about me, he's just trying to keep me up to date." She sighed, why had Mark gone to Matt, that should have been the last place he looked for information.

"Are you sure there's nothing to worry about? I miss you Alex, come home leave this to us." He begged.

"I can't do that Matt you know I can't, I miss you too. I'll be home as soon as I can."

"Oh the latest news, Lee is on remand now, they decided there was enough circumstantial evidence against him, he's still saying he's done nothing though, I was hoping he'd have talked by now but he definitely knew Dominic.

"That's a start I suppose, do you think he's capable of murder?"

"Yes, he has a hell of a temper on him, I don't think he'd have any problems taking a man's life." Matt replied sounding certain they'd got the right man. "Have you heard from Mel?"

"No but I know Summer's keeping her eye on her, I hope you're right about Lee." They talked for a while longer about how much they were missing each other before they hung up and went about their business. Alex was missing him more than ever now, she was starting to realise that what started out to be an adventure could quickly turn into a nightmare, she would be pleased to get out of Bangkok it was a place that certainly wasn't for the faint hearted yet she'd hardly seen any of it. She thought maybe it was her being oversensitive and so focused on Michael, maybe if it was a holiday she could relax and enjoy herself but she was still tense and eager to move on.

Next she phoned Jasmine, she'd not been in touch for too long and Jasmine needed to know what was going on, she answered and still sounded quiet and sad. "I'm pleased to hear from you Alex."

"I'm in Thailand Jasmine, still no news yet but I'm not giving up, he's here somewhere, I've just got to find him. I need you to try to remember anything you can about him and Dominic Waite."

"What do you want to know about Dominic, I read in the paper that the body that they found was him, he was a nice enough old guy." Jasmine offered.

"You knew him?"

"Yes, I drew up contracts for him with Michael." Jasmine sounded alive again talking about her world and Alex could have kicked herself for not phoning Jasmine sooner.

"What was he like?" Then Alex added. "Were they friends?"

"He was okay, Michael had known him since he was a boy, Dominic taught him to draw and paint, he always wanted to be a Pre-Raphaelite revivalist but as well as Dominic taught him, he just never had that edge, that added bit of style that he needed. Dominic reminded him of it every time they met." There was a smile in Jasmine's voice now, they must have been fond memories for her, and then her voice grew darker. "The last contract I checked for them was a bit odd, it seemed stacked in Michael's favour... more so than usual but Dominic didn't fight it, I remember him just shrugging as he left the meeting."

"Why was it different?" Alex was all ears now.

"The percentages were small for Dominic, he didn't seem to care much though so I didn't pursue it, also it made him exclusive to Michael which rarely happens."

"Did you ask Michael about it?"

"Of course and he said something like, it's all he deserves, or something like that and the way he said it was like he meant end of conversation."

"So he didn't think much of Dominic then?"

"I'd never seen any animosity between them but it certainly felt that there was something not right."

"Did Lee have anything to do with them both?" Alex was in full journalist flow now.

"Lee had something to do with everyone, always had his nose in other people's business on the off chance there might be some money in it for him. I suppose he must have known Dominic for a long time too but beyond that I don't know."

"That's a great help, thanks Jasmine. I'm moving on tomorrow but I'll ring you as soon as I can, just one last question. Do you know about any links to Thailand with either Dominic or Michael?"

"Yes of course, Dominic lived out there for a while I can't remember the name of the town and Michael has a gallery out there too."

"Can you email me the address of the gallery? I'll check it out in the morning,"

"Of course, it'll take a few minutes for me to find it, I'll do it now." They finished their conversation with a little chit chat and Alex waited patiently for an email.

She packed up as much as she could so she could focus on this evening and just relax. The email came through from Jasmine, it turned out the gallery wasn't too far from where she was now, in fact it was in the shopping complex she had been in earlier so on her way out she would take a look. By the time the evening came she walked through the streets of Bangkok, the heat hadn't abated much but the lights and the bustle was enthralling her, she walked along the Chao Phraya River and instantly fell in love with Thailand, she found the place where the gallery was but it was all closed up and dark, maybe she could try again tomorrow. Everywhere around her was lit up and alive, she crossed the river on a shuttle boat and found a market selling just about everything under the sun and it was packed with people, she took another boat along the river and the city looked so beautiful, she wished Matt was with her now, temples shining golden under the full moon and the bustle of people cooking, eating and selling everything you could dream of. She was amazed at how different the night was to the daytime, everywhere seemed so alive, this city was spectacular, the temples were lit up and people were thronging around them making offerings and wishing for good health and happiness. There were markets on almost every street corner, food, clothes, flowers and gifts. Then there was the calm of Lumphini Park where there was a small group of musicians playing traditional instruments, she stopped for a while to enjoy the music before venturing to another market which seemed aimed at tourists, full of souvenirs of Thailand. She spent the evening exploring Bangkok and all it had to offer and now wished she didn't have to leave the following day.

Chapter Forty Five

Mary's house was full today, she couldn't remember when there had been so many visitors in one day. Janet had come over to see if anyone had heard from Alex, all she'd had from her daughter was a message a couple of days previously. Once she'd been assured that everything was fine, she returned home, after that there was Mark still hard at work, checking social media for any clues for Alex to follow but coming up empty. Alex had sent him an email telling him in passing about a murder in Thailand, which seemed to give him something else to follow for a while. Mary was beginning to wonder how many batches of brownies she was going to have to bake before he decided to go back to the tunnel, he seemed to love her baking every bit as Alex did. Jack was enjoying having Mark around and it was nice that Mark could keep Jack involved with all of the gossip of what was happening, Jack seemed to be in his element with Mark almost living with them and Summer popping in often. Mary loved all of them but would be glad to get the house back to themselves at some stage. It hadn't been so long ago the house had been quiet and she could sit back and do a puzzle in her favourite chair and now it always seemed busy, she loved having everyone around but sometimes it would be nice to just sit and be with her Jack.

"Jack, come here." Mark shouted, he went to see what Mark was shouting about. "Look at this... a photo fit of the men they are looking for in connection to that murder in Thailand." Jack looked at the computer screen in front of him.

"Okay, what am I looking at? I can never make these things look like real people." There were three men pictured, one bald, one with dark cropped hair and one with longer hair and a goatee beard, all medium build, average everything from what Jack could see.

"The one with the small beard, don't you think he looks like Michael?"

"Oh, I don't know Mark." He looked towards the kitchen. "Mary, come here." She walked over to the men huddled over the screen. "Do you think that looks like Michael?" He pointed at the third picture.

"Yes I suppose so but it could just as easily be anyone with a beard, sorry Mark but I'm not great with these, I think it may be a bit of wishful thinking." She drifted off back to the kitchen.

"Maybe she's right, she knows him better than either of us." Mark went back to checking the social sites still following his hunch but keeping it to himself at the moment.

Mary eventually came into the lounge and sat down with Jack, she couldn't do much wedding preparation whilst Mark and Jack were constantly around so she switched the TV on and put her feet up, just as she got comfortable the phone rang. It was Alex she updated them on what she was doing, it sounded like she had had a lovely evening in Bangkok but she hadn't come up with any news yet, she was moving on tomorrow. They chatted for a while and then she handed the phone to Mark, he told her what he thought and again warned her to be careful.

Mary was woken up an hour later from a doze, there was a banging on the door, 'what now' she thought. She opened the door and Mel was stood there, looking ruffled and unkempt. "Is Alex here?" She asked sharply.

"No Mel, she's away at the moment, come in?"

"No Thank you, I just wanted to talk to her, I understand now why she acted the way she did, I just wanted to tell her." Her voice was clipped and her speech to the point.

"She's been really worried about you, she'll be happy you've come round are you sure you don't want to stay for a while, I can put the kettle on?"

"No I'll try and ring her, thanks Mary." With that she turned around and walked off up the road.

Mary shook her head and silently wished for the rest of the evening to be quiet and uneventful, it looked promising, Mark was getting ready go back to the tunnel and she could hear Jack whistling in the kitchen, she went through to tell him about Alex's phone call and Mel turning up on the doorstep. She walked into the kitchen to find Jack cooking; he looked up at her and smiled. "I thought you needed treating, it's been a hectic week." She smiled and walked up to him and gave him a peck on the cheek.

"Thank you."

Chapter Forty Six

Michael had been in Prachuap for a couple of days and was already starting to like the place, he'd kept himself to himself and the only problem he seemed to have at the moment was trying to convince the owner of the guest house that his passport had been stolen, so he couldn't prove who he was. The owner, whose name he hadn't caught yet was threatening to throw him out if he couldn't find some form of ID. This town didn't seem to have the same bustle that was in Hua Hin, there was little chance of finding any Europeans here who might help him out, in fact he hadn't seen any Europeans yet and after his last experience he was pleased about it even if it was inconvenient.

He decided to try and find somewhere else to stay, he needed to avoid hotels but there may be some small places that wouldn't ask too many questions. First he wanted coffee and there were quite a few coffee shops to choose from in town, he walked down to the sea front and ambled along for a few minutes just enjoying the view and the warm breeze, he was shocked to see that he knew this view, he hadn't noticed it last time he had walked along the sea front, he had seen it in a painting that Dominic had done and it was even more stunning in reality, he took a few quiet minutes to take in the view. Moving on he turned into the next road and walked towards the market to get himself some fruit for breakfast. Continuing along the road he found a book store with an English language newspaper in a rack, he picked it up, he could pass an hour with this and a cup of coffee. He walked back to a quiet, small open fronted coffee shop and sat under a fan, flicking through the paper whilst he waited for his coffee.

He opened the newspaper and saw the photo fit pictures loom large before his eyes, they were not photographs but he recognised himself immediately, he needed a haircut, his wavy hair could be a giveaway, also a shave and to hope that the owner of the guesthouse didn't read newspapers. He started to feel a small knot of panic in his stomach, he really needed to find a new place to stay, he had expected a relaxed visit to this town but this was turning into a nightmare, a girl placed a cup of coffee in front of him he looked up and said. "Do you know anywhere I can stay?" She looked at him and smiled but he got no reply, it seemed no one here spoke much English, it looked like he was on his own. He went back to the newspaper, the three faces looking out at him were all familiar, one of the men had already been picked up, and he wondered where the others were now. He also wondered if he would have to move on to somewhere more remote but he didn't really want to, he'd seen a barbers shop in this area on a previous walk, it was time he went and had a haircut and a proper shave, if nothing else he would feel better. He finished his coffee and left, the heat had intensified in less than an hour, with any luck the barbers would be air conditioned. That was where he lucked out again.

Feeling clean and fresh albeit very hot Michael went in search of a new place to stay, there were enough hotels but that was out of the question but he didn't know where to start looking for small guest houses, he walked around until he was exhausted in the heat, he returned defeated to his room and packed his things up, it didn't take long, all he had was a new bag and a change of clothes to put in it. He put the newspaper in too thinking at least it was one copy less to be seen, he really was grasping at straws now. He threw his bag over his shoulder, put more than enough money to cover the remainder of his stay on the bedside table and left. His host was nowhere to be seen as he left and he had no idea where he would be staying tonight.

He made his way down to the beach, keeping his head down as he passed the police station. It was nice to feel the sand beneath his feet, it calmed his mood and he thought if nothing else he could sleep on the beach, it was warm, what else did he need.

Chapter Forty Seven

Alex awoke, the bright sunshine trying to creep into the room through the cracks in the curtains. She had arrived the previous evening when it was already dark, the hotel was warm and welcoming and everyone smiled at her when she checked in and they all smiled at her when she sat by the swimming pool to have a drink and relax after the long drive down. She could see why they called it the land of smiles, it hadn't been quite like this in Bangkok. She had gone to her room and fallen asleep almost immediately, she was glad she hadn't had to do the driving but still she felt exhausted.

    She got out of bed and pulled the curtains back, the sunlight almost blinded her, she opened the door to the balcony and stepped out, the sun was up high over the mountains, those mountains she'd seen them before, they were beautiful, she had a feeling of deja vu. The breath caught in her throat, she couldn't believe she was actually looking at the real mountains that she had been looking at on her wall at home. Dominic had painted these and they were even more beautiful in the morning sunlight than on her wall, she stood looking at them for a long time, it was the heat that finally drove her back into her room, it was only nine o'clock and already incredibly hot. She was hungry, she got dressed to go out and find whatever it was that passed for breakfast in this country, and she wasn't expecting bacon and eggs here. She stepped out of the cool lobby of the hotel into the intense heat of the street, everywhere was busy there were people selling things on the side of the road who were already beginning to pack up, they must have been here for hours. Alex walked along the road looking at everything that was for sale, most of it was edible but little that she recognised. There were people everywhere and as she turned a corner the temperature ratcheted up a notch as she entered the market, there was every type of food you could imagine. The sweat tickled the back of her neck as it ran freely, she spotted a stall selling fruit already peeled and cut up and it looked fresh, that made up her mind. She got her fruit and headed straight back for the hotel, the heat was too much for her, how did they work in it. She retreated to the cool of the lobby and nibbled on her breakfast.

Once Alex had cooled down she returned to her room to check her computer, hoping that someone may have some news to help her look for Michael, she was sure this was the place and at some stage she would have to brave the sun drenched streets and look for him. She needed to get to know the town too, it gave the impression of being a small town but she was sure there was more to it than the tourist leaflets and websites showed. There were no important emails for her just a lot of junk mail and it was too early at home to start ringing people. Her only alternative was to go out and take a look at the town and try to stay in air conditioned shops.

She spent the next two and a half hours hopping from coffee shops to supermarket and back again until it seemed like an appropriate time to ring England.

After catching up with her Mum she rang her Nan, who after bringing her up to date on the local gossip started telling her what she wanted to hear. "Have you heard from Mel?"

"No, should I have?"

"She came here Saturday night, to find you, she said something about understanding why you did what you did. I asked her in but she wouldn't stay."

"Oh so you didn't get that gossip then?" Alex teased. "She hasn't been in touch with me, how did she look?"

"Tired, older but that could have been the lack of make-up, I'd never seen her looking less glamorous,"

"I hope she's okay, I'll ring her later. How's Jack? Is everything organised for the wedding of the decade?"

"Jack's fine, worried about you though. Don't tease me about the wedding Alex I just want it to be perfect, we've waited fifty years for this, it's worth waiting for just a little while longer."

"Sorry Nan, you know I love you both. I've got to go and do my sleuthing now, have a lovely day Nan."

"Alex hang on, Mark and Jack were looking at some pictures yesterday, Mark was looking into that murder you told him about in Thailand, have you seen the photo fits?"

"No, I haven't seen a paper today."

"One of the guys looks like Michael…" She went quiet for a second. "We're not sure but check it out for yourself, Mark found the pictures online." Mary paused again. "If you think it is please drop this Alex, come home, we don't want you to get hurt."

"I'll check it out Nan, don't worry, thanks for telling me."

They said their goodbyes and Alex scoured the internet to find the photo fit pictures, it came as quite a shock when she did, one of the men certainly looked quite a lot like Michael but with longer hair and a small beard. So that's what you look like now she thought, thank you Michael, you've just made it easier.

The next call was to Matt and she was missing him, when he picked the phone up she could tell he was smiling, she could hear it and in the background she could hear The Killers 'Mister Brightside' blasting out, it was his favourite song. "What's up with you?" She asked smiling back at him, knowing he would be dancing around the kitchen playing air drums.

"Just happy, when are you coming home?"

"Soon, I promise. Matt I need your help again."

"Why what's wrong?" His voice changed completely from fun to business like in a split second, she could picture his face, the sudden appearance of those small frown lines and the loss of his lop sided grin.

"Nothing wrong, something has come up I need your help with. Can you look into a murder in a place called Hua Hin."

She spelt it out for him. "There was a photo fit in the news and one of them may just be Michael but I can't get much news about it here."

"Alex come home, I don't want you out there looking for him."

"Hang on, it probably isn't him, I just want to know what you think and if it is he's not here he's a hundred kilometres away, sometimes you sound like my Nan." She smiled.

"Okay, email me any links to do with it, I don't want to flag up that I'm looking into something that's nothing to do with us here. Alex... do I really sound like your Nan?" He was putting on a high pitched woman's voice. They laughed and she knew the frown lines had disappeared, replaced by his lop sided grin, they chatted for a while longer but Alex was aware that she had worried him, Mister Brightside had been turned off even though he was trying to sound happy. She felt bad ruining his mood.

"You can look at that view on the painting and think of me Matt because I'm looking at the same view from my balcony, I miss you."

"Come home Alex, it sounds far too nice out there for you to be on your own and I would be jealous if I didn't know how much work you were doing." He added sarcastically.

Alex sat back on her bed, all she could do now was wait until Matt got back to her, whilst she was waiting she sent him an email with some photos of the mountain, she was glad she had her good camera with her, this view deserved more than a snapshot.

Chapter Forty Eight

Michael had spent two nights on the streets already and it was an easy life, he had encountered no problems, no one bothered him, in fact the previous evening a man had bought him some food after he saw him sitting with his belongings on a sheltered part of the beach. He had tried to say he had money but the gentleman hadn't been able to speak English and it seemed rude to refuse, the food had been delicious, there was no shortage of food here, there were food markets that went on until ten at night and noodle bars that served throughout the night. When the town went very quiet about midnight he had found a nice little spot down by the sea wall, there was a fresh cool breeze at night and no one tried to move him on or bother him in any way, he would never of believed he could be so content with so little, it was the total opposite of his other life. The market started opening up at five o'clock in the morning and he would go and watch the monks collecting food from the stall holders until about six o'clock, they looked resplendent in their saffron robes amongst the dullness of the market before the sun came up, this morning a monk had approached him and pointed for him to sit in front of him, the monk had proceeded to chant over him for a couple of minutes before moving on to collect some food from another stall holder. Michael had no idea what that was about but it had felt special, it made him feel like he was meant to be here.

He had decided today he would get a motorcycle taxi to take him to the next village, he wanted to see more of the area and there seemed to be these little taxis hanging around outside one of the bigger hotels, he could hire one to show him around the area. He couldn't just hang around town much longer, someone might notice him and then inform the police, a day away might be a good thing. He hadn't seen anything else in the newspapers, he bought one daily now just to keep his eye on the news but it all seemed to have gone quiet, he felt immensely sad for Oli and couldn't get that image of him lying on the kitchen floor being pecked at by those chickens. He hadn't realised until that moment that he hadn't eaten chicken since and he didn't think he ever would again.

He walked towards the hotel and noticed a few holiday makers in their shorts and t-shirts milling around, he wanted to get to the motorcycle taxis before they did, he had a growing feeling he ought to get out of town, he jumped into the crate on the side of the motorcycle, the driver looked at him. "Just drive anywhere." He said.

"Where you go?" The driver asked, obviously not understanding Michael's English. Michael knew there was an air base not too far away so mimed an airplane, the driver instantly smiled and they went on their journey that turned out to be no more than five minutes away, not quite what he expected but he thought he could walk here now he knew where it was. He jumped out, paid the man and walked onto a beautiful beach, here there were lots of tourists, eating and drinking, it was the most white faces he'd seen since he'd been in Hua Hin. He could lose himself amongst them for a while and aim for a fairly normal day, he went to one of the roadside stalls and bought himself a pair of shorts, then went to find the communal shower block, he got changed and relaxed for a few hours just like any other tourist.

Feeling much better about life he decided to walk back into town and get some food, the afternoon heat was cooling and he was feeling good, he wanted to go and look for Dominic's house, he didn't know why he hadn't started looking for it before, there would be a perfectly good empty house somewhere, he didn't have an address but he had a rough idea what it looked like. Dominic had been possessive about his privacy and had never revealed his address to anyone as far as he knew. He walked back along the main road that was bustling with people doing their shopping. All he knew about the house was that Dominic could hear the sea and it had a small front garden, it was the only things he remembered him ever saying about the place. Michael was sure it would be empty, Dominic wasn't the kind of man to share his property, he didn't think he would have rented it out and hoped that he hadn't sold it. How he wished he'd got this information the last time he saw him. He couldn't even check his bank statements from here to see if there was any regular income from anywhere. It would have stuck out like a sore thumb, Dominic spent from his inheritance, he rarely had income except from the odd painting here and there, as good a painter as Dominic was most people wanted more modern works, his old fashioned style with lots of detail and colour were just out of fashion. Michael shrugged in acceptance and started looking. After an hour he began to realise that this would be a difficult search, there were houses everywhere, tiny tracks between shops and around corners would lead to an area of often ten to twelve houses that from a glance you wouldn't have realised were there and then there were all of the obvious houses too. He didn't know how he would ever find anything in the jumbled way this town was put together; he would have to rack his brains to remember anything else Dominic may have told him about it. He walked back into the centre of town, past a large colourful temple and found a small restaurant with great Thai food, where he ate before he made his way down to the beach to settle down for the evening.

Chapter Forty Nine

Alex still hadn't been able to contact Mel, the phone would just ring out without an answer and Mel certainly hadn't tried to get hold of her. She'd been sat around the hotel for a couple of days now with no news and no leads to follow she was beginning to think this might have been a crazy idea altogether. She didn't know how to move forward now. Matt had sent her an email with some news from Thailand. The Thai police had caught one of the men on the photo fits pictures connected to the crime and he had been taken to Bangkok prison awaiting trial. Apparently he had admitted to the crime but saying he hadn't meant to kill the man, just to frighten him enough to hand over his money, he admitted to stealing from another man too. The police will go through his belongings to try to discover who the other man is. At the bottom of the email he admitted that the one picture did look like Michael but he didn't add anything else. She had nowhere else to go now, there was just nothing she could think of left to show her the way. She sent the photo fits to Jasmine in an email but only because she couldn't think of anything more productive to do, Jasmine may have already seen the pictures for herself, Alex had already convinced herself that the picture was Michael. There was no news from Mark beyond how he was getting on with Summer and their encounters with Mel, which made her smile, she prayed that Mel was calming down now.

   She needed to go out and get a Thai mobile phone because her bill when she got home would be horrendous and Charlie would have a fit at her as he paid most of it. Charlie…. Oh hell she thought, he's going to be firing me on my return. She hadn't spoken to him or sent any work in since she'd arrived here, so that was her day sorted now she'd have to stay in and work on the Paris story that had gone totally out of her head. To buy some time she sent some of the photos she'd taken in an email whilst she put together the last of the interviews. She also put together a sketchy story on the murder in Thailand maybe something from here would ease his mood although she could only repeat what she had read from other papers.

The work took longer than she expected and she had to work late into the night to pull it all together, it was quite harrowing work but at least it might calm Charlie down, she could picture him going purple in the face with anger at her and she really didn't want to lose her job. Looking on the positive side she was too far away to take the brunt of his temper at the moment.

She had fallen asleep finally at three thirty in the morning but was woken up at four thirty by her phone, she fumbled for it in the dark and looked at the display, it was Mel, she touched the answer button, immediately awake now.

"Mel, how are you?"

"Alex can you come round?" She was crying.

"Mel I'm in Thailand, it's four thirty in the morning, I'd love to pop round but I can't, just talk to me."

"I'm sorry, why do I always get it wrong? I knew you were away, I just didn't know where." There was an uncomfortable silence between them, Alex waited for her to talk. "I'm sorry I didn't believe you, but you were so cruel and I loved him, I trusted him, I was a fool. He's going to go to prison for murder and I don't know what to do."

"It's okay Mel, this isn't your fault or even your problem."

"But it is Alex, I was going to marry him knowing he was up to no good but not wanting to believe it."

"Do you want to tell me about it?" Alex coaxed.

"You know, you were right, he wrote to me from prison to tell me he just wanted to be left alone, I wasn't to visit and he was only interested in me whilst I had money in my pocket. He was never going to marry me. I even bought my own engagement ring.... Did you know that?" With that statement she dissolved into floods of tears, Alex wanted to reach out to her but there was nothing she could say to make any of this any better.

"At least you found out before you got in any deeper, just be glad you're away from him."

"I guess, but Alex could he really of killed a man, do you believe he could do that?"

"I don't know Mel, I didn't know him as well as you, do you think he could have done it?" Alex's mind drifted back to the time her and Matt had met them at the pub for a drink and how quickly Lee's attitude had changed when they turned up, he had certainly known how to turn on the charm, she had the feeling that he could actually be cold and calculating enough to really hurt someone. Her Nan had been right, he had a streak of spite running through him.

"Never." Mel's voice cut through her thoughts. "What are you doing in Thailand?"

"Looking for someone, don't worry I'll be home soon."

"Thank you and I'm sorry for the way I acted."

"Me too Mel, Me too." There seemed little else to say. Alex felt better having spoken to Mel, at least they were talking again. With that thought she fell asleep, this time undisturbed.

When she woke up and checked her phone there were messages, emails and calls waiting for her, Charlie had been trying to call her several times, she would deal with that later, she at least needed some breakfast before she was prepared to take on Charlie.

There was a thank you message from Mel that made her smile and emails from Jasmine confirming that she also thought the picture was Michael. There were also two emails from Matt and one from Mark; she needed coffee and something to eat before she went any further. She popped down to the market and got some fruit and sticky rice and went to a little coffee shop to get a take away and picked up a new sim card from the local phone shop. She had finally got back to the room, hot and bothered but it was nice that it had been cleaned and tidied whilst she was out, she settled in front of her computer to find another email had joined the queue, Charlie again, she was dreading that one along with the ones he had sent earlier, wondering if she still had a job to go back to. She checked Marks message first, nothing much to report, he didn't have an address for Dominic's house and he couldn't find any reference to it anywhere. Matt's emails were much nicer but not any more helpful and he had sent a selfie with the painting on the wall behind him with caption 'better view now?' These emails weren't so bad after all. She knew she was putting Charlie's email off, she didn't want to read what he had to say, it couldn't be good, with trepidation she clicked on the message. It started 'where the bloody hell are you!!!' and it got worse from there, he hadn't sacked her but he was obviously furious at her for just taking off, maybe he was waiting for the sacking to do it in person. She wondered if she should do a travel piece for him and then reprimanded herself for being flippant, just as Charlie would have. She decided against replying in haste, another day and maybe he would have calmed down enough, she could hope.

This evening she was going out with one of the girls that worked at the hotel, called Pet, they had got talking one afternoon whilst Alex had a coffee overlooking the swimming pool, Pet's English was bordering on good and in exchange for a few English lessons Pet was going to show her around the town and give her an insight into Thai life, at least it gave her something to do whilst she waited for news on Michael which she hoped would come soon.

After a lazy day she got ready to go out, she was looking forward to seeing more of the town, they met in the lobby and Pet handed her a helmet, they were going out on the motorbike so Alex could see the town beyond the hotel area. Pet drove slowly up and down roads, Alex made a mental note of places that looked interesting so she could return, then they stopped at a local restaurant that served only Thai food, Pet ordered and within ten minutes a banquet was laid out before them, there was so much food she didn't know where to start. Alex started asking questions about the area; what she really wanted to know was where the ex-pat community lived. They drank local beer and got to know each other, Pet only looked about twenty years old but it turned out she was thirty six and had three children, her husband had left years ago with another woman. Pet and her family all lived with her mother towards the back of the town. "Haven't you wanted to find anyone else?" Alex asked.

"No, men no good." She smiled as she said it. "I wait for rich foreigner." She laughed.

"Where would you find a rich foreigner here? I haven't seen many tourists at all." Alex was pleased the conversation had naturally come round to tourists.

"Not many here, a few live here but no nice ones."

"Is there an area where they live?"

"No, just buy land and build houses, anywhere."

"Do you know these foreigners?"

"Some, not all." Their focus returned to the food for a while and it wasn't long before the Thai desserts were being brought to the table, the food was incredible, Alex had never tasted anything like it. Now she was feeling comfortable she started asking the questions she really wanted some answers to.

"Did you know a man called Dominic or maybe just Dom here?"

"What he look like?"

"Does. What does he look like." Alex corrected Pet's English.

"Thank you" Pet thought about it then asked again. "What does he look like?" Alex gave her the thumbs up.

"Older man, dark grey hair, quite fit for his age, looked younger than he was." Alex could see this description was getting confusing for her. "He used to paint pictures."

"Yes, yes." Pet's eyes lit up. "He go away, not here now."

"Yes that's him, where did he live?"

183

"The house by the sea, big house. I take you." They finished off their desserts, Alex was stuffed, she'd eaten far too much but the food was too good to leave, whilst she paid she hoped Pet would take it easy driving back, she wasn't sure her full stomach could cope with stopping and starting too much. They drove down to the sea front and past the hotel and there it was, a house that looked reminiscent of a western built house, three floors and very tidy, it was a big house because it went up three floors but it didn't cover a large ground area. It was a lovely building, if this was it Dominic must have been doing well for himself. They got off the bike, sat on the sea wall and looked at it, it was in darkness but Alex could see why someone would like to live here. "No one live here now, he go to England, he was a kind man, I not know his name. He smiled a lot but never get drunk like other foreigners." They walked up to the house and had a look around but there was nothing to see, it was dark and everything was closed up. "Would anyone have a key?" Alex asked.

"Yes his cleaner, I know her, I can speak with her tomorrow." Pet smiled seeming happy to help.

"Thank you." Alex was over the moon. They had had a lovely night and she had learnt so much about not only Dominic but about the hospitality of the local people. Pet went home, she had offered Alex a lift but Alex fancied a walk back to the hotel, it wasn't far she could see it from where she was now, she enjoyed the cool sea air as she walked. She could see why Dominic had chosen to make this place his home; although she couldn't think why he would want to leave it behind.

Chapter Fifty

Michael was starting to get used to the area, he had been all over the town by foot and was getting to know it well, however, finding Dominic's house was turning out to be more of a challenge with every corner he turned. What he thought of as a small town was turning out to be like a rabbit warren, he needed to focus instead of running around like a lunatic, but he couldn't think of any other details. He would have to start asking around but he didn't want to draw too much attention to himself and sleeping by the beach was already starting to get him noticed, people had started bringing him drinks and food as it was. He sat down heavily on the sea wall and tried to replay in his head everything he and Dominic had ever spoken about, the more he tried the less he could recall; this was impossible.

He'd read the newspaper as usual this morning and had seen the report that one of the men in Hua Hin, had been arrested, which meant they must still looking for him too, they had not given up yet, it said as much in the article. He couldn't run anymore, he had lost his identity and didn't know which way to turn. He raised his head and looked around, there were more tourists turning up by the day, now he was looking he noticed that this part of town seemed to have a few white faces milling around, he was getting past caring about being spotted, although because he was living on the street the tourists tended avoid him, terrified they may catch some misfortune, he needed a lucky break. What started out to be an adventure was turning into a depressing game of hide and seek, he had put himself into this position and it had stopped being exciting, now he was beginning to feel frightened. He had no idea how all of this could end.

He took an alley way that he knew led onto the main road and sauntered down to a coffee shop to pass some of the day, he had nothing else to do. He picked his paper up and read the rest of the news whilst he waited for his coffee, his name was no longer mentioned and the world seemed to have forgotten about him, he wasn't sure how he felt about that anymore. He'd had the highs and the thrill of the chase and now he was just another loser bumming around Thailand and when the police caught up with him they'd send him back or worse he could end up in prison, that couldn't happen, life wasn't feeling so good anymore. The waitress approached him with his coffee and smiled her perfect white smile, he smiled right back at her, the door opened and her attention was taken away to the next customer. He went back to his newspaper and reading about all of the trouble in the world. The door clanged again, another customer, this was obviously a popular coffee shop, he looked up and immediately ducked behind the newspaper again. No, this couldn't be right, he was just feeling a bit freaked out today, he inched the paper down and peered over it not believing what he was seeing. Could it really be Alex the woman he gave an interview to, what should he do now, if she could track him the police would have no problems. She was sitting at a table with her back to him, he was sure it was her, he'd always been good at remembering faces, how else would he remember his first love, Janet, after all of this time, he needed her to turn around a little just to confirm his thoughts. Why had she bothered to track him down? He was nothing to her, the only connection they had was the interview which she never even used. He was aware he was sweating now, he could feel his body going into a panic, and his heart was racing. He would have to follow her and find out where she was staying, he needed to know why she was here, it had to be more than coincidence and the only way he could find out was to follow her around, he couldn't approach her. Everything he had done this for would unravel and he couldn't cope with that.

She obviously wasn't in a rush, she sat there reading a book and drinking coffee for nearly an hour, whilst he sat there wishing the wall would open up and swallow him, when she eventually got up to pay he waited for her to leave before he did the same and headed in the same direction following her across the road and down to the market. She picked up some fruit from the same stall he used most mornings and walked down to the sea front, she sat on the sea wall just enjoying the sunshine whilst he hid in the shade of an alley between two shops watching from behind a wall, a couple of locals walked past him and gave him an enquiring look but kept moving without causing him any grief they were more interested in each other.

He watched her enjoying the sea breeze as he himself did every day, after fifteen minutes two girls approached her and stood talking to her for a few minutes before she walked away leaving them chatting to each other. He slipped out of the alley and walked behind her following her along the road, he was startled when a girl came running past him shouting Alex's name, Alex stopped and turned around, Michael ducked down and sat on the wall averting his face, hoping she hadn't seen him, he was lucky she was so wrapped up in conversation with her friend she didn't even give him a second glance. The two of them walked a little further and turned into one of the larger hotels. Michael didn't know if that was where she was staying or if they were having lunch there, now they were together he decided just to keep an eye on the main door in case she came out again.

After almost two hours in the sun he decided enough was enough, he would have to keep his eye open for her but at this time of the day there were few places outside to get any shade in front of the hotel, he would have come back later when it was cooler and see if he could find her again. At least now he knew to be careful and vigilant, a wakeup call, the chase wasn't over yet.

Chapter Fifty One

Lee was sitting in his cell still wondering how he had got himself into this mess. He'd written to Mel trying to sort that part out as he was certain she would be feeling terribly hurt but what could he do, he had strung her along and it had backfired on him, he'd needed an alibi and almost ended up with a wife. He felt awful about that but even if he'd have gone through with it he couldn't have coped with her clingy personality. They were well rid of each other. He hadn't heard back from her and he hoped he never would.

Now he needed to find a way to prove his innocence, he hadn't killed Dominic, the police weren't believing him and there was no way of proving it, the closest he could get would be to tell them about Michael and the way he treated Dominic and he didn't want to cause any trouble for Michael, he cared too much about him, even after all of this mess that he found himself in. He looked down at his hands with their bitten fingernails and flaking skin and had no idea what he should tell the police, surely they would have to let him go eventually, after all he hadn't done anything and he had a good idea who had but he had no proof and couldn't be certain, so why would they believe him.

He couldn't live like this he was a mess, he kicked at his cell door, out of frustration more than anything, an officer was outside the door in seconds. "What's the problem Lee?"

"I want to speak to the police."

"So you can waste more of their time?"

"No, I need to talk to them." He'd said all he was going to say to this officer. He went back to his bed and sat down and waited. Two hours later the officer returned to take him to see the police. He arrived at an interview room and he saw Matt Jones, why did it have to be him. "Hello Lee, got something to say to us?" Matt leant back into the hard plastic chair and smiled. Lee sat down opposite him and started to tell Matt what he had come here to tell him. "I went to Michael's flat to find some letters, that's what I was doing there."

"You got me out here just to tell me you wanted to find some letters! Lee you're going to have to do better than that."

"It's the truth, Michael had a bunch of letters I had written over the years and was blackmailing me with them, I thought when he disappeared it would be my chance to try to get them back."

"So all of this is about letters? You need to spell this out for me Lee because I'm not seeing the link between a murder and your letters." Matt was watching Lee closely and he was acting very differently to the Lee that he had interviewed in the police station, quieter, he'd lost his arrogance, he hoped he would get some answers now.

"There is no link, Michael had been blackmailing me for years... hell why do you think I was living in a tiny flat in the back of nowhere, I'm a fairly successful artist."

"Okay so you went to find the letters, did you find them?"

"No." He looked down into his lap "No, you know I didn't, you saw the note he left in the car too."

"We're meant to believe that you're the victim in all of this?"

"I am, can't you see he's stitched me up."

"No, I'm afraid I can't see, we have a dead body and a disappeared multi-millionaire and we happen to have you at the bottom of it all. Can you see how it looks?" Matt had had enough. "What was in these letters?"

"They were love letters." Lee's face coloured.

"Love letters!" Matt had to stop himself from smiling. "Now I have to believe that you, who were going to marry Mel not a week ago are now telling me you sent Michael love letters, come on Lee you can see how this looks."

"I've been in love with Michael most of my life, he didn't care about me but that didn't stop me, I was stupid enough to put it in writing. He kept the letters and threatened to go public with them if I ever tried to go it alone, so I was tethered to him, I thought that was okay at least I got to see him regularly. He drew up a contract that gave him most of the money I earned, I even put up with that. I thought he would have kept the letters in his flat so I went to look for them. That's the truth. He made me feel ashamed of loving him, like it was something dirty. That's what he meant in the note he left. He said I'd never find them." That was when Lee broke down, Matt had seen a lot of people's reaction to interviews over the years but this was unusual.

"If that's the truth Lee where could the letters be now, any ideas? We need to see them."

"I don't know where they are I didn't find them and his note said I never would."

"So that leaves us with you having a stronger motive to get rid of Michael than we thought. How can we believe you Lee, you've lied to everyone, as far as we know you were in love with a woman a week ago. This is turning into a farce; you will stop at nothing to get out of here. We will check every piece of paperwork in the flat and we will check out your story." Matt couldn't believe Lee had just made sure it was even tougher for him to get out of this mess. "Anything else you want to tell us now we're here?"

"Michael had Dominic in an unreasonable contract too, I don't know what he had over him though, there might be something in the flat. I don't know if he was being blackmailed too."

Lee looked at Matt not believing what he was hearing, he hadn't thought of it from the point of view of the police only that he was desperate and needed to tell the truth. He'd just given them even more reasons to keep him in prison.

"So you both had a reason for revenge on Michael. Seems Michael isn't the likeable guy we all thought."

"That's the truth."

"Is he dangerous?"

"I don't think so he's just a con artist, it doesn't matter what he does he always comes out smelling of roses."

"Thank you for talking to us, we'll check out his paperwork and see what we can come up with." Matt got up to leave, the other officer whose name Lee didn't catch followed him. He couldn't do anything else now. He'd put himself in a worse position but hoped they might discover something from his information that would get him out of this place.

The prison officer returned to the interview room and led Lee back to his cell. Not a word was exchanged between them.

Chapter Fifty Two

Matt hadn't managed to tell her anymore about the incident in Hua Hin than the papers had but he was keeping his ear to the ground for her. It seemed from the emails that everything was fine at home although she hadn't had one from Mark today but at least she felt she could relax a bit and enjoy her surroundings, she felt like she'd been running on adrenaline since she left the UK.

Pet had introduced her to the lady who took care of Dominic's house, her name was Dam and she had been his cleaner for several years and even though Dominic hadn't been here she still took care of the house unpaid because he had always been kind to her. Now she just went in once a week to make sure everything was safe, she didn't know whether he would be back or not. Alex hadn't told her about his demise yet but Dam had readily agreed to show her around the house. Alex didn't know what good this would do but she wasn't going to refuse an invite, it may give her more of an insight into the man who created her amazing picture. She would meet up with her a little later today at the house. Right now she was psyching herself up to speak to Charlie, she had the impression it wasn't going to be a pleasant conversation. She went out onto the balcony and took a good long look at the incredible view that really did look like a Buddha reclining, she hoped it would help relax her. She dialled Charlie's number, he answered and she listened, for at least five minutes he ranted at her for being unprofessional, after two minutes she stopped listening and just focused on the view, when he finally stopped she simply said "Sorry Charlie but I had to follow the story up, you'll benefit from any news I get whilst I'm here." She could hear him steadily breathe out trying to control his blood pressure.

"Okay, there's nothing I can do now anyway, make sure it's a bloody good story otherwise you'll be picking up your P45 when you get back, none of this goes on expenses either, you fund it yourself!"

"I won't let you down, I'll write up a story about Michael and the art world, just to keep people interested, I'll include a few quotes from him."

"Alex, how would you get quotes, you told me you didn't have an interview with him." She smiled, yes that's exactly what she'd told him.

"I didn't Charlie, I'll treat you to a bit of personal chit chat, no extra charge."

"You'll be the death of me, I should have sacked you last year, you're always trouble Alex." He didn't wait for the goodbyes he just put the phone down on her. She had to smile, that mountain must be lucky for her because she thought she had handled that quite well. She spent the next hour working on a story for Charlie giving him some background on Michael Masters, she sent the rough draft off to Jasmine first as she promised she would and added a footnote about finding Dominic's house.

She went off to meet Dam outside the house, she was already there when Alex arrived, sitting on the sea wall waiting, she smiled as Alex approached and got up and walked towards the house, Alex followed her. The house was quite imposing, narrow but tall compared to those around it and it was in a European style, built with light stone, there wasn't another building like it along the sea front. Dam turned around to face her and spoke to her in Thai and held out the keys to her, Alex took them not understanding why and shrugged her shoulders at Dam, with a lot of arm movements Alex managed to understand that she was trying to tell her something about her children. Dam pointed to the keys then towards the hotel "Pet" she said. Whatever was going on she understood that she was to give the keys to Pet when she was finished here, with that Dam walked off up an alley that ran alongside the building. Alex stood at the door, she was a little nervous entering the house alone. She kept telling herself, I'm a journalist it's fine, just go inside. Eventually she put the key in the lock, it turned easily and the door swung open. She was straight into a lounge area, there were cloth covers draped over some of the furniture, to keep the dust and she assumed the damp off the settees. It wasn't a huge lounge but there were windows all around her, no one could see in because of the heavy net curtains that had been hung over them. There were paintings around the walls, there was one similar to her 'Buddha Mountain' that must have been a predecessor to hers, this one was just the mountain, there were no people or activity here, it was every bit as beautiful with more of a feeling of serenity about it. There was no television but there was a radio perched on a small table and beside it a large square box with a carving of an elephant in the lid, she opened it and found a pile of magazines and paperwork. She moved through to the rear of the house and found a small kitchen with a staircase beyond that, the kitchen was basic but very clean. She walked through and went up to the next floor, there was a bathroom with huge mirror tiles across the walls and a large bedroom that had double doors that opened onto a balcony. Alex pulled aside the full length net curtains and looked on the view of the mountain. She didn't go out, apart from a deck chair on the balcony there was nothing of any interest, the bedroom however was furnished with beautifully carved teak wardrobes and a dressing table. There was no doubt that Dominic lived well here. She took the stairs up another short flight and was in an attic space, there were canvases, paints and boxes of all shapes and sizes, at the far end of the room there was another smaller balcony, she randomly opened one of the boxes, it was full of paints the smell of oil paints almost overpowering her in the heat of the room.

Back downstairs she turned on the only air con unit she could find and the overhead fan, within a minute the room had cooled. She pulled a cover back from the settee to sit down only to find a pile of sketches, these are good she thought, flicking through them, she wished she had that sort of talent. Her focus moved to the box on the floor, she put the drawings down and opened the box pulling out magazines, she couldn't read most of them, they were in Thai, there were one or two in English, there were also newspapers and some letters. She was in no rush, so thought she would have a flick through the paperwork, it wasn't long before she saw a pattern to the magazines and the newspapers. Where she had assumed that he read Thai maybe he didn't the connection between the majority of the saved magazines were Michael's shops, the Thai papers showed photographs of the new shop in Bangkok and Michael stood in front of it or works of art that were being sold by him. Maybe he had exhibited in the new shop opening, which would explain keeping these as mementos. She turned her attention to the letters, these were still in their envelopes but had been opened, if she thought she would find anything here she was disappointed they were mainly bills. She put everything back in the box and closed the lid. There was a lot of furniture in the bedroom maybe she could take a look round in there, she was pleased that Dam hadn't stayed here with her, she'd have felt terrible rummaging through his things with her watching, as it was she felt free to look wherever she wanted to now. She got her phone out and took a few photos of the house, it always helped her focus on a story and she went back upstairs. The bedroom furniture was beautiful it would certainly have cost him a fortune, he must have had plenty of money and that was why he never fought over the details in the contract he had with Michael. She looked through the room, opening wardrobes and drawers but there didn't seem to be anything to find, he had a drawer full of receipts and scraps of paper but nothing that seemed particularly interesting. Alex had seen enough and the upstairs of the house was getting too hot for her to continue there was no air conditioning in these rooms and she didn't want to open the doors to the balcony and draw attention to her snooping, she took a few more photos and decided to go back to the hotel. She'd like to have another look in the attic space, maybe she could come back tomorrow she'd check it out with Pet when she took her the keys. She walked out of the front door pulling it to behind her.

Pet wasn't working when she got back to the hotel, Alex decided to go to her room and ring Matt, she would catch Pet later when she came down for dinner. Matt was at work when she phoned and it was awkward for him to talk but he told her to check her emails, he had sent her one an hour ago. She promised to call him back later. She connected to the internet and got her emails up on her phone. Matt had sent her a short email that said,

> *'the police in Thailand have found a bag which contained a couple of passports and a tablet computer, the passports were in the name of D M Waite, Shaw and Southwell, all with Michael's photograph, they're going through the computer but I haven't heard anything about that yet. It looks like it had been dumped behind a bar. It was the guy they arrested for the murder in Hua Hin that told them where to find it. Don't get involved!'*

Chapter Fifty Three

Michael couldn't believe it, he thought he was finished with no idea how to continue and then he caught sight of Alex, she was talking to one of the ladies he saw her with yesterday as they walked towards a house, he watched the woman as she handed Alex some keys and walked away. So that's where she's staying, in a nice big house on her own by the look of it. He moved a little closer so he could see as she went inside but it had looked dark inside, it was just too bright on the street, he ambled down the alley to the side of the house where it was more shaded and looked at the windows, they were covered with net but one window had a gap in the netting as if something had knocked it out of place, maybe just the breeze, he hoped it would be just enough to see through. He looked around, he was totally alone in the alley there didn't seem to be anyone around, he walked up to the house and opened the side gate and stood close to the wall, he just had to hope she wasn't looking out of the window when he looked in. He listened carefully with his ear to the door but he couldn't hear any sounds coming from inside. He sidled up to the window, still checking there was no one on the street watching him, he looked quickly through the gap in the curtains, he couldn't see her, where was she? He backed away, then feeling a little braver looked again, she definitely wasn't in that room, he took a second and looked more carefully at the room, he saw a movement to the left of his vision, he ducked back breathing heavily now, his nerve endings tingling, all of his senses seemed to be on alert. He looked again, no movement, this time he crept back to the window and through the small gap he could see a part of the room, it was enough to convince him that this was the very house he had been looking for, there was a painting on the wall, the one that Dominic had shown him as a prelude to Buddha Mountain, Michael had held that particular painting in his hands, carefully checking the brush strokes, the hues, the quality of the canvas. He couldn't believe his luck, this was Dominic's house but what was Alex doing here? He didn't need to see any more, he slipped away from the house and back down to the seafront without being noticed by anybody and he waited, smiling to himself.

It had been quite a while until Alex had come out of the building, pulling the door behind her and confidently strolling down the sea front. He watched her and followed a good distance behind, she walked down as far as the hotel again and slipped inside, this time he followed her up the stairs and into the lobby. He stood in the lobby entrance and enjoyed the breeze whilst he watched her approach the reception area and speak to someone behind the desk. A shake of the head from the receptionist and Alex walked over to the bank of lifts, he moved closer to watch which floor the lift went to, one, two, three then a pause, she was on the third floor, he went back outside and looked up at the balconies and waited. She hadn't left the building but he wanted to be sure she was staying here and not at Dominic's house. After twenty minutes of him patiently waiting he was rewarded, there she was pulling up a chair on the balcony and it looked like she was alone, he couldn't be sure but there was only one chair on the balcony and he hadn't seen her with anyone apart from the Thai girls since he had been following her. He felt happier than he had in days; he was finally having some luck.

He went to find something to eat, he didn't need to hang around anymore and he didn't want her to catch sight of him, he had all the information he needed. He sat in the noodle bar and found his appetite had returned and he ordered enough food to feed a small army, he hadn't realised how hungry he was.

As the light went out of the day and the temperature dropped a few degrees footfall along the sea front increased, he'd been around here long enough to know that by nine thirty all of the tourist would be making their way back to their hotels to get some sleep before another hard day on the beaches tomorrow, nothing happened in this town after ten o'clock in the evening and by then things would already be quiet. He just needed to wait for a while until everyone had had enough to eat and drink then the night would be his, the only thing he would need to watch out for were the regular police patrols along the front. Having watched them for long enough he now knew their routine. He treated himself to a bottle of beer and sat on the wall watching the tourists walk by, some hand in hand, others chatting and laughing, not one of them took any notice of him, he just blended into the background. Occasionally someone would walk past and say hello and he would nod and smile at them.

Ten o'clock came around quickly or so it seemed to him, he could feel his heartbeat quickening in anticipation, there were a few people milling around down by the hotel but there was no one around where he was, he slipped into the alley and through the gate belonging to the house, he was nervous but being as quiet as he could. He checked to see if there was anyone around and had to duck below the level of the small wall as a couple of local boys on a motorbike screeched down the alley, talking loudly and laughing. He managed to duck before the headlights picked him out. He gave it plenty of time after they had gone, he took a deep breath to calm himself and slow his heart rate down, the last thing he needed now was to panic, approaching the door he pushed it but he knew that would be a long shot, it was firmly locked, he picked a half brick up from behind the wall that he had placed there earlier and wrapped a rag around his hand. Suddenly he was very aware that the night was silent, this would make a lot of noise and as if God was listening to him a bunch of lads on motorcycles came roaring past playing music, they were larking around and the only thing they were interested in was having fun. As they approached he launched the broken brick at the small pane of glass. Even he had barely heard it over the noise of laughter and music. He shook off the rag from around his hand and dipped into the inside of the door and flipped the lock, he was in. He cleared up the glass and looked around for something to put in the small pane, if he left it like this someone would surely notice, he saw a cardboard box in the corner of the small garden and ripped a piece off it and jammed it in the gap. Hoping if anyone saw it they might think it was in the process of being fixed. Once inside he looked around at the covered furniture, just grey shapes in the dim light, one half of the settee had the covers pulled back. He sat down and for a moment enjoyed the luxury of the soft seating, he looked around, yes this was definitely Dominic's house, his work on the walls and a pile of sketches on the settee, Michael cast an admiring eye over what he could see with just the street light to illuminate them, these looked good. He started to relax, to be safe he went to both of the doors and clicked them to double locked and he curled up on the settee exhausted and slept.

Chapter Fifty Four

Alex spent the early morning checking her emails and being distracted by funny cat videos online, she was feeling more light hearted than she had in days. The emails mainly were chatty, Jasmine has agreed to the quotes in the piece she had written for the paper. Mark was keeping her up to date on his relationship with Summer and how Mel was doing, also that he'd had word that Georgie was back in town and was going to try and find him before Matt did. Her Nan and Jack were fine and still warning her to be careful, as she thought about her Nan her stomach rumbled, she wished she could get some of her Nan's baking out here. She would eat at the hotel this morning and she had nothing else to do this early in the day, the time difference meant she couldn't ring home until this afternoon and she needed to see Pet to hand the house keys over to her.

She found a seat by the swimming pool and ordered her breakfast, Pet was working this morning, Alex would talk to her when she wasn't so busy, she took her time over her breakfast enjoying the sun and watching the fishing boats come and go from the pier. Pet eventually came over to talk to her, Alex handed the keys to her. "You keep them." She said.

"Dam told me to give them to you."

"Dam's daughter not well, you keep the keys." Pet insisted. Alex didn't argue.

"Okay, do you want an English lesson this morning?"

"No time today, busy. Many tourists. Tomorrow?"

"Sure." Alex replied. They chatted for a few minutes before Pet had to get back to work.

Alex looked at the keys, maybe she could go back and take a longer look at the paperwork in the house. She knew she shouldn't but those keys were a temptation, she pushed them deep into her bag and tried to forget about them. She went back to her room and sent Charlie the article she had written and tried to relax but her mind kept wandering back to the keys. The room phone rang, which made her jump, she picked it up and Pet was on the other end, she wanted to take Alex to a local beauty spot tomorrow afternoon with her and her children to show her more of the area. Alex was happy to accept, the more she knew of this town the more she was liking it although she would have to think about going home soon, there didn't seem to be much more she could do here and there had been no sign of Michael, she was beginning to realise how big this country was and there were so many places he could be and now he was involved in a crime here he would be being extremely careful. She was starting to give up hope of ever finding him.

The afternoon was creeping in and the heat was too much to go shopping around town, she relaxed on the balcony with a cool drink, it was almost time that she could phone round and talk to everyone at home, she really needed to speak to Matt, she was missing him like hell and she wanted to speak to Mel and make sure she was okay too. The phone rang out at home, she knew it was a little earlier than usual but still Matt would answer the phone even if it woke him, she let it ring longer but still no answer. Where would he be at this time in the morning unless something had happened and he needed to go to work. She rang his mobile, still no answer, she started to worry. She sent a text and phoned Mel instead. Mel answered groggy from sleep but she was fine and they chatted for a few minutes, she was still worried about Lee but she was beginning to accept that it was one relationship that was never going to work out. Alex was just relieved that they were talking again. She also phoned her Nan, Jack answered he was pleased to hear from her, he hadn't seen anything of Matt for a couple of days but told her not to worry. They were all fine but her Nan was still in bed and he didn't want to wake her, she enjoyed the occasional lie in. Alex smiled, she hoped her and Matt's relationship would be as warm as theirs when they were seventy. Jack said Mark wouldn't be around until late today, he'd gone off to try to find 'Georgie' and see what he knew. Alex was taken aback at how helpful everyone was being, she thought maybe Mark was still trying to prove himself to Jack after he had alerted her to their tunnel last year, it was true she probably would never have found them without Mark interfering, that was ancient history now though and everything had turned out for the best. After they had chatted and she had told Jack her news to be passed on to Mark also to tell him not to worry about Georgie any longer, now they knew who the body was, it was something that the police would have to deal with. Georgie wouldn't be able to help her with finding Michael. She tried Matt one more time, still no reply. She hoped he was okay, he was probably in the middle of an investigation, which would be the only reason he wouldn't answer his phone.

The thought of the keys in her bag were still nagging at her and she knew if she went back she would have the whole afternoon to check out all of the paperwork in the house, there may be nothing to find but she wanted to know that for herself and she had nothing else to do today, it was too good an opportunity to overlook. Before she had a chance to talk herself out of it she grabbed her bag and left the room.

Chapter Fifty Five

She walked confidently towards the house as if she had every right to be there, she needn't have worried no one was taking any notice of her. She walked up to the front door and let herself in. Straight away she thought something was different, she was sure the drawings she had been looking at were on the settee but now they were on the floor and hadn't she thrown the cover back over the settee. No, she had left the cover half off the settee, then she must have moved the papers too, she accepted her own explanation and knelt down to pick up the papers whilst looking through them. He was so good, why had he not been more well known, some of these sketches were works of art in their own right, she tidied them up and set them on top of the box, she would come back to that later, she wanted to take a look around the attic most of all, if he had anything to hide maybe it would be up there, out of the way. She walked through to the kitchen and felt something crunch under her foot, as she looked down she caught sight of the piece of cardboard in the small window pane, someone had smashed a window, who would do that? From what Pet and Dam had said he had no enemies here, he kept himself to himself, everyone seemed to think well of him. She pulled the cardboard away from the door frame and saw that some jagged pieces of glass were still clinging to the frame, she grabbed a cloth from beside the sink and pulled the shards out and looked around for something more substantial to put in the window. The cardboard box was on the floor with a chunk of cardboard pulled from the side of it in exactly the same shape as the piece she had found in the door. Someone had been inside, so she hadn't left those paintings on the floor. "Hello..." nothing.

"Hello is there anyone here?" There was not a sound from inside the house, her skin prickled and she broke out in a sudden sweat, the back of her neck feeling the fear first. If it was thieves they were very bad ones, apart from the sketches being moved everything else looked the same as it did yesterday, unless they knew exactly what they wanted and it was something she hadn't seen yet. She walked back to the kitchen and picked up a heavy meat cleaver that was hanging from a hook on the wall and went upstairs, creeping up every step, wildly alert, trying to keep her breathing regular. She was conscious of her hearing and vision being acute as she entered the bedroom but nothing looked like it had been disturbed and so she climbed the final flight of stairs to the attic, if there was anyone on the premises then they had to be up here, she raised the cleaver noticing her hand was shaking, she put both hands on the metal grip and entered the open area that had boxes strewn around the floor, this area also looked just the same as it had looked yesterday. She put the cleaver on top of one of the boxes as she heaved a sigh, she thought she might cry with the relief of finding nothing, it must have been kids messing about, it didn't look like anything had been touched.

She went back downstairs returned the meat cleaver to its rightful place, switched on the air con and sat down to take a look through the box by the side of the settee, now she had more time she could start to relax and have a proper look. Yesterday she had been too nervous to take in even half of what she had looked at. There were all the magazines she had seen yesterday with Michael's face smiling out from the pages and there were a few that looked like bills although they were written in Thai so she could only guess at what they were for. There were a bundle of newspapers at the bottom but they didn't appear to have any link to Michael, they just seemed to be random newspapers, she put them all back and closed the box, she wanted to have a proper look through the bedroom. She went back upstairs and her eyes took in all of the beautiful furniture. She started at the carved dressing table, most of the draws were empty, the ones that did have anything in them contained only a few headache tablets, indigestion tablets and sun cream amongst other bits and bobs all probably out of date by now. There was nothing else to see and she moved to the wardrobe, he obviously didn't go much for new clothes, all that she could see was old jeans and shirts and a couple of waistcoats all of the clothing looked well worn, on the base of the wardrobe were two boxes which she pulled out to find an old pair of leather shoes and a pair of deck shoes, they were so well worn Alex had to wonder why he would bother putting them back in their boxes. He was obviously solitary for a reason, she smiled to herself. Then what sounded like a board creaking above her head, she froze, was there someone up there? No there couldn't be she'd looked. Another unknown noise followed, she was on alert again, her ears amplifying every sound, she crept up the stairs and looked around the attic, nothing seemed to be out of place. A rustle again, it made her jump and she stifled a scream as she ducked down and a large bat flapped around the room. She nervously laughed and left the bat to it, the wildlife was not her problem, he would settle eventually.

She went back into the bedroom and looked on top of the wardrobe, under the bed and ran her hand under the mattress, her hand felt something under there she pulled out an envelope, there was nothing written on it but when she opened it there was money inside, she pulled the cash out and counted one hundred thousand Baht that was a lot of money to leave lying around, it was roughly two thousand pounds but in Thailand that would buy a lot. Alex guessed that that was just where he had chosen to keep his money. She slipped it back in the envelope and put it back where she'd found it, she didn't know what she was hoping to find here but money wasn't it. There was nothing else to see in the bedroom and the sun was going down she decided that she would go back to the hotel, get changed and go out for dinner, tomorrow would be soon enough to tackle the attic. If she got here early she could still get the keys back to Pet before she finished her shift. Before she went she wanted to put something more secure in the door to cover the hole, she found a piece of thin board and cut it down with a kitchen knife, it fitted perfectly, that would have to do until tomorrow, she would ask at the hotel if they could organise someone to come and fix it properly.

Chapter Fifty Six

Michael had woken early, found the shower, cleaned himself up and left the house, he left some money under the mattress in the bedroom thinking it would be safer in the house than carrying it around. He had slept well and was in a far better mood for it, the settee had proved to be comfortable, he touched as little as he could, he had no idea whether anyone would come to the house today and he really didn't want to be discovered there or to bump into Alex. He walked back to the lovely beach he had been at a couple of days previously, on the way he stopped to feed peanuts to some monkeys, it was a relaxed day, and he was feeling good. During the afternoon he thought he had seen the man who owned the guesthouse he had run out on, he decided he should make his way back to Dominic's, at least he would be out of sight there, he still had no idea who was looking for him, if anyone but he wasn't ready to take any chances. He tried to pick up a newspaper on his way back but the shop had sold out, he thought it was time he got hold of a new computer, it would be an easier way to keep up with the news. He knew there was a computer shop on the main road, he eventually found it, went in and bought himself another tablet, it was also a great excuse to spend more time in the coffee shops where he could get internet connection.

He got back to the house as the daylight had almost gone from the sky, checked there was no one around and walked up to the door, the cardboard had gone and been replaced with a piece of board, from the inside, he stepped back, someone had been here. He walked away from the house not knowing what he was going to do next, there may be someone in there, he would watch and wait. After more than an hour of watching and seeing no movement he decided to take a chance and walked back to the door, someone walked down the alley and smiled at him, he was feeling nervous but he tried his best not to show it, he smiled in return and kept walking past the door and along the alley until the man had gone, he turned around and came back, he walked up to the door and touched the board in the space where there should have been glass, it gave a little, he was relieved. He gave it one good push and it fell to the floor inside allowing him access to the lock, once inside he closed the door and replaced the piece of board. He looked around, the pictures he left on the floor had been tidied up and the cover pulled across the settee, he ran up the stairs taking them two at a time, thrust his hand under the mattress and was relieved to find the envelope of money still there, he put it in his pocket, he wouldn't make the mistake of leaving it here again. He sat on the bed, the room was now almost completely dark and he suddenly felt tired. For the first time in what felt like forever he undressed and got into bed, he couldn't remember when he had ever felt so tired, the sheer luxury of a soft bed lulled him. Within minutes he was asleep.

It was still dark when he opened his eyes, he revelled in the feeling of lying in between clean sheets, for a moment he had forgotten where he was, he was so comfortable. He eventually got up at the same time the sun was putting in an appearance, there was little in the kitchen, not even a bottle of juice, only water. He threw his clothes on and went out to get some coffee, juice, and fruit, within ten minutes he was back and feeling quite at home in the lounge watching the sun come up through the net curtains whilst sipping a hot coffee. He would go out in a couple of hours but first he wanted to take a look at more of Dominic's artwork, from what he'd seen yesterday the work he had been doing looked well up to standard. He also needed time to set his new computer up but he would have to do that later at a coffee shop.

He took the cover off the settee and spread the sketches around, pulling out the really good ones, these could be worth a fortune, he knew exactly why Dominic had kept them away from him, Michael didn't mind, he'd got his hands on them now anyway. He was enjoying checking the art out after all it was what he had done since he'd been at school.

He sat up startled, he heard a key turning in the door, he dived behind the settee, not knowing what would happen next. He heard the door open, the key being slid out of the lock and then quietly closed, there was an intake of breath followed by the padding of feet the other side of the settee. Whoever it was in the house was rustling paper presumably tidying up the pictures. He was holding his breath and the quieter he tried to be the more he had an urge to cough, his heart was racing. The footfall went towards the back of the room, towards the kitchen, stopped, then carried on out into the kitchen and up the stairs. He stood up and looked around, he wanted to know who it was. If it was a cleaner he could explain that he was stopping there for a while as a guest of Dominic's if it was Alex he had no idea what he would do. He moved silently up the stairs, when he reached the top he could see movement as someone walked in front of the window. He walked into the room. It was Alex, he stopped, she was focused on something under the mattress or as he thought the lack of something. He walked up behind her, not close enough to touch her but close enough that she couldn't run when she turned around. He whispered "Hello Alex." She spun round dropping the mattress and made for the door but he grabbed at her and caught her arm. "Where do you think you're going?" His tone was even and cold.

"Michael." She gasped trying to pull herself together but failing, she was breathing hard and looked scared. She tried to pull away but he had a strong grip on her.

"You look like you've seen a ghost." He laughed, a cold hollow noise, still not releasing her arm. "What are you doing here Alex?"

"Looking for you." She managed to say, the look in her eyes was wary.

"Oh Alex, why couldn't you just print the story and forget about me, that was why I gave you the interview. Why did you have to come here?" He pushed her down the stairs, she stumbled awkwardly but her feet managed to stay underneath her and then through into the kitchen, he picked up a sharp knife that was hanging next to the meat cleaver on the wall. "I don't think you'll give me any trouble but just in case." He thrust the knife towards her. She flinched. "I don't want to hurt you Alex, just tell me why you're here."

"I'm, I'm looking for you. You disappeared, I was a suspect." She stuttered her way through the sentence.

"That interview would have made your career, you could have been a famous journalist but that wasn't enough for you was it, greedy girl." He took a breath. "Who are you here with?"

"No one."

"Oh all alone in Thailand. Now do I believe you…?"

"It's true Michael, I just wanted to find you."

"Sit down and shut up!" He pointed to the settee with the knife. Alex sat down.

Chapter Fifty Seven

Alex was in shock, she'd gone upstairs to check that the money was still under the mattress, she had slept badly last night worrying about it. She found more than she bargained for when she got there but the money had gone.

Michael had been there, in the house and was holding her captive and no one knew she was there. He had startled her and fear had left her helpless. He spoke to her in a cold, calculated way almost as if he was expecting her, this was not the charming, thoughtful Michael she had met before, now he sounded dangerous. As the time moved on he made her go from the bedroom, downstairs into the lounge, he had grabbed a knife as they came though the kitchen and was waving it around. Her knee hurt from her stumble downstairs, he had pushed her, she didn't have time to worry about it now, her adrenaline was dealing with the pain.

The longer he stood over her the more she was starting to feel in control of her emotions, her heart rate returning to below heart attack levels, the knife was a threat but she somehow got the impression he wouldn't use it, she prayed she was right, if she misjudged him she could be dead. The fog in her head was starting to clear and her knee throbbed but she didn't take her eyes off Michael. He stalked around the room muttering to himself and occasionally to her but never taking his eyes off her. "Why…" Her mouth was so dry she could hardly speak. "Can I have water?" It was just the fear that was making her feel like this. He walked backwards into the kitchen and grabbed a carton of orange juice, not once taking his eyes off her. "Here." He threw it to her.

"Thank you." She said, greedily drinking the cool, sweet liquid, her throat absorbing every last drop. She looked up at him. "Why are you doing this Michael?" She noted that she sounded a lot braver than she felt. He didn't answer for minute, he just looked at her.

"You really don't know do you?"

"I know you disappeared, I know you left me as a suspect and I know you may have been mixed up in a death when you arrived here." She noticed his eyes widen a little. "You thought no one knew about that?" She asked, feeling braver by the minute.

"That was nothing to do with me."

"Okay." She needed to tread carefully, he still had the knife in his hand and was waving it around whilst he was talking, it didn't feel like a threat any more though, it was almost like he was conducting his own speech. "What happened?"

"I met some guys in a bar, drank too much and stopped at their place over night and when I woke up, Oli was dead and the chickens were pecking at him, my stuff was stolen and the others had gone, I didn't kill him, I didn't even really know him." He was talking quietly, Alex believed him, he didn't know that his things had been found.

"Chickens?" She asked curiously. "You know the police are looking for you."

"Of course they are." He ignored the chicken reference.

"But you said you didn't ..."

"Not for that, you really are stupid aren't you." He snapped, she looked down into her lap she didn't want to antagonise him while he still had the knife. They were silent for a while, nothing was said, he just sat on the arm of the settee watching her. "Who sent you to look for me Alex?"

"No one."

"I've been thinking and I just don't believe you. What do you want?"

"I want you to contact people in England, Jasmine and your family in Australia, let everyone know you're alive and well."

"Why would anyone care about me?" He laughed an empty laugh. "No one cared when I was there, unless it was for the money."

"What about Jasmine, she cares."

"Ah yes the lovely Jasmine, she wanted to live the high life, it would drive her mad that I just wanted to sit in that house and look across the fields, she deserved better."

"Yes, she did. She loves you, still, even after everything she still loves you Michael."

"No, she's a tough one she'll be fine without me, we weren't even that close."

"Maybe it was you that wasn't, she needs to hear from you." Alex was feeling more confident with every sentence, if she could keep him talking she might be able to get out of here.

"Michael why did you run, why did you leave a note in the car in Paris for Lee? I found it."

"So you tracked me down to France too. Alex much as I like you, it's none of your business."

"But you've made it my business."

"Shut up, I'm not to blame for you being here, you should mind your own business." He sounded like he was getting angry, Alex stopped asking questions and just watched him, he looked like he was getting agitated, the calm, cruel exterior that he had first shown has now gone, now he seemed more erratic. Alex wondered at exactly how unstable he was, his moods were swinging, was there any record of mental health or was this just the pressure of running away now telling on him. She could try and overpower him and run for it but she would have to wait until his guard was down, she needed to keep him talking but her mind kept running into blank spots, it's just panic she kept telling herself. She started to try and regulate her breathing, to make herself calm down; Michael was just sitting watching her. They didn't speak for at least half an hour, then Alex said "What are you trying to do? Someone will come looking for me eventually."

"Maybe they will but I'd guess no one knows you're here." They sat in silence again for a minute.

"How long did you know Dominic?" Alex made a stab at conversation to keep him occupied.

"Since I was nine years old."

"Do you know where he is now?"

"Of course I do, he's in hell where he should be." He had a bitter, twisted grin on his face.

Alex sat up straight, was he saying what she thought he was saying, if so she could be in more danger than she thought. "Have you spoken to Lee?"

"Why would I want to, he's just a twisted old queen." Michael's face was angry, his voice once again turning hard and cold. Alex changed the subject.

"This art is really good." She picked up one of the sketches pretending to look at it whilst still watching where the knife was. She was running out of topics of conversation to change to.

"He was a great artist, he could have done better for himself."

"What do you mean?" Alex was confused by the statement, Michael had taken him on, that was what most artists wanted. They sat in silence again for a while, Alex not knowing what to say and Michael not wanting to talk.

Chapter Fifty Eight

Matt was happy to finally have arrived, it had been a gruelling trip, he walked up the steps and to the reception area. The girl behind the desk was expecting him, he had phoned ahead to arrange for Alex to be in the hotel when he arrived. It seemed the receptionist hadn't seen Alex since early this morning and she had no idea where she had gone. He would have to hang around the hotel until she came back, the hotel wouldn't give him a key to her room and he was glad they were careful with their clients.

He went to the swimming pool and sat down, he ordered a drink and relaxed, it had taken him a long time to get here and he was tired and he really wanted to see Alex. It had taken him an awful lot of arm twisting to get the time off work but with Lee already locked up and more than one force looking for Michael he had managed to pull in a few favours, he looked around and took in the view already he was liking this place, the view was every bit as good as Alex had said it was, every second of the journey here was melting away. The waitress who brought his drink over looked at him, turned away and then turned back to him again. "Hello, are you Matt?" She said with a heavy accent.

"Yes."

"I saw picture of you, Alex's husband." She had a beautiful smile.

"Yes, well no, not married but yes with Alex." That sounded confusing even to him, he sat back and smiled.

"She not say you were here."

"No it's a surprise. Do you know where she is?"

"No, not seen her today." Pet put her tray down and stuck out her hand. "I'm Pet, Alex's friend." With that she wandered off back to her work. Matt relaxed, she'd be back soon enough and then she could show him around. He had a sip of his drink and leant back in the chair, the heat was enough to send him to sleep. He was woken by Pet, gently shaking his arm "Matt, wake up, too much sun, you should move." He awoke startled, for a moment he had no idea where he was.

"Oh okay, thank you." It all came back to him and he looked up at Pet. "Is she back?"

"No, no-one saw her leave today." Pet had asked around the staff. "You look tired, wait here." She walked off, Matt must have been sound asleep his head felt muzzy, he looked at the still full drink in front of him, he didn't fancy that anymore, he needed water.

Pet came back over to him with a bottle of water, he must have looked hot too. "Drink." He did. "Come with me." He followed her to the reception, she had got the manager who thankfully spoke English well. She talked to him in Thai, Matt had no idea what was going on. Pet turned to him "You need to sleep, I told them who you are and that I know you." With that she nodded to the receptionist who handed Matt a key. "Go and sleep Matt. I'll look for Alex. I finish work now."

"Thank you Pet." He smiled at her, she was right he really needed to sleep even though it was still the afternoon. The manager accompanied him to the room and left him to relax. He walked out onto the balcony, and saw the view, she was right he thought it's beautiful. He pulled up a chair and stretched out in the shade, within minutes the sound of the sea and the warm breeze had lulled him off to sleep.

Chapter Fifty Nine

Hours had passed and nothing had happened, Michael kept watching her and Alex had given up making conversation, the few things she had tried to talk about had come to nothing, it was obvious he didn't want to talk. She had no idea what would happen now and she got the impression Michael didn't know what to do next either, she wondered if there was any chance someone may realise where she was by now. On a positive note she thought she was safe, he still hadn't let go of the knife, not for a moment but she did not sense any threat now, maybe he just didn't know how to go about backing down. She thought maybe if she could get him talking again they could end this thing. It was midday now and the house was getting warm. "Michael could we put the air con on, it's too warm."

"Yes, do it." He sounded gruff, she got up, and her knee squealed with pain, she had been sat down for too long. He watched her as she hobbled across the room.

"I'm sorry." He said quietly.

"What for?" She replied

"Hurting your leg." He may have been sorry but he didn't for one second take his eyes away from her. He hadn't softened enough that she could try and make a run for it.

"Can I get a drink?" She knew Dam kept fresh water in the fridge, in case Dominic came back unexpectedly. Michael nodded yes. She opened the fridge and filled two glasses with cold water. She handed one to Michael. "What did you mean Michael?"

"About what?"

"You said I was stupid, I didn't know... What don't I know?" She knew she was pushing her luck but she had nothing to lose by asking and he seemed to be much calmer now.

"Nothing."

"Okay but maybe I can help."

"No one can help me now, all I wanted was a quiet life and you had to follow me. Why couldn't you have just left me alone?"

"So this is my fault? I just wanted to make sure you weren't dead, there's a lot of people who are worried about you. Why would you run the way you did?" She watched him, he didn't seem to be reacting badly to her question.

"I'd had enough of the whole art business, I told you that when we spoke at the exhibition, it wasn't a lie. It's not the high life that you think, there's always someone waiting for you to fail, waiting to stick the knife in and get you out of the way so they could take your place."

"So why not just sell up and go quietly, why did you have to run?"

"Because of Dominic." He looked carefully at Alex for her reaction.

"What's all of this got to do with Dominic, you know he's dead don't you?"

"Of course I do, I killed him." He said this so matter of fact that Alex couldn't believe it.

"You... but why, you employed him, you looked up to him, he taught you how to paint. Why would you kill him, it makes no sense." There wasn't a word spoken for the next ten minutes as Alex absorbed what she had been told.

Michael eventually looked up at her and held the knife in the air and made a big show of dropping it on the floor. "Go Alex, get out, this is not your problem."

"No." Was all she said, she had thought all along that he wouldn't hurt her and now she wanted the story, she wasn't going anywhere.

"GET OUT!"

She moved to a seat closer to him. "What made you kill Dominic, and why let Lee take the fall?"

"Ahhh Lee, yes that was just a bonus, I should have known he could never be trusted to keep his nose out of my business, I kept telling him to get lost and he didn't listen, eventually I just locked him into a contract with me that would cripple him financially, almost every penny he made was mine. I wasn't proud of myself but he wouldn't listen, he wouldn't go away and I gave him every opportunity but still he hung around like a love sick puppy. Since I was a teenager he's followed me and I hated it but he wouldn't leave, well he won't find me here."

"No he won't, he's in prison for the murder of Dominic." Michael looked up and smiled, then he started to laugh, it was a hollow, haunting laugh not filled with happiness as a laugh should be but just a sound, totally emotionless. Alex just watched not believing what she was seeing.

"I always told him to keep away from me, that he'd never do any good following me around, he's had to learn the hard way hasn't he." He laughed again.

"So what happened with Dominic? People who knew him here liked him, said he was kind and generous. Why would you want to hurt him?"

As they were talking there was a sound at the door, a key being slotted into place a creak as the door slowly opened, Alex looked at Michael who was already standing up and making his way to the door. It opened up and Michael somehow grabbed someone and pulled them into the kitchen, throwing them against the refrigerator, then everything went silent. "Nooooo." He shouted. Alex rushed into the kitchen, there was Dam lying on the floor strangely twisted in an unnatural way with a ribbon of blood running from the side of her mouth. "Get back in there." He grabbed Alex and pushed her into the lounge. From where she was she could see him standing over Dam's broken body. Dam who had never done any harm to anyone, she was just the housekeeper. If Alex had ever thought Michael was not capable of murder, that swift movement had changed her mind. He walked into the room and grabbed the covers from the settee and took them into the kitchen presumably to cover Dam's body, he must have thrown her against the fridge with an incredible amount of force. Now she knew what he was capable of Alex was terrified.

Chapter Sixty

They were both crying when Michael told her to sit still and listen, he would give her his story and then he would go, she was to leave him alone and stop following him, he needed to get away. "I didn't mean to hurt her, she shouldn't have come here, I didn't mean it, oh God what's happened to me. I'm so sorry." He dissolved into tears again, Alex moved as if to comfort him, an instinct more than anything but he held his hand up. "Stop, just listen, don't move, don't speak." As he said that Alex could hear her phone vibrating in her bag, a low buzzing, Michael hadn't noticed it. She moved back from Michael as he had told her and she sat as close as she could to her bag, she needed to get to her phone. As she was thinking of her next move Michael started talking, he had a glazed look on his face, his eyes still wet with tears and he was no longer looking at her, he just started talking, with no emotion just cold hard fact after fact, Alex moved closer to her bag and put her arm out she thought she could just reach it from here, he stopped immediately. "Forget your bag, or your phone or whatever you're after, just listen." She looked up at him, and saw the glint of the blade in his hand again, she did as he said, she had seen what he was capable of. She was feeling caught between sorrow and fear.

He spoke quietly. "I met Lee at school, we were both interested in art, Lee was good, he could really sketch and paint, sadly I wasn't and that was how I met Dominic. He came to an art class which we did after school every week, I don't know why, maybe he was looking for new talent, that's what I like to think anyway. He wasn't very old himself back then but we thought he was, he was everything we wanted to be, a successful artist, his work was sought after for everything from traditional paintings to album covers. He could see how desperate I was to be a painter, he would give me tips on my work but I never really had the natural talent for it, it was always hard work for me." He reached for his glass and took a long drink.

"So how…"

"Don't talk Alex, just listen." There were still tears in his eyes but he continued. "When I was fourteen Lee declared his undying love for me, I was never interested, I liked girls not boys well not like that anyway. In fact my first crush was your Mum, she was so beautiful." He looked up and smiled at the memory, the smile didn't last long but at least it had been a real smile. "You are very much like her but you know that…" He paused reflectively. "Lee used to follow me around everywhere, he hated your Mum because I liked her but it was just a schoolboy hate, no real malice in it just jealousy. Lee tried to teach me to draw but I didn't want to be around him all of the time so when Dominic offered to teach me to paint I jumped at the chance. It was a way to step away from Lee, which was when Lee started writing me love letters, it was creepy, I wanted him to leave me alone so I tried to distance myself from him. The letters stopped after a while and I thought he had got the message, I burnt the ones he had sent in a gesture of friendship and we managed to build our relationship again. I didn't realise that as he got older he would try again. When I started my stall I used to sell a lot of Lee's work, it was good. We went out to celebrate one night when I had sold a particularly nice painting of his for a great deal of money and it all started again. Even the letters started again, I don't know why, I never once encouraged him." He drifted off into his own thoughts for a minute, Alex looked longingly at her bag she wanted to get to her phone but she didn't want to stop him from talking, she resigned herself to ignoring it and then suddenly he continued. "Before all of that happened I used to go to Dominic's house whenever I could, his work was incredible, well you've seen it, you know how good he is... was." The last word he added in a whisper." He liked to paint in the style of the Edward Burne-Jones and Rossetti, lots of depth and intricate design, he had a good name in the art world and was well known, I was honoured that he wanted to take me on and teach me what he knew, he knew that the Pre-Raphaelites were my preferred choice of art and he believed he could mould me in that school. He had a flat just outside Blunsford back then and I would go as often as I could, any spare moment I had, it was only a bus ride from Charmsbury. I believed he could teach me to be a great master. I dreamed of painting masterpieces that would hang in galleries all around the world, that's what he did, he made me believe." He took another break from his story and played with the knife in his hands, he had a faraway look on his face, as if he was replaying his younger self in his head. It wasn't a happy look. Alex sat still not wanting to jolt him from his memories; the phone in her bag was long forgotten. She looked over to the kitchen but she couldn't see Dam's body, just a trailing edge of the cover that had been thrown over her. When would all of this end, she had no idea what to do next. Michael started speaking again. "Dominic was good at making people believe anything he wanted them to believe, he was manipulative but he was also brilliant. I looked up to him, a bit of hero worship I suppose, he asked me to keep quiet about the lessons he was giving me, he said he didn't want anyone to know otherwise there would be lots of people who would want the same tuition and he didn't have the time. I felt even more special then and it spurred on my enthusiasm. I had lessons with him whenever I could find an excuse to get away from home, maybe three times a week sometimes an afternoon at the weekend too. I thought I was doing okay, my painting improved in leaps and bounds, I was happy, I believed my dream just might come true. It took me six months to get to that stage. Dominic would guide my hand and help me create all sorts of beautiful work, he taught me how to hold the brush, how to stand before a canvas and he never once asked me to paint a still life, we only did the fun stuff, there were no boring lessons. I liked him for that. When my work got better he would stand behind me with his hand on my shoulder studying the work, it made me feel a little uncomfortable but I was learning so much I could forgive him that and push any discomfort out of my mind and just keep doing the lessons. Then on one occasion he started massaging my shoulders, I shrugged him off but he said I wasn't to worry I just looked tense and he wanted me to relax, I remember him saying you'll never be a great painter unless you learn to relax." Michael stopped there, Alex was beginning to feel uncomfortable about what she was hearing, he took a swig of water. "He carried on massaging my shoulders, I can vividly remember the overpowering smell of his aftershave as he leaned in close to me, I turned around to face him to ask him to stop, he just stood there smiling, I tried to move towards the door knowing something was wrong but he was too quick for me, he grabbed me and threw me against the canvas I had been working on. It was my best work to date too." He gave a hollow laugh. "I tried to fight him off but he was just too strong, I didn't have a chance… He took what he wanted." Michael started crying again, reliving this had taken everything he had; he didn't look like there was any strength left in him. Alex still didn't say a word even though she wanted to, this was his story to tell. She knew she could run now, he wouldn't stop her but she needed to hear his story. He took a deep breath and wiped his eyes with the back of his hand "From then onwards Alex I was bitter and I wanted revenge, Oh sure it took its toll for a while but once I was over the shock of it, all I wanted to do was to bring him down, by then I was already making a name for myself selling art and I focused on that. I should have thanked him for that focus because it was all done to get back at Dominic. Lee got in the way again and as we grew up he was determined that I should fall in love with him, he wrote me some very explicit letters, which I put away in a very safe place, they're still very safe. I suppose this is why

I've never had a serious relationship with anyone, I could never trust anyone again, the only people I had let close to me had let me down in the worst way, nobody was going to abuse me again in any way. Lee tried one night at a party but I threw him off, he still never stopped trying. I think that was why I had the lifestyle I had, nothing deep and every relationship only on my terms." He stopped for a moment and seemed to be back there, then lifted his head and continued. "I lived a hedonistic lifestyle but that was my choice, no strings, just fun. I screwed it all up Alex, my whole life I just screwed it up, if I hadn't had the money to do it I would probably have killed myself, I hated everything I was. Now look at me. They made me this way, how else could it end." That was where he stopped.

Chapter Sixty One

The temperature woke him up, he was sweating, he wasn't used to this fierce heat, Matt looked at his watch he had been asleep for nearly three hours, he stood up and stretched, admiring the view. He turned and went into the cool room, it was basic but with Alex's things strewn around it looked kind of cosy too, he smiled when he saw the photograph of the two of them on her bedside table and her make up lying on the desk.

She still wasn't back; he decided to go down to the reception to see if anyone had seen her yet or maybe she would be sitting overlooking the bay having a drink. As he went towards the door he noticed a slip of paper had been pushed into the room underneath the door, he picked it up. It read 'sorry, cannot find her – Pet', so that was it, he could do nothing but wait, he was sure she'd be sunning herself on a beach somewhere enjoying her time here until he managed to get her some news on Michael. He didn't have much to tell her, she seemed to be getting closer to finding him than anyone, with or without his help. It was one of the things he loved about her and infuriated him in equal measure, she wouldn't let something go until she'd got to the bottom of the story. He had been worried about her being out here on her own that was half of the reason he came out to join her, the other half was that he had missed her like crazy, so much so he hadn't been concentrating properly at work, especially once he'd heard about the murder.

He went down to the restaurant but she wasn't there, nor was she sat by the pool, he asked at reception but no one there had seen her, they said they would ask some of the staff who had been working earlier in the day. He took a seat in the lobby, it was cool and comfortable. A girl walked across the lobby and said hello, she had seen Alex leave this morning, it had been early but she didn't know where she had gone. Matt thanked her and thought he may as well go for a walk around town and see what this place was like, Alex must have gone out for the whole day. He also wanted to find a nice restaurant for this evening, somewhere special he could take her.

He walked through the market and across the main road, he was already incredibly hot, when he spotted a cool looking coffee shop he ducked inside and he wasn't disappointed it was cool bordering on cold inside and the coffee was great. It looked to him like a fairly normal busy town, lots of shops and cafés and clusters of market stalls along the road. He was enjoying watching the world go by, then he saw a familiar face walk past the window, she looked in and he waved, she came in and sat down, Matt ordered her a coffee. "I'm sorry I couldn't find her for you." Pet said. "I've spoken to my friend Dam and she thinks she may know where she is, she said she would go and look. She will ring me soon. My family and Alex were supposed to go out this afternoon, she must have forgotten,"

"That doesn't sound like Alex." Matt frowned.

"It doesn't matter, we can go another day, I suppose Alex was so wrapped up in her work."

They sat together drinking coffee and chatting about the town and all the things that Matt should take Alex to see whilst they waited for Dam to ring. Matt was feeling a little concerned that Alex had let Pet down, it really wasn't her style, if Alex didn't want to do something she was never afraid to say so. He promised Pet they would make it up to her when Alex got back from wherever she was now. It had been a pleasant way to spend an hour but there had been no call from her friend. "Where did your friend think she might be?"

"At the house, I think, it's okay she will look."

"What house?" Alex hadn't said anything to him about a house.

"Dominic's house, my friend is the housekeeper."

"Dominic's house! She didn't say." He had a strange feeling that something wasn't right, since Alex had arrived here she had rung him saying there was nothing to do, no leads and that she barely left the hotel and now all of a sudden no one had seen her all day. He was starting to feel uneasy. "Where is this house?"

"Down by the sea." Pet looked as if she wished she hadn't said anything.

"Can you show me?"

"Yes, but there's nobody there, Dominic hasn't been there for a long time."

"He won't be coming back Pet, he died about a month ago." He was immediately sorry he had said that, it was obvious that Pet didn't know this news.

"Alex didn't tell me that, I didn't know, he was a nice man."

"I'm sorry." Was all Matt could think of to say. He paid for the drinks and sat with Pet until the news had sunk in, then she walked with him down to the sea front and down towards the house. Still Dam hadn't rung.

Chapter Sixty Two

She sat there watching Michael carefully not knowing what he had meant by 'how else could it end' she was praying that she didn't have to witness anymore violence, there were already too many bodies, too much misery and she didn't know what to do next. Michael was still sitting on the arm of the settee turning the knife over in his hands, totally focused on the blade. She still wanted to know how he ended up here and why. She just watched him until he finally looked up and looked at her wondering why she hadn't got out yet, he wouldn't hurt her and he thought she knew that. "Why don't you just go Alex?"

"I won't leave you here alone Michael, we can sort all of this out."

"Yes I'm sure we can but they'll still send me to prison."

"What happened after the letters and how was Dominic involved?"

"Lee continued to periodically send me letters, some were just friendly but some were explicit, I kept them all, they're safe, he'll never find them. It was only a few of years ago he discovered I had kept them all, he started to try and keep even closer to me to find out where they were obviously I never told him, I guess he'll just have to keep looking. Eventually I realised I needed to keep my enemies close it was the only way I could stop them from continuing to hurt me, I needed to control the situation. I signed Lee up to a fresh contract, I thought he would fight back at the conditions but he accepted them so easily, he trusted me. How stupid was that?" Michael seemed to have drifted off into telling his story again, a glazed expression came over his face, no emotion showing this time, cold, calculating, he continued as if talking to himself. "It was all in my favour and I'd got it sewn up so tight he would never get free of it, I ruined him, his work became popular but the money was coming to me and very little to him, I kept telling him his profile was growing and he only had to wait for the big time, he never seemed to worry until the money ran out and by then it was too late, I no longer accepted his work for exhibitions, he had to live off the back of other people and he got a reputation for being a leech. Yes I got him back properly, he even lived in that horrible little bedsit in the end. You should have seen his houses in the early days he was used to the high life." He laughed, a cold sound, no light found its way to his eyes. "It worked so well I decided to do the same with Dominic, he had been in many previous contracts and I needed to be cleverer so I was, I dated the woman who checked all of the legal details on the contracts, you met her, Jasmine. It was easy, I contacted Dominic and told him the contracts were changing and he needed to sign a new one, he smelt a rat almost instantly but when I told him that there were many people who would be very interested in him having raped a minor he just signed the paperwork and returned it to me. As I said, easy. He didn't want to come and join my company but what choice did he have? He could take less money and keep things quiet or he could take the risk of me spilling the beans and ruining his career, it was on the slide anyway because for years he hadn't been out in public, many people in the art world thought he was dead already. I'm not even sure that anyone else wanted to sign him, his work is good but has been out of fashion for many years, he came here for a long time to try and escape any publicity, I got him back for a couple of exhibitions, I wanted him to know that I pulled the strings now. Jasmine tried to protect him, she didn't understand why I would do this to him but when he told her to leave it alone and just do the paperwork, she did. It took me years to totally take over his life, I got access to his bank accounts and as you know I got hold of his passport. Once I had all of that he was of no use to me, I wanted to get rid of him. The night of the exhibition in Charmsbury he came to me and asked if we could talk, I said yes but it would have to be after the exhibition had closed, that was when I saw you, Janet's daughter it was as if you were a gift from the gods and a journalist, it was perfect, I knew I was moving on that night, I had it all planned. I was going to France to drop out of sight and live out my life in peace and quiet, where no one could find me, what I told you when we talked was true. I hoped you would put out the interview, I had always seen journalists as pariahs of society, put there just to tear people apart. I hadn't accounted for you though, I thought you'd print and take the money and fame, I didn't expect you to have a conscience. Anyway you gave me an alibi for the evening before I disappeared. When I came out of the building after you had left, I was ready to go and pick my car up, I'd left it at the hotel but Dominic was waiting for me at the back of the car park by the road, he asked if we could walk and talk. I agreed, we walked along the road and down towards the river, there was no one around just the two of us." Again he went quiet, reflective, he sipped at the water which was no longer cold. Alex saw a shadow out of the corner of her eye, Michael hadn't seemed to have noticed, if it was anyone trying to come in she hoped they wouldn't, she didn't know what Michael would do, they already had one body to account for. He carried on with his story. "He demanded I rewrite the contract, my terms were crippling him, we argued. I told him that if he hadn't raped me I wouldn't have sought to ruin him, the argument got out of hand and he tried to hit me, silly really he was no longer the man he once was, he was still fit to look at but he was slower than he used to be and this time I turned the tables and grabbed him and didn't let him get away. Do you know he didn't shout or scream, he barely made a noise at all when he died, I hit him, hard and then I picked up a smooth rock, I remember thinking how smooth and silky the stone felt in my hand, then I pushed it with as much force as I could muster into his skull. I pushed him down the bank and into the water, it seems he didn't get back out. That just made my life easier, then I went to get my car and left Charmsbury." Alex couldn't believe that this man was the same one she had laughed with and sat opposite whilst drinking with him. She heard a noise from the kitchen, she hoped it wouldn't be Pet looking for her, Michael looked around sharply and got up moving towards the kitchen. "Alex, come quickly." She jumped up, a pain shooting through her knee and as she got to the doorway she saw Dam trying to pull herself up to a sitting position, she grabbed a bottle of water and a tea towel and started trying to clean Dam up, Michael stood over them both and watched, passing the knife from hand to hand almost nervously. Dam managed to take a drink and Alex had to make sure she stayed where she was although she wanted to get up and get out of the house, unsurprisingly. After a while and as Michael continued to look on but do nothing she looked like she was going to be fine, she would have a nasty bruise on her head but she seemed conscious and it didn't look like there were any broken bones, Alex was relieved. "Michael we have to get her to a doctor."

"No, take her in there and sit down." He pointed towards the lounge with the knife.

"But she's hurt, please Michael." She helped Dam up and slowly walked her through to the settee where at least she could sit comfortably, Alex tried to smile at her, at least show her some comfort but her eyes were flicking around looking for an exit. Michael strode around the room watching them settle onto the settee.

"I went to France and stayed out of the way in a quiet little town, it was too easy Alex, just too easy to disappear." Alex couldn't believe he could just continue his story like nothing had happened. "I knew Lee would look for the letters, it was obvious, it seems that's what got him into trouble, stupid man."

"That stupid man is in prison taking the blame for a murder he didn't commit." Alex seemed to have found her voice again, protecting Dam had snapped her out of feeling sorry for herself.

"Lee's being done for Dominic's murder?" Michael began to laugh almost manically. "Perfect, it's perfect."

"Not when I tell the truth to the police, he will be free and it'll be you in prison."

"I'm not going to get caught Alex, how will you get me back to England, they may find out the truth but they'll never find me." Whilst he was talking she was sure she saw a shadow at the window again, it could only be Pet and she didn't want her to get involved too, she looked at Dam and could tell from her eyes that she'd seen something as well, Michael seemed oblivious to anything happening outside.

Chapter Sixty Three

They walked along the sea front, Pet pointing out things along the way that she thought Matt might be interested in. All he was really interested in was finding the house, he had a feeling once he found that he would find Alex, he wished she hadn't got herself involved in this case but she was stubborn and if she wanted to find out anything nothing could stop her, he wondered what she'd discovered this time. Pet pointed towards a building that seemed out of place compared to the others around it, it was modern looking and three storeys tall, a nice looking house with balconies at the front overlooking the sea. It seemed Dominic had been doing alright for himself. As they approached the building he noticed how well kept it was, Pet had said her friend was the housekeeper, it looked like she was doing a good job. Once she knew about Dominic he didn't know what would become of the house, thinking about it he hadn't yet discovered if there was a will in place.

They walked up a small side road and the house proved to be bigger than it looked it went back a long way, Matt noticed a broken pane of glass in the door he pointed it out to Pet. "How long has that been done?"

"I not know, not there three days ago."

"Does your friend know?"

"She did not say." They looked at it and Matt walked towards the door, the glass had been removed but there was no cover over the hole. He moved to a window and tried to see inside but the net curtains were too dense and he couldn't see anything. The house seemed very quiet. They returned to the sea front to sit on the wall. "Dam said she would come. We should wait."

"We could let ourselves in." Matt added.

"No, Dam looks after it, we go in with Dam." They sat and waited, enjoying the breeze coming in off the sea. Pet told him all about her family, he promised to spend some time with them as soon as he had found Alex, they also watched the house but there was no movement. Pet didn't know why Dam was so late getting here, even she seemed to be getting somewhat concerned. "You are a policeman right?"

"Yes." He wondered where she going with this.

"You could get us inside."

"I'm not a policeman in Thailand Pet."

"But we should look, Dam is never this late, she has a family to be at home for." Matt thought this through, he could get into trouble but if there was a reason there was a broken window and something had happened to Dam surely it was his duty. He didn't think for too long, he looked at Pet, nodded and they both strode across the road towards the house. He took a look through the windows again but still couldn't see anything, he went to the door. "Pet, stay here." He left her at the gate, he didn't want her to get into any trouble. He gently tried the door so as to make no noise but it was locked so he hooked his hand through the hole in the door and reached around until he found the lock, it turned smoothly and quietly under his grip. He pushed the door open and immediately saw what looked like blood on the fridge door and on the floor. "What can you see?" Pet called after him. He spun around with his finger to his lips to silence her. She went silent and from the look on her face she realised he was being serious. He pulled the door to a few inches and slipped around it to get inside, using it to lean back against, he stood behind it waiting to hear something, anything. He heard a man's voice talking and laughing, he looked at the blood but there was no clue as to where it had come from, there was a blood stained tea towel on the floor and a small bottle of water. The man's accent was English and he heard him mention Lee and Dominic. He knew in that moment that he was about to face Michael, Alex had tracked him down. He moved from behind the door and closer to the doorway in the direction he could hear the voice coming from, from this angle he could see Michael's arm and shoulder, he had his back to the doorway, he was moving his arms as if he was passing something from hand to hand. Matt didn't take his eyes from him and he inched forward, he didn't know who else was in the room for sure but he guessed that it would be Alex and Dam and he hoped that the blood on the floor belonged to Michael. He moved a little further forward and saw more of Michael and beyond him Alex, the thing he was passing from hand to hand looked horribly like a knife. He looked at Alex but she hadn't seen him, she looked unhurt but her attention was being taken by someone else in the room. He kept inching forward until he could get the whole picture, then Alex looked up and saw him, her mouth opened but just in time he motioned to her to keep quiet and at almost the same time he lunged forward grabbing Michael and forcing him onto the floor. For a moment everything was in mayhem and then Michael stopped struggling, Matt was kneeling on his arm which forced his muscles to release the knife and it fell to the floor. Dam moved forward quickly and grabbed the knife taking it out of reach of Michael, she quickly retreated. "Alex, are you okay?"

"Matt, Matt what……." Realising there were more important issues "Get Dam out she's hurt."

"Pet" Matt shouted, Pet came running through the door and gasped at the scene in front of her. "Get her out of here." Pet grabbed Dam and supported her as they stumbled through the door into the fresh, warm air. "Alex are you okay?"

"Yes." She replied, watching Michael carefully. Matt turned his attention to the body he was holding down and shifted his weight to allow Michael to move.

"Are you going to give me any trouble Michael?"

"No." He replied with a gasping breath. Matt stood up holding Michael's arm behind his back, Michael wriggled a little but gave no fight, he looked like he'd had it all knocked out of him, he almost sagged into Matt's body exhausted. Matt pushed him down onto a chair.

"What's going on?" He demanded sitting down next to Michael. "Alex go and tell Pet to get Dam to a doctor." Alex stood up a little unsteadily. "Are you okay, what's wrong?"

"Nothing I've just hurt my knee. It's okay." She went out of the room.

Then there were just the two men. "What the hell have you been up to Michael?"

Chapter Sixty Four

Alex couldn't believe what was happening, Matt had come rushing through the door, she had no idea where he'd come from or why he was here and in that moment she didn't care she was just so pleased to see him she could have cried with relief. There had been a scuffle in which Matt had somehow got Michael on the floor and disarmed him, Dam had rushed forward to grab the knife and got it out of the way. Matt was totally in control, she'd never seen him in action before and he was truly a force to be reckoned with. Before she knew what was happening she had been ordered outside to take care of Pet and Dam. When she got outside the sun was bright and she had to squint to look around, she spotted them both on the wall talking, Pet with her arm around Dam's shoulders. She walked over to them, her knee still tender but not as bad as it had been. "Are you okay?" Pet looked worried and Dam looked like nothing had happened, apart from the blood on her you wouldn't have thought it was anything but a normal day for her, she was tough. "You need to see a doctor Dam." Pet translated and nodded in agreement. Dam shook her head and said something to Pet.

"She said no, she's fine."

"She was knocked out, we thought she was dead! Can we send a doctor to her house?" Again after the translation Dam shook her head but looked up at Alex and said "Thank you." In her heavy Thai accent. Alex could have cried she felt the lump rising in her throat, this woman was possibly the bravest woman she had ever met and the thank you had been meant, she could read it in Dam's eyes, how could she mean that, Alex didn't understand, Dam should never have been there and Alex had done nothing to stop her getting hurt.

The three of them sat together in silence just looking at the house and waiting to see what would happen when Matt and Michael finally emerged. They eventually started to talk everything out and were beginning to calm down, Dam was upset that Dominic was dead she had liked him, he had been kind to her family and she seemed genuinely upset by the news. Alex looked up at the sun slowly tracking its way into evening then glanced down at her watch not realising how long they had been sat out here. They'd heard nothing from the house and neither of the men had left, she felt a wave of panic rise in her chest. She stood up and stretched her legs out, her knee was feeling much better, Pet and Dam were talking and looking after each other. She started to make her way back towards the house, she needed to know that Matt was okay, she still couldn't believe he was here but they could talk about that later. She slowly walked towards the house and went back in through the open door into the kitchen, she stood there and listened for a moment, Michael was telling Matt about how he had set up Dominic and how Lee had got himself involved, exactly the same confession he had made to her. Something in her felt sorry for Michael, for all of his wealth and fame his life had been so full of misery and empty of love. She wondered how she would tell Jasmine all of this news. She walked into the lounge, Matt looked at her but didn't tell her to leave, he was listening intently to Michael's confession. She sat silently and listened as Michael told Matt all of the grim details of his crimes and sat and watched Michael cry whilst he told his tale of abuse and revenge. He asked to see Dam but Matt refused, she had been through enough but Michael insisted. "Alex go and see if Dam would come in, she doesn't have to, make that clear." She went outside, they were still sitting on the wall, when Pet translated what Alex had said Dam got up immediately and stood next to Alex. "Yes." Was all she said. When they walked into the room Michael looked up at her, placed his hands palms together and deeply bowed his head keeping his head low until Dam approached him and touched his shoulder, when he raised his head his cheeks were wet with tears but his hands stayed together, she understood. "I'm so sorry." That was all he could manage before he dissolved into a flood of tears. Dam turned and walked back outside with her head held high. Alex was astounded by the strength of the woman.

They could do no more in the house, Matt took Michael to the police station, Alex fixed the door as well as she could and locked the house up and handed the keys back to Dam, who shook her head, she refused to take the keys. Pet said "He's dead, he does not need a cleaner now." Pet took her home and made sure she was okay. Alex wandered back to the hotel, she checked her phone on the way, nine missed calls from Matt.

Chapter Sixty Five

That night Alex had never been so grateful for Matt, he pulled her close into him and held her like he would never let her go. They were together but there would be little sleep tonight with everything that had gone on through the day.

He hadn't returned from the police station for almost four hours, they had to get a translator and the police had agreed to hold Michael until a deportation notice could be arranged for him, he would be travelling back to the UK with them, Matt still needed to arrange things with the Embassy in Bangkok and it would all take time but it should be straight forward, for now Michael was giving the Thai police the details of what he knew about the murder of Oli in Hua Hin, the one thing he wasn't responsible for. He would stay in the cells until they could sort out the travel arrangements.

It was three o'clock in the morning that Alex got out of bed and went and sat on the balcony, as she expected she hadn't been able to sleep, she wanted to make some phone calls and hear some familiar voices. She could hear Matt moving around inside the room but she picked up her phone and listened to it ringing out. "Hello."

"Hello Nan." They talked for more than twenty minutes, Matt brought her out a drink and sat next to her and after she put the phone down Alex thought she might be able to get some sleep in fact now she felt incredibly tired. Matt was already peacefully asleep in the chair next to her, she still had to pinch herself, he was so handsome and he loved her, she leaned in and gently kissed his head.

The following five days were taken up with Matt spending a lot of time with the police and trying to arrange paperwork for

Michael. Which meant that Alex had time to write up everything that had happened, it seemed that none of this news had leaked to the newspapers back in the UK yet so Alex wanted to get her story to Charlie with promises of more details to come, how Matt had managed to keep all of this quiet was beyond Alex but she was grateful for it. Charlie was over the moon and yet again forgave her all her misdemeanours as soon as he received her story. Once the writing was done Alex had plenty of time to relax, there was nothing else she could do. The only thing she hadn't done yet and it was playing on her mind was ringing Jasmine, she picked up her phone and dialled her number. "Jasmine, it's Alex. We've found Michael."

"Thank God."

"There's a story going to print today, you're not mentioned but there'll be plenty of people who want to talk to you when it goes public."

"How is he?"

"He's a mess, there's so much I need to tell you I barely know where to start." Alex told her what had happened and Michael's side of the story, which fitted in with everything she had already told Alex, the only thing she asked was if she could meet them when they got off the plane, Alex promised to do her best to arrange it but it wouldn't be her decision. Alex felt bad for Jasmine, she had no idea how she would cope with all of this she wasn't as tough as she liked to portray herself.

For the next few days they relaxed and would go out for meals in the evenings after Matt had finished working to help Michael and they found a lovely small restaurant overlooking the sea where they had the best Thai food they had ever tasted and it was friendly, they soon became treated as regulars there.

Michael was staying in the town, Matt had fought to keep him here, if he went into a Bangkok prison it could take months to get him out and back to the UK because there would be so much more paperwork, as it was if they kept it local he could return with them and be handed over at Heathrow to the police.

Alex had been to see Pet and Dam and arranged to meet them when they both had a day off, they were to bring their families too, it was going to be a big day out for everyone and a chance to relax and forget about everything that had happened.

Chapter Sixty Six

The day dawned hot as everyday did in Thailand, today was going to be special for all of them, Alex was going to make sure of that. Matt had hired a van and was ferrying the kids to the beach, the adults made their way there any way they could, there were plenty of family members coming to their day out, there was Dam and all of her brothers and sisters and their children and Pet and her children and her Mum with a couple of Aunts and Uncles, it was a real get together. Alex had arranged for a local restaurant to do a huge barbeque on the beach and for all sorts of games to be played watched over by a local sports club, when Alex got there with Matt's final run and the last few people, the beach was already buzzing with excitement. They stood with their arms around each other watching everyone laughing and having fun.

Pet and Dam were the guests of honour and thoroughly spoilt, after an hour Matt received a phone call and had to return to the hotel to check some paperwork which had been sent from the embassy in Bangkok, Alex hadn't taken a lot of notice when he had said it was paperwork, she was having too much fun with the children on the beach, he gave her a peck on the cheek and told her he'd be back really soon. She looked up and watched him walking away feeling like the luckiest woman on the planet, the warm sand between her toes, laughter and she was in love.

An hour later Matt returned smiling, he called Alex, Pet and Dam together and they wandered over to the bar and got a cool drink, they sat around the table and Matt thanked Pet for her help in finding Alex and asked her to translate to Dam, he turned to Dam. "I have been in touch with Dominic's solicitor and in his will he had left the house to you." Alex and Pet gasped in delight, Matt grinned and held out the house keys to her, she shook her head and then Pet told her to take them and why. She took the keys but a tear slipped down her cheek.

It was turning out to be quite a party, as the sun set people started heading towards home, no one expecting Matt to drive them but he did anyway and by seven o'clock there was only him and Alex left on the beach, walking hand in hand, watching the sky darken before them, in the shadow of Buddha Mountain. It had been a perfect day.

Epilogue

Alex and Matt managed to get Michael returned to the UK without too many problems, Michael had resigned himself to having to pay for his crimes and gave them no trouble. Jasmine met them from the plane and had a few minutes to speak to Michael. Alex didn't know what would happen between them in the future but Jasmine was adamant that she would wait for him, whatever the outcome would be. They held on to each other until the police turned up and took Michael away. Alex hoped there would be some happiness for Jasmine with or without Michael.

Dam and her family moved into Dominic's house and settled in with no problems and from the emails Alex received from Pet the whole family were happy there. Pet was trying to arrange to visit the UK, she would stop with Alex and Matt for a while and practice her English and the manager at the hotel had offered her a promotion if she would return before the next holiday season.

Lee was taken to court for breaking and entering but as he had been on remand the judge let him walk out of the court a free man. He didn't hang around in Charmsbury, no one knew where he went but he wasn't seen at his flat again. Mel was pleased he wasn't around anymore and picked herself up and got back to living her normal life, stating that she was thoroughly embarrassed by the whole episode.

Mary is still teasing Jack with outlandish plans for their wedding in the Spring.

Acknowledgements

Thank everyone who took the time to read my second novel 'Pictures Of Deceit' I know how precious your time is and I'm grateful that you gave me some of yours. I hope I entertained you.

I would also like to take a moment to thank everyone who helped me along the way and gave 'The Community' such great reviews, making me want to continue Alex's story. As always thank you to my husband who put up with me throughout the whole process, my Mom for inspiration and grammar tips, Kirsty Prince for her proofreading skills. Thank you to everyone for your kind support especially Alysa Blackwood-Bevan who inspires me to continue when I doubt myself, I am grateful to all of you and couldn't do it without any of you.

If you would like to contact me or leave a review you can use Facebook page 'SC Richmond' (facebook.com/scrichmond3/)

Or visit my blog at
https://scrichmondblog.wordpress.com

I'd love to hear from you.

'The Community'

S.C. Richmond

A mystery and love story that spans fifty years.

Jack still mourns his lost love but now he has more to worry about. His friend has died and Charmsbury's local journalist, Alexandra Price, is getting closer to discovering The Community.

Alex has no idea as to the identity of the woman's body that has been found in the park, but it leads her on a journey of discovering more about her home town than she could ever have imagined.

What connection could an unknown body, an abandoned baby, missing people and a triquetra have? She sets out to find some answers, unaware of how it will affect the people she loves the most.

Available now at all good bookstores.

Reviews included... Brilliant, enchanting, romantic, intriguing and enthralling.